AF414093

STARLITE PULP REVIEW #4

Pulp done right.

Michael Bracken ✦ Alec Cizak ✦ Eric Esquivel ✦ Jean-Paul L. Garnier ✦ EB Hunter ✦ Meagan Lucas ✦ John McNally ✦ Greg Mollin ✦ J.D. O'Brien ✦ Daniel Pyne ✦ Alex Slusar ✦ Manny Torres ✦ Jim Towns ✦ Brian Townsley

Starlite Pulp

Starlite Pulp Review #4 Copyright © 2024 by Starlite Pulp

Cover art is 'Peace Offering' by the amazing Danny Galieote

All rights reserved. Printed in the United States of America. No part of this book may be used or reproduced in any manner whatsoever without written permission except in the case of brief quotations embodied in critical articles or reviews.

These stories are works of fiction. Names, characters, businesses, organizations, places, events and incidents are either the product of the author's imagination or are used fictitiously. Any resemblance to actual persons, living or dead, events, or locales is entirely coincidental.

These stories were chosen by the editors at Starlite Pulp through submissions sent to our Submittable page.

For information, contact : editor@starlitepulp.com
Site : www.starlitepulp.com   Instagram : @starlite_pulp
Youtube channel : youtube.com/@starlitepulp

Book and Cover design by Tristan and BT
Executive Editor : Brian Townsley
Associate Editor : Jake Naturman

ISBN: 979-8-218-43106-8

first edition: June 2024

"If love could die along with death, this life wouldn't be so hard."

Andrew Vachss

"My lifestyle/determines my death-style."

Frantic, Metallica

"For the sum of everything was a circle, and the sum was labelled Zero."

Shoot the Piano Player, David Goodis

STARLITE PULP
REVIEW #4

Liner Notes/1

Nothing to Worry About by John McNally/3

Toronado by Manny Torres/23

Outlaw Country by JD O' Brien/49

Supper's Ready by Jean-Paul L. Garnier/69

They Light Themselves on Fire by Meagan Lucas/75

The Sweet Science Blues by Brian Townsley/95

Dog Eat Dog by Greg Mollin/127

Genius in a Bottle by Alec Cizak/137

The Stowaway by Alex Slusar/173

Marked by Michael Bracken/201

Dead Man's Muse by Daniel Pyne/211

Neon Gods by EB Hunter/233

Ghost Stories by Eric Esquivel/253

The Cannibal of Space City by Jim Towns/257

LINER NOTES

There were *so many* good stories that were sent to us this time around, and the fruits of that labor, well, it's now in your hands.

John McNally, who has written 19 books to date, starts the Review off with a twisted, psychological stone bruise to the soul in 'Nothing to Worry About,' and following that is a fun, funny, and Florida-filled escapade by Manny Torres. 'Outlaw Country' by JD O'Brien also has a humorous twist and an absurdist bent (whenever a guy commits crimes wearing a Nudie Suit it must fall into that category), but is also a serious crime yarn. 'Supper's Ready' by Jean-Paul L. Garnier falls into the Sci Fi category, but is as funny as anything else. Great, simple concept, well done. What more do you need?

'They Light Themselves on Fire' is Meagan Lucas's debut with Starlite, and she hits it out of the park with this crime/psychological/relationship thriller. 'The Sweet Science Blues,' is one I won't go into much detail about—since I wrote it—but it does serve as the Sonny Haynes debut in the Review, who has been featured in both *Outlaw Ballads* and *A Trunk Full of Zeroes*, both released from Starlite Pulp. 'Dog Eat Dog' by Greg Mollin follows, and it's a gritty crime drama...that involves werewolves. Right up our alley, and full of heart, to boot.

'Genius in a Bottle' is next, and we're very familiar with Alec Cizak here, as he was included in the 2nd Review, and was featured on our podcast

(Starlite Pulpcast) as well. This story may be the best thing we've seen from him. 'The Stowaway' by Alex Slusar is next, and, I'm not gonna lie, this one pissed me off. I've thought of writing a 'western' on one of the large steamboats that crept up and down the Mississippi for years. And then Alex went and wrote one. And a really good one. 'Marked' by Michael Bracken is a short, concise, classic noir tale, that hits in all the right moments. Michael's a pro, and this reads like it.

'Dead Man's Muse' is perhaps the least 'pulpy' of the stories here, but certainly one of the stronger narratives. Daniel Pyne has a unique voice and an ability with language that leaps off the page. I don't want to get into 'Neon Gods' much—just sit back and enjoy it. Written by EB Hunter, it involves Egyptian Gods and Atlantic City. 'Nuff said. 'Ghost Stories' by Eric Esquivel, is our first venture into 'graphic' shorts, and this one-pager is a blast. The art is by Scott Godlewski and Ryan Cody. Enjoy. Last, the Review finishes with a Cyrus Major story by Jim Towns. It involves Cape Canaveral, 1960s Florida, the Everglades, a missing girl, and...maps (!), which make the 13-year old Middle-Earth nerd in me very happy. The last issue is one we're very proud of, but was dark in tone, this one...not so much, from a pulp outlook. I mean, there's still dark alleys, bad decisions, and guns involved, but if you listen close, you can hear some laughter in here as well.

BT, Starlite Pulp, Spring 2024

NOTHING TO WORRY ABOUT
BY JOHN MCNALLY

The Physician's Assistant from the dermatologist's office called and, without a hint of concern in her voice, said, "We got the results back. It's basal cell carcinoma. Nothing to worry about. We've already called the surgeon to remove it. You should be hearing from his office soon. His name is Dr. Reynolds."

Jenny said, "Okay." She was having difficulty reconciling the word carcinoma with the casual tone in the voice of the women delivering the news. She had questions, but it wasn't in her nature to ask them.

Before hanging up, the PA said, "Don't think twice about it. It's the good cancer."

"Oh," Jenny said. "All right."

Ten minutes later, a woman from Dr. Reynold's office called to schedule an appointment for the surgery.

"We had a cancellation. Can you come tomorrow?"

"Tomorrow?" Jenny said. "I guess."

"Great! So here's what's going to happen."

Everyone was so chipper, Jenny thought as the woman explained about a procedure called MOHS, where the surgeon, Dr. Reynolds, would remove an area of skin, examine it for cancer cells, and then either stop removing skin if the margins were clear or continue if they weren't. Jenny would be charged each time the doctor had to remove skin.

"Can you be here by six a.m.? Dr. Reynolds likes to start early."

"I guess," Jenny said. "Sure."

The next day, Jenny pulled into the medical complex, a series of identical-looking buildings, and parked in the nearly-empty parking lot, but the lot was pitch-black when she turned off her headlights and stepped out of her car, and she had difficulty finding the correct building. When she illuminated her phone and saw that she was already ten minutes late, she started to panic. Why couldn't she find the damn place? But then she turned a corner and saw ten cars parked near the only illuminated building.

"I'm sorry I'm late," she said to the receptionist as she caught her breath. She offered a look of contrition, but the receptionist merely handed over a clipboard and said, "Fill out these forms. Here's a pen." Before Jenny could even get settled in a chair, a young woman in nursing scrubs opened a door and loudly called her name despite the fact that she was the only person in the waiting room.

Jenny stood and picked up everything – her bottle of water, her cardigan, and the book she had brought to read in case the surgeon had to keep removing skin, a new book about the extrajudicial killings of suspected drug dealers in the Philippines – and she followed the woman into an exam room where the surgery was to take place.

Jenny didn't have any friends in town, so she hadn't told anyone where she was going. She had lived in Louisiana for a year, and it hadn't been easy making new friends. She went to work, came home, ate dinner, watched TV, and then read a book until she fell asleep, usually with the bedside lamp still on. She worked at the university library in the Acquisitions Department, inventorying books as they arrived while following up on orders that were never fulfilled. The books she read at night were books from orders she hadn't yet inventoried. It was like stealing but not exactly since she always brought the books back. Even so, her heart sped up each time she stepped through the sensor on her way out of the library. It gave her a strangely satisfying thrill, a rush, but lately she'd begun to wonder if something was wrong with her. *Why* did it give her a thrill? A rush?

As she placed all of her belongings in yet another chair, she saw that one of her old scars on her forearm was showing. In high school, she had been a cutter. She was only self-conscious about the scars in medical settings. She didn't want lengthy lectures, but she also didn't want to alarm anyone. The cuts were from a lifetime ago. She rarely thought about them, the way people with old tattoos hardly ever thought about their old ink. To hide the cuts now, she put on her cardigan and pulled down the sleeves. She sat down in the exam chair and tried getting comfortable, but the headrest was positioned wrong and a muscle in her neck felt pinched.

The exam room door opened. A voice ruptured the silence.

"So, you think your time is more valuable than mine?"

Standing in the doorway was a boy no older than eighteen, but as he stepped closer she realized he was older than his boyish features had suggested. The nearer he got, the older he became. She settled on thirty-eight – twenty years older than her initial guess. How was that possible?

"You should see the look on your face," he said. "Hey, I'm just teasing you. We've got plenty of time." He held out his hand. "Dr. Reynolds," he said. "You've come to the right man. This is what I do all day long. This and only this. Nothing else. What a life, right?" He looked over at the book she had set on the chair. He scanned the title. He quit smiling. He looked back at her and then down at the clipboard she was holding. She still hadn't filled out any of the forms. "Tsk-tsk," he said and winked at her. He took the clipboard from her and moved in toward her face, as though he was going to kiss her. He examined her temple and then leaned back, sizing her up.

"What's your first and last names?"

"Jenny Falls."

"And which side of your head was that pesky bump on?"

She pointed to her left temple, where there was an obvious biopsy scar, still sore and angry.

"Bingo," he said. "We're in business. My assistant will come in and numb your temple, and I'll be in shortly after to remove the first layer of skin. And then we'll see where we're at. Sound good?"

Jenny nodded.

Dr. Reynolds glanced over one more time at her book and then left the room.

***

Jenny could feel only the pressure of the scalpel pressing into her temple, not the pain. She kept her eyes averted, however, to avoid distracting the surgeon while he worked. Having skin cancer removed from her head was more intimate than she'd imagined. There were two other women in the room, one on either side of her. The woman on her left massaged her shoulder to keep Jenny relaxed while the woman on her right absorbed the blood as the surgeon cut.

"I don't think that's a bad thing," the surgeon said. "Killing drug dealers." Jenny wasn't sure to whom Dr. Reynolds was speaking until he added, "Your book."

"Oh," Jenny said. "Yeah. I..." She wanted to explain the issue at the heart of the book, that the killings had occurred without due process at the behest of the country's president, but she didn't want to disagree with the man cutting on her face with a scalpel. "Actually, I haven't started reading it yet," she said.

7

"Honestly? I think I'm becoming a fascist as I get older," he said and laughed. Was the laugh meant to reveal that he was joking or to convey the surprising turns that life takes? "The other day," he said, "I saw a man spit on the sidewalk and then get into his car. The car had Indiana license plates. I thought, how dare you come to my city and spit on my sidewalk! I served my country. I came back home and went to med school. I could have gone to med school at Northwestern or Harvard, but I didn't. I went here. Tulane. I help people. *My* people. And then someone who doesn't even live here spits on the land where I grew up? I take that personally. Where is it that they cane people for spitting? Singapore? You ask me, *we* should start caning people. When you give people too much freedom, they become fat and complacent." He paused. "There!" he said, stepping back. "I'll go look at this sample and see if I got it all."

Jenny felt dizzy from the lack of food and the endless talking. She smiled, tight-lipped, and nodded. She felt an unexpected wave of sadness and thought she might start crying, but she held back the urge.

"You're doing great," the surgeon said and stepped out of the room.

***

It took one more removal of skin before Dr. Reynolds was satisfied he'd gotten all the cancer cells.

"Come here," he said to Jenny after he had stitched her up and placed an extra-large bandage across her temple. "Let me show you what I did."

On the back of an empty prescription form, he made a drawing.

"This was the first layer of skin I removed."

Then he drew another line, widening the area.

"And this was the second. In six months, you won't even have a scar. That's how good I am." He smiled. He patted her arm and said, "When you're done gathering your things, you can pay at the front desk. Take your time." He looked like he was going to crumple the drawing, but then he handed it to her. "Here. In case you want to frame it."

Thirty minutes later, Jenny was sitting in a booth in Waffle House, waiting for her order. Twenty years ago, she'd have been horrified at the thought of going out in public with a giant dressing on her head for a wound, but she didn't think twice about it today and no one even looked at it. The world was full of so many absurdities that a woman alone in a Waffle House fresh from skin cancer surgery didn't even register. She was just another person with a story no one wanted to hear.

***

Sunday night, as she dozed in a chair with a book in her lap, Jenny's cell phone buzzed. She answered the phone even as she desperately tried placing where she was and into which part of her life she was waking.

"Hello?"

There was nothing. Only the silence of someone on the other end listening. She remembered an old boyfriend from when she was in her early twenties. She'd broken up with him but he wouldn't move on. He would call her and not say anything. She knew whenever there were long silences that it was him. His oxygen – what kept him alive – was listening to her breathe.

"Mark Ellis?" she said now.

"Dr. Reynolds," the voice said.

"Dr. Reynolds?" She was still disoriented from her nap. It took a moment to remember who Dr. Reynolds was.

She heard ice clink in a glass and then liquid pouring over ice. She heard the ice breaking, sighing.

"How's the wound healing?" he asked. "Any problems?"

"No," Jenny said. "It's good, I think."

"You're not running a fever?"

"No. No fever."

"Good."

She heard him take a drink. He swallowed and sighed.

"This is what I do," he said. "I spend Sunday nights in my office calling my patients."

Did he, Jenny wondered, keep liquor in his office? Where did he get the ice?

"That's thoughtful," Jenny said, because she couldn't think of anything else to say and because the silence needed to be filled.

"It's my job," he said. His reply sounded like a reprimand, but then he said, "I downloaded that book and read it."

"What book?"

"The one about the Philippines. The quote-unquote *extrajudicial* killings of drug dealers. Have you finished it?"

"Yes," she said, though in fact she hadn't even started it. She had come to the disturbing realization that although she read books, she mostly carried them around as props. This was one such book. She'd already returned it to the shelf on the library cart with the rest of the order that still needed to be inventoried.

"I didn't care for the tone of it," he said. "You know what I mean?"

"I guess," Jenny said.

"If you write a book," he said, "be objective. It was clear to me that the author disapproved." He took another drink. "They're drug dealers, for chrissake."

"Have you been to the Philippines?" she asked.

"No," he said. "No interest. I don't know why." There was a long pause, and then he said, "Can I ask you a question?"

"Okay."

"Who's Mark Ellis?"

"Mark Ellis?"

"When I called, you thought I was Mark Ellis."

"Oh yeah. He's just an old boyfriend."

"He still calls you?" the surgeon asked.

"He hasn't called in eighteen years."

She heard him take a long drink and then she heard the ice clinking together. He must have finished whatever was in the glass. Whiskey, she imagined. Something expensive.

"This Mark Ellis character," he said. "Was he a good guy?"

"No, he wasn't."

"See?" the surgeon said. "You seem like a nice woman. Why did you put up with a guy who wasn't nice?"

Jenny flinched. Why was it *her* fault?

"He hid it," she said. "He was nice at first. I thought... I don't know what I thought. I thought his cruelty was an aberration, I guess."

"Fair enough," the surgeon said, as though this concluded the matter. "Well, you have a nice night. And don't hesitate to call me if you start having problems, okay?"

"Sure. Okay."

The next day at work, Jenny searched the cart for the book about the extrajudicial killings in the Philippines, but a coworker had already inventoried it and sent the book along to be processed for shelving. The coworker took extra-long lunch breaks and left fifteen minutes early each day. He also wrote bad poetry and published it in obscure online magazines, which was fine, but he treated the rest of the staff like his inferiors by quoting unknown authors and frequently dropping French idioms. Jenny secretly sought out his poems and read them for her own amusement. She also established that he had never been to France.

"The cart," Jenny said to him, "was sitting by my desk. I was going to inventory them."

"Slow day," he said and shrugged. "*C'est la vie!*" He swiveled back toward his computer screen, probably to compose a poem about their tense exchange.

Jenny knew it was unreasonable, but she hoped he would die soon. She didn't want to spend the rest of her career sitting near him. It was unlikely he would ever change jobs or, for that matter, departments. He had brought to work his own Tiffany-style lamp for his desk, cementing his permanence.

The degree of specificity Jenny conjured of her coworker's fictional demise disturbed her – and yet she couldn't stop letting it play out. On more than one occasion, she had imagined him taking an Ambien for sleep, covering himself with a weighted blanket, and wearing a sleep mask to block out any light – and then one night, inside his walls, bare wires touch, a spark ignites a fire, and the poet, deep inside a pharmaceutically-induced sleep and while wrapped inside a cocoon of his own making, can't move his own limbs as carbon monoxide chokes him out, killing him even before the first flame touches his hair, igniting his head.

The only other person whose death she had fantasized was her ex-boyfriend's. She had imagined Mark Ellis dying in a terrorist attack, the victim of an explosion of nails would leave him in dozens of unidentifiable body parts.

Jenny eventually went to a therapist to help her move past these fantasies. Her breakup with him had happened shortly after 9/11, and the therapist believed that Jenny was conflating two fears – the fear of random violence with the fear of personal violence.

Jenny knew that most people had dreams of violence against people they knew, even if they wouldn't admit it, but what was unusual was the guilt she had felt over things that would never come to pass. Her guilt struck her as a particular type of narcissism. Instead of laughing off her silly thoughts of retribution and comeuppance, she wallowed in her own shame for thinking such things.

And here she was twenty years later wishing her silly coworker would perish in a house fire for thinking he was an intellect and a good poet, but she no longer felt any guilt. It was, she had decided, no less valid a way to pass her time than posting photos of her meals on Instagram. It didn't mean anything. It was just a way to fill the hours.

So why did she recoil over her surgeon's glee over the murder of suspected drug dealers? Drug dealers were surely worse than bad poets. Was it necessary to draw a line in the sand to assure the world that she wasn't a sociopath? Jenny had in fact drawn a very clear line between herself and the surgeon, so why couldn't she say out loud to him where her line was? Why couldn't she just tell him he was wrong?

On her break, she walked to the designated smoking area of the campus, a wretched area near a Dumpster, and bummed a cigarette from a short, old man she didn't know. She hadn't smoked since she was a teenager, but the first taste of nicotine immediately settled her nerves. She shut her eyes and let euphoria overtake her. Smoking the cigarette didn't make her happy, but it certainly brought her closer to happiness than she'd been in over a year since moving to Louisiana, a place she feared she would never understand and whose dirt she would one day be buried under.

***

Winter hit Jenny unusually hard.

Southern Louisiana could get surprisingly cold, especially since the houses were so poorly insulated and sat only inches off the ground. Even the alligators that lived in the campus swamp burrowed under water to hibernate. It was a cold, gray season that only exacerbated her loneliness, and the colder and greyer it became, the longer she went without having a conversation of any substance with anyone.

One Saturday evening, as she sat flipping through a biography of Frida Kahlo, feeling guilty for looking at the photos instead of actually reading the book, her phone buzzed. The number came up unknown.

"Hello?" she said.

She could hear a faint noise but couldn't identify it.

"Jenny?" a man said.

"Who's this?" Jenny asked.

"It's Dr. Reynolds," Dr. Reynolds said. It had been months since his last phone call.

"I'm sorry," she said. "I didn't recognize your voice."

There was a long silence. Was he angry that she hadn't recognized his voice?

"This is hard to admit," the surgeon said, as though he hadn't heard her apology.

"Yes?"

He took a deep breath in and then let it out. "When I performed your procedure..." He paused.

"Yes?"

"There was a cancer cell on the margin of what I considered acceptable," he said. "Another doctor would have been okay with it. But not me. Normally, that is. Except for that day with you. We were overbooked, and I..." He paused again.

"Go on."

"I decided it was good enough. Ninety-nine out of a hundred doctors would have accepted those margins as clear, so I thought..." He breathed heavily through his nose again, expressing his frustration with himself.

"Where are you?" Jenny asked. "What's that noise?"

"I'm in my car."

"You're parked somewhere?"

"I'm in your driveway," Dr. Reynolds said.

Jenny's heart sped up but not in an altogether bad way. She'd found herself thinking more about him lately. She had regretted not pushing back on some of his ideas. She had found them revolting. Unacceptable. But she had also imagined a playful back and forth – their disagreement as a kind of flirtation.

"Do you want to come in?" she asked.

"Is that okay?" he asked, but before she could assure him that it was indeed okay, she heard his engine cut out, the ring of keys jingling as the ignition key was removed. The car door opened.

She put down her book and hurried to the front door. When she heard his footsteps, she opened the door. He was holding an Army-green tackle box in one hand and a small Igloo cooler in the other. She imagined him coming home after a long day fishing, but the gloomy expression on his face told her that he hadn't caught anything.

"Coffee?" she asked when he stepped inside.

He nodded.

Jenny shut the door behind him.

"The kitchen's this way," she said and led him through her house. It was a shotgun home that required barely more than five long strides to cross the living room. There was something about this moment that felt eternal, as though he had been coming to her house this way for years, and she experienced a familiarity about it all, even in the way his shoes sounded right behind her, the heavy footfalls of a man dejected but hoping for a moment of grace: salvation, if he was lucky.

"Let's do this first," he said when they reached the kitchen. "Please. Sit here?" He motioned to one of her own chairs, as though it were now his. He looked up at the kitchen's fluorescent lights and said, "This should work." He looked back down at her face and then up at the lights and then back down again. He said, "Okay then."

He opened the tackle box and removed square packets of disinfectants. He peeled one open – Jenny had to hold back a sneeze from the assault of the smell – and then he wiped the area where there was now a scar. Next, he removed a needle from the tackle box to administer the local anesthetic.

"I'm sorry," he said. "The first few injections are going to hurt. But you know that already."

"It's okay," Jenny said.

"Ready?" he asked.

Jenny nodded.

The surgeon inserted the needle multiple times into her temple until that side of her face felt numb and weird.

"You're crying," he said.

She shook her head to indicate that she was okay, that it was nothing. When she was a child, she would sometimes become overtaken by an emotion. Even her parents were speechless by her sudden and frightening expressions of joy – joy that was usually flanked by a bottomless sadness. She had never felt she belonged in this world, let alone in her parents' bungalow with a room full of toys made in countries she would likely never visit.

Dr. Reynolds tore open another disinfectant wipe and cleaned her face, and then he removed the scalpel. On a wall, framed, was the drawing he had given her. She had hung it there as a joke, but he stared at it now, as though trying to place where he had seen it.

"My wife left me last month," he said.

"Oh God. I'm sorry to hear that," Jenny said.

"It's funny how things happen, isn't it?" he said. "Who knew when you walked into my office that I'd be standing in your kitchen today." He stared vacantly past her, as though unsure where he was. He cleared his throat and said, "I need you to hold this gauze against your cheek." He handed her a pad of gauze from his tackle box.

"I brought ice," he said. "I'll take the sample back to the office tonight."

"Not before I make you coffee," Jenny said.

"A cup of coffee sounds good," he said. "Especially on a night like this. Now hold that gauze right here." He guided her wrist up so that her hand was higher on her cheek. But then he twisted her wrist, hard, causing her to flinch. "What the hell's this?" he asked. He pressed his fingers harder into her arm.

Her sleeve, she realized, had crept up, exposing new cut marks. She hadn't cut herself since high school, but lately she had begun again. The first new cut had been out of curiosity. She had wondered if it would conjure the same feeling she had experienced when she was a teenager experimenting with a box cutter. It hadn't. When she had cut herself all those years ago, it was because the pain of living in this world was too much to bear and she didn't know what to do with such a strong emotion. What she discovered this time around was that she liked the act of cutting. Furthermore, she liked the pain.

"Don't do that to yourself," Dr. Reynolds said. "Do you hear me?" His loosened his grip and ran his fingers across the fresh cuts, almost too lightly, causing an unexpected shiver to run through her. "These are sloppy," he said. "You don't even know what you're doing." He pushed her sleeve all the way up. He picked up his scalpel and said, "Here, let me show you." He held the tip of the scalpel against the bony part of her forearm. "Notice how my hand is positioned," he said. "Now look at the position of the blade. Are you looking?"

"Yes."

He pushed in and, slowly, drew a line across her arm. For a moment she wasn't even sure he had cut her except for the fact that she could see the clean incision. The cut was deep enough that it took longer than normal for blood to appear...even longer for her to feel the pain. When the cut began to pulse, she shut her eyes.

"Another?" he asked.

She nodded. She felt an emotion, but she couldn't put a word to it. It eluded her, residing in the margins of vocabulary, a grainy figure in the shadows.

"I could do this all day long," the surgeon said. "It's what I'm good at."

He cut her again.

"Another?" he asked.

She opened her eyes. She nodded.

"Just one more," she said, and because she had been taught to be polite, she added, "Thank you."

She heard rain hit the tin roof of her shotgun house as he cut into her arm. The wet streets would likely turn to ice by morning. Jenny believed that the window to fall in love had passed her by, but this thing that was happening between her and Dr. Reynolds tonight was better than loneliness. She was grateful for it, whatever it was. As with everything in her life, the situation was complicated.

As the surgeon soaked up blood from her arm, she felt tears on one side of her face, but on the other side she felt nothing at all.

TORONADO

BY MANNY TORRES

Thank you, Whitney

"They call you the car whisperer," Snowman said.

"Never heard that one," said Gallo.

This was a repair shop in Miami. Salsa blasted from a boombox sitting on the supply shelf.

"You fix cars, but you drive them too," Snowman said. He'd casually strolled into Diamond's Auto Repairs and the other mechanics lowered their heads or went about their work. Whenever one of Mambo Saviano's men walked in, it was either to collect, or to ask a favor.

Someone lowered the volume of the music.

Gallo Devita was elbow deep inside a white 1958 DeSoto Firesweep seeing if the backbone of the engine was structurally sound as sometimes a minor fracture was wont to disable an old relic. Sharp tailfins anticipated spaceflight, or at least rocketlike acceleration.

"Gotta test drive my work," Gallo said. "Don't I?"

23

"But you *drive,* right? Cars. People. You make deliveries."

Gallo looked at him from an angle. "Not anymore. I don't coyote, I don't transport illegal substances, or illicit packages. No getaway driving, or diamond heists."

"Diamond heists? That's still a thing?"

Gallo's face was stone. "Just laying it out for you right now."

Snowman chuckled. He was a tall, linebacker of a black man, wearing a striped blazer, slacks, bucket hat and boat shoes. *Polo* boat shoes from what Gallo noticed. He could smell his cologne from where he stood.

"Mr. Saviano knew you to have a soft touch when it comes to certain cars," he said.

Gallo spoke while working. "You have to treat your machines with kindness if you want them to work for you. Treat them gently. Speak nicely to them. You'd be surprised how motivating that is. They'll get you home safely and not breakdown when you're at the grocery store."

Snowman shook his head. "All that whispering shit sounds like magical realism."

"We Colombians invented magical realism."

"You sure did. I'm more of a pussy whisperer myself."

Gallo kept working. His face was sharp and angular, squinty eyes, with a neat mustache and soul patch. Hair kept short. Naturally tanned.

Lean and muscular. Wearing a tank top, with a gold crucifix tight against his throat. No tattoos.

"Mambo Saviano is dead," Gallo said.

"While we sort out his effects, we need to relocate his assets."

Gallo nodded. Wasn't the first favor he'd been paid to do by the Saviano family.

Snowman went into his jacket pocket and pulled out an envelope and a key on a ring.

"What kind'a repairs we talking about?" said Gallo. "Like, *repair* repairs, or *something else?*"

"Car's working perfectly. I mean, it needs a good tune up."

Gallo pulled up from under the hood. He looked over Snowman's shoulder, past the other mechanics and to the exterior of the shop. He could see where Snowman had parked his big, black Cadillac Escalade.

"Oh, it ain't here," Snowman said. "It's gathering dust at an impound yard."

"The Feds confiscated it?"

Snowman laughed. "Don't try me, man. The car needs relocation. It's over at Dan's impound. I need you to drive it up to Odyssey where a collector paid a lot of money for it. Just like last time, only you don't have to drive out of state."

He handed Gallo the envelope. Gallo looked inside: registration papers, and cash.

"Odyssey?" Gallo said. "Why don't you just hire a car service? Probably cheaper than what you're paying me."

"Like I said, it needs a tune up. We want to keep this transaction in the family."

Gallo wiped his hands, closed the hood of the DeSoto and limped around it, inspecting it. Admiring it. There were rust spots he'd sanded over and patched up. It needed a lot of love, but the thing was a tank that would outlive them all.

"How's the nub?" Snowman pointed at his leg.

Gallo flipped him off. "How'd it get impounded?"

"Fuck if I know, man. Hard to keep shit organized since Mambo died and I'm handling his estate. You should see the wine cellar I gotta relocate. The car went missing a few days ago but was found illegally parked in Palmetto Bay. Mufuckas couldn't just put a boot on it. Have I ever misled you?"

Gallo didn't answer. This is what happened when you accepted a favor from the Saviano family, and they kept coming back for reciprocation.

"I'm checking that car, top to bottom," Gallo said. "I told you, I don't do courier work anymore. Talk to Baron about that if you need to. I'm not transporting any *thing* or any*body*. If the car's not clean, it stays in the impound yard. And you don't get your money back."

Snowman cleared his throat.

"Gallo," he said. He pronounced it *GAL-OH*.

"I told you before, it's pronounced *GA-YO*. Like a rooster. A cock."

Snowman grinned and shook his head. After stroking his chin, he said,

"Just a car, man. You can't miss it. A 1966 Oldsmobile Toronado. Slick, shiny, and black. Just like me."

"That's a sweet ride," said Gallo. "Mambo brought it in once for service."

"Just drive it from point A to point B. Easiest two grand you ever made. Per diems included. Make sure you clean up before you go. Don't wanna fuck up the interior."

"Yeah, I'll wear a tuxedo."

***

"Bitch, you said you'd never come back to Dade County," Layla said. She was one of those skinny model types with big, bright, blue eyes, golden hair extensions, always complaining about her kids, her ex-husband, or the new guy that wouldn't text back. Toned arms from weekly gym visits, tattoos, and stars in her eyes. "You swore on your mom's grave you would never come back here."

Every Florida bar was a ratchet hot mess of bad service, watery drinks, dancing cougars and MILFs, sports TV, loud, shitty nu-metal from twenty years ago, and wall-to-wall gorilla juiceheads. There was a row of high-top tables stretching the length of the bar, overstuffed with drunk but enthusiastic sports fans. Darling Penny stood and stretched as if coming up for air, her face pinched with disappointment. Not at how much the place had changed, but how she'd changed and everything and everyone around her was still the same.

"But, I'm glad you're here, baby," Layla said. She wrapped both arms around her and squeezed. "Yay! Sisters, back together again!"

Darling was shorter than Layla, had a lot more curve to her hips. Her hair was a cardinal shag of waves and curls on the brink of messiness. She tried her best to hide the bruise under her eye. Tomorrow it would turn black.

"I said I'd come back, but only for a funeral," Darling said. She snatched a tequila shot from one of the passing mouth breathers. That was shot number four and she promised herself she'd stop after the tenth one. The place was a notorious date-rape environ. She kept a close watch on what was being served to Layla and her.

Layla propped herself close to Darling, nodding to emphasize that she was listening. Darling never knew her to be so concerned; it was performative, to say the least. But Layla was the only friend she had left in this town and the only person she trusted to share a bed with, even if for the night.

"How was the funeral?" Layla said.

The crowd erupted, fists pumping in the air. Darling got pushed and shoved by cheering lunkheads and had to read Layla's lips over the din of sports and music.

"Didn't get to go," Darling responded. She shouted and repeated every other sentence. She would have preferred to shut down the conversation all together, but Layla was her ticket for the night. Darling had slouched into town a few days ago. In her purse were five singles, a spent Visa gift card and an ATM card from an overdrawn account.

Layla said,

"How's Nashville? You make your record yet?"

"Just demoed some songs," Darling said. Already, she felt drained. The pulse of the bar and the drinkers had depleted her. "Too much talent already there. If you spit, you're bound to hit a singer in cowboy boots and hat hoping to be discovered in some tourist honkytonk."

Layla shook her head. Unclear. "Thought you were getting the inheritance."

"I kind of spent it already."

"You two ever get married?"

Darling shook her head.

"How much did he leave you?" said Layla.

"Not much. But the bastard had promised me *the* car. At least, he *should* have left it to me. He knew it was my favorite."

"The Mustang? Ooh, that's hot."

"No. The Olds. From the sixties. The big black one. Looks like the fucking Batmobile."

"Well, that's hot too. I'm sure resale will bring in some serious cash. And how'd you get that black eye? You think I didn't notice?"

Darling bit her thumbnail. She stood intimately in front of Layla, *tete-a-tete.* One of the brutes Layla had set her up with turned from the TV screens and grabbed her by the waist. The troop of man apes all had unibrows, rippled muscles, and studio tans. Made her stomach rumble. Darling pulled away. He turned back to the TV screens.

"Funny you should ask," Darling told Layla. She pointed her middle finger at the crescent bruise beneath her eye. "This and the Olds go hand in hand."

"Oh my god, did you take it?"

"I kind of drove it off his yard, then went to celebrate...instead of going to his funeral. Ran into some guy I used to date. Next thing I knew, I threw a punch at his ugly girlfriend, stuck a knife in his leg and took off."

"So, you got it parked outside? Let's cruise the beach, girl!"

"It's no longer in my possession, hon. You see, I kinda got arrested. DUI, assault. So, I had to bail myself out. That's where my inheritance went."

"Girl," Layla said. "Was it true? He was, you know, a *gangster?*"

"He was a lot of things: my mom's ex-husband, my stepfather, my boyfriend, *an asshole*. Now he's dead. He was always just a fucking bastard."

Layla shook her head, rolled her eyes. Finished up her vodka and tonic. Ordered another one. Took a shot of tequila while she waited.

"Dang, girl," Darling said. "You're too skinny to be drinking like this."

"Fuck you." Layla laughed. "Drink some more."

They got caught up in the festivities and Darling Penny couldn't help but indulge. Platter after platter of fried appetizers, more drinks, beers, and shots. Was this day four or five of her bender? In a few years she'd marry a nice guy and have several kids with him. But she'd crawl there on a road paved with debauchery and vomit.

"*This* girl's crazy, boys," Layla announced to the table. It was Darling, Layla, two gorilla juiceheads, and two random girls who'd driven down from Tampa for the weekend. Tampa girls were a special breed of privilege. Bleach-blonde hair, fake tits, fake asses, often in their forties, sometimes in their twenties looking like they were in their fifties. Their mantra was, *I want to speak to your manager.*

The game ended, their team lost. Half the bar cleared out, but they kept getting drinks. The juicehead tightened around her waist again. His name was Dax Breaushel, but they called him Breau. His buddy was Dick Ireland. One blonde, one brunette. Lots of muscles, fading hairlines, crisp studio tans.

"You ladies coming to the afterparty?" Breau said. Layla smiled and laughed, standing so small and fragile between them. Made Darling sick to her stomach. Layla wasn't the same person she'd been an hour ago. Or a year ago. She was the same performative, two-faced bitch though. Darling hated that.

The server came over to clear the table. Breau pressed against Darling.

"*I ordered us another round,*" he said.

Darling nodded and gently felt the bruise under her eye with a middle finger aimed at Layla who had been swept up by Dick. The lamp over their table was warm. She looked green underneath it. Darling's eyes bulged and her vomit extravasated over the table.

***

"Maybe it's something I ate," Darling said into the toilet. Layla looked over her from the stall door.

"I can't believe you did that," she said.

Darling wiped her mouth and cackled like an old witch. "*I* can."

"I've been trying to get with that guy for three weeks!"

"You said you already fucked him."

"I did, I just want to cuff him, you know? Let him get to know my kids."

"Uh huh," Darling said. "Where are they now?"

"With their dad."

"Huh. Where you working now?"

"I'm not. That's another thing," Layla whispered. "*He owns a yacht*. That's why I said, *let's go*."

Darling got off her knees and went to the sink to rinse off. She gargled and spit, fixed her face, fixed her hair. Her eyes were wide and sad, eyelashes fluttering like flytraps.

"Here." Layla handed her a stick of cinnamon gum and they walked back to the bar.

***

Those steroid freaks were well into their 30's. Layla and her were both 25. They crammed into Breau's silver Honda Accord where the music was deafening. They'd lost a man. Went off with the Tampa girls who'd taken a cab elsewhere. The mating call of a Tampa girl was to flash her tits before handing out her number, so it hadn't taken much convincing. Now it was Layla in the backseat with Dick, and Breau with Darling up front, touching her knee while her guts bubbled.

"I got some Molly," Breau said.

"So passé," Layla said. Again, perpetrating a different persona. "I just want some coke, man."

They drove into one of those gated condo complexes that used to be a resort. Stumbling drunkenly out of the car, Breau kept trying to kiss Darling. They struggled up to the second-floor landing. The apartment was two doors down on the right. When they entered, the place was neat and smelled of Axe Body Spray. Sports team posters on the walls, workout equipment crowding the living room, and a minibar by the faux fireplace.

"Make yourselves comfortable, y'all," Breau said. He went for Darling, who pushed past him.

"Thanks, I gotta go take a shit," she said.

***

Gallo walked from his apartment to the impound lot the next day. He brought along a set of tools in a canvas zip-up bag that he slung over his shoulder. He also brought a small bag with a change of clothes, since he was going out of town. The Olds occupied his thoughts a lot. He was looking forward to seeing this machine, a relic from a time when Americans drove tanks on newly paved highways, a time before monster truck SUVs, minivans, and Honda's with lawnmower engines took over the road.

***

Since they couldn't score any coke, and didn't want Molly, Layla thought it'd be great to crush her Adderall into powder and pass it around on a plate for everyone to snort.

Hanging out at the minibar, Darling took a shot of some cinnamon vodka that reminded her of toothpaste. Then she transitioned to tequila. The squeeze of lime was as close as she'd come to eating a salad all day. On the couch, Dick groped and kissed Layla as she perused through her phone. Darling glanced at a photo of them together that popped up from several years ago where they were both dressed in high heels and urban camouflage. Both giving the finger to the camera. Darling realized how much Layla hadn't changed. And that she no longer wanted to take on the personality traits of her cunt bestie.

***

Dan Camel's Towing Yard. The logo on the metal sign was a winking cartoon camel towing an old junker. Gate was chained. Guardhouse empty. A lone pit bull barked at him, nervously circling and pacing on the other side of the gate.

"Fuck," Gallo said. He was early.

Was your standard impound car lot, but not the place where a majestic vintage car should sit among tired, busted autos that'd been here for decades. Gallo knew exactly where it was parked because it was the only car on the lot covered with a blue tarp. He circled the fence line for a better glance, making out the shape under the cover. E-body, as most sporty autos from the early 60's had. Body size and style would reach fullness with the '67 Eldorado, though that car wasn't as slick as a '66. There was no body style quite like an Olds Toronado; it was shaped like Link Wray's slick back pompadour and tough enough to bounce at a roughneck

35

bar. The car had turned a lot of heads in 1966, and still did now. Sleek lines, hidden headlights, big ass interior; Gallo imagined the rogue shenanigans its previous owner got into in his day. A car that powered smoothly, even with a heavy front end. Rocket V8 was standard, hauling ass at 385 horsepower. He followed its sexy curves with one continuous glance. He'd never associated a piece of machinery, even a vintage car, with anything sexual, but that's how people liked to describe this antique. No doubt, it was a sexy beast.

An SUV turned the corner into the gravel parking lot and parked. A blond musclebound man and a small redheaded woman climbed out and waited for the yard to open. The man couldn't keep his hands off her and she frequently complained about it.

***

Last night.

"What's wrong?" Layla said.

Darling leaned her head in her open palm, elbow against the couch. "I'm bored."

"Oh my god! How can you be bored? I'm having such a great time here."

True narcissist says what? Darling thought. They didn't even put music on in the apartment. Just the TV to get more sports highlights.

"Did you want them to sing and read poetry to you?" Layla said. "Let's do whip-its and run up and down the hallway!"

Darling thrust her face into hers. "Let me just get my time machine and go back to *WHEN WE WERE IN FUCKING EIGHTH GRADE!*" She got up from the big leather couch and walked to one of the bedrooms. It was quieter in there. Once she laid down on the unmade bed, she managed to sleep.

When she woke up, the apartment was dark and quiet. She'd woken because Breau had his arm around her, cupping one of her breasts.

"Hey, fuck off!" She pulled away and sat up. He was dead asleep, drooling and snoring into the pillow. When she felt fully awake, she walked to the living room and saw Layla lying face down on the leather couch wearing only her thong. Darling stood over her, shaking her head. She covered her with a serape that was draped over one of the chairs. There was a condom wrapper on the floor. She recognized the brand Layla carried in her overnight hoe bag. Darling checked to make sure she was breathing, leaned in and kissed her forehead. She headed out when Breau stopped her.

"You just gonna take off without a goodbye?" he said. "Let me buy you breakfast."

"I gotta be somewhere. Think you can afford me a ride? It's on the other side of town."

"Afford you a ride?" Breau's smile was too big and too fake but fitting for his stupid face. "I'll afford you whatever you want, sweetheart."

This turd ain't from around here, she thought.

"You think so, huh?" she said.

He followed her outside, one hand on her shoulder, his other arm wrapped around her, bringing her in for a squeeze.

"Get off!"

Downstairs in the parking lot the sun was bright and happier than it should've been. She brushed herself off. His essence clung to her like dry sweat. She bunched her shoulder-length waves and curls with both hands to make them spring. The thing about having bushy, shaggy hair was that it never looked messy. Or perhaps, in her case, it always looked slept in.

***

Gallo stared at the lot, arms folded, the muscular edges of his biceps prominent under his tight black t-shirt. Darling stared at dozens of cars, arms out at either side of her, hands opening and closing, fingers twiddling to keep her blood flowing. Or in case she had to punch somebody.

Gallo was attractive, but she was too tired to be attracted to him. Plus, she didn't *feel* attractive right now, looking like a ragdoll someone had slapped around all night. But, hey, at least her makeup hadn't smudged. Her eyes were bright blue and maybe a little bloodshot.

Ugh, she thought. *Too early for this shit. I picked the wrong year to quit smoking.*

A pickup truck drove up close to the fence, having entered the parking lot from the opposite entrance. A young, skinny, pale kid jumped out wearing greasy overalls, wiping his crusty mouth on his sleeve. He walked to the guardhouse without saying anything and unlocked it.

"We open at ten," he said with his back to them.

"Not what it says on your sign," Darling said. "Kind of in a hurry."

"Dan has a hangover and I'm the only other one with keys," the kid said. "Let me get straightened out here. Takes my computer like five minutes to warm up. Plus, I gotta feed the dog."

Breau came up to her, putting his arm around her waist.

She growled,

"Stop it!"

Breau moved from her waist to her neck and clenched. She broke loose and went to the guardhouse and leaned on it impatiently. Gallo looked at Breau. His face tightened to a squint.

The kid walked out of the guardhouse on the other side of the gate, holding a clipboard. Darling followed him along the fence.

"Careful," the kid said. "Dog hasn't been fed yet."

On cue, the pit bull ran and slammed her face into the fence, barking and drooling. The dog was beautiful. Velvet gray with bright eyes and a fierce snarl. Her head was as big as Breau's helmet skull.

Breau reached for Darling. "Watch it, babe."

Darling twisted away from him, moving toward Gallo.

"Boyfriend?" Gallo asked as if Breau wasn't there. "He put that mouse under your eye?"

She found his sardonic tone at once appealing but beheld him with diffidence.

"That's the lady's business, buddy." Breau towered over her while staring hard at Gallo.

"Well, that answers that," Gallo said. "Which one's yours? The car, I mean."

She perused the yard. Couldn't find it right away. If it was even here. Why couldn't Saviano just leave it to her?

"It's an old one," she said. "I don't see it though."

"I'm here for an old one too," Gallo said.

The dog got riled and barked. And barked. The kid walked back to the guardhouse and came back out carrying a large bowl filled with moist kibble.

Breau let Darling go, and Gallo swore he heard him grunt. Breau stood impatiently, unsure of his next move. Unsure if he was going to lay Darling after all this.

"So, what kind of name is Darling?" Breau said.

The dog buried her face into the food bowl. The kid worked the locked chain. He clipped a questionable rope to the dog's collar that linked to the fence.

"Were you like, a porn star or something?" Breau said. He blew a kiss and made crude gestures with his hands.

"Ew." Darling held herself. "It was my grandmother's name."

The kid slid the gate open all the way and lazily invited them into the lot. The dog slopped up the remaining gravy in her bowl.

Gallo went in first, waved at Darling, and made a sharp left, walking the cluttered maze between cars. Three rows over and two rows back. Cars were parked closer than they should've been with only mere inches of space to pull out with. Among the rusted junkers, and confiscated pimpmobiles was a Belair, a Javelin, and plenty of tricked out Toyotas. They deserved better than being packed like sardines in this messy lot. The blue tarp told him exactly where he was going. Next to it was a 1987 Oldsmobile Toronado, and perhaps this was their own special filing system, keeping all the makes and models grouped together. This newer Toronado was a Trofeo. *Si, feo,* he thought about one of the dullest, most plastic looking auto failures he'd ever seen. An embarrassment they referred to as a Toronado. He could hear Darling saying,

"Let go of me, asshole!"

Gallo pulled the tarp off and stared. The black 1966 Oldsmobile Toronado glistened with chrome trimming, even if it was a little dusty. Tires muddy. But not neglected. Sleek fastback, low headroom, elongated doors, flat floor, and headrests. Red leatherette interior. Transmission combined a three-element turbine torque converter to a geartrain for three forward speeds. This car was the first front-wheel drive vehicle ever developed, with the intake manifold's unique shape depressed to allow for engine hood clearance. Cruising made easy with the manual shift option eliminated. All front-end torque responded easily, glided smoothly. 0-60 in 7.5 seconds.

Gallo admired it for a moment, whispered to it, remembering that this beauty had started out as a pencil sketch on paper, but Oldsmobile executives were hip to its futuristic styling. The name derived from a portmanteau of a bull, and a hostile weather pattern. He lifted the hood and looked around underneath. Adjusted a thing or two. From the smell of it, the Florida humidity was doing its thing to these innards. Sea air would do worse in time. It would easily make it to Odyssey, where he could really get greasy with it before turning it over to the new owner. He inspected the trunk, checked the tire hubs, under the chassis, under the hood door.

He called the kid over and showed him the registration and ownership papers. The kid looked clueless, clicking his teeth as he read. He read and read, not understanding. Gallo showed him his driver's license and his military ID.

"Well, thank you for your service, but this ain't your car." Took all of three minutes for the kid to clear his head to tell Gallo that.

Gallo heard Darling and Breau again between the other aisle of cars. Breau's verbal exchanges were of late-night desperation. Casting a net and seeing what he pulled in.

"I know it's not my car, genius," Gallo told the kid. "I've been paid to drive it out of here so I can give it a tune up and turn it over to its new owner."

"I'm gonna have to call my boss before I can release it."

"You're calling the guy with the hungover? Are you kidding me?"

"Sorry. Rules is rules." The kid walked back to the office.

Darling and Breau rounded the corner and stopped at the rear of the Toronado. Darling gasped.

"What, this?" Breau said. He laughed. "That's a grandpa car. Looks like a toupee."

"Sorry." The kid came back. His voice cracked with pubescence. "Can't reach my boss. But I left him a message. He'll call back later. Maybe this afternoon. You can wait at the guardhouse if you want. I'm gonna go grab some donuts and coffee."

"Listen," Gallo said. He yanked the kid's collar. He took the clipboard from him, did a quick onceover, signed the bottom of the page, and handed him several folded hundred-dollar bills. "Release is signed. Here's the fee, plus tip, and my business card if you need to reach me."

"I don't think that's kosher, sir," the kid said.

"Yeah?" Gallo got in his face. "The fuck you know about kosher? I got a key, and the title."

"This is my car!" Darling stomped past the kid. She got between him and Gallo, giving them each a shove. The kid threw a fit and walked off.

"This is Mr. Saviano's property," Gallo said. He could see Breau coming up behind her and prepared for the beating he was going to give the big jock if he stepped up disrespectfully.

"He's dead," she said. "And I'm his next of kin."

Gallo gave her a quick once over. Mambo was Cuban-Italian, with a very serious tan.

"Not biologically. He was my..." she looked down for a moment shaking her head.

"Sugar daddy don't count," Gallo said and put the key in the lock and opened the door. The red leather interior smelled fresh and recently polished. Double delta-shaped horn ring, speedometer like a slot machine. He sat inside and Breau pushed past her, clenching his shoulder, yanking him out. Breau was a brute, but Gallo had speed. He elbowed Breau's face, just as the pit bull rounded the corner. The dog went for Gallo's leg and chomped. That bite was no joke, tearing his jeans and revealing the below-the-leg prosthesis underneath. Gallo shook his leg and kicked the dog, and then got back inside the car, slamming the door shut. The dog turned around with little hesitation and lunged at Breau's balls. The big man struggled and hollered, slapping the dog's face as it tore his jeans, and gobbled the family jewels.

"Hey!" the kid called out. Not at the dog, but Gallo, who'd already shoved the key in the ignition. He cranked it. The engine was tired. He gave it several tries. The car groaned, like it was waking up from hypersleep. Again. Didn't catch.

"Gimme." While Gallo and Breau fought, Darling had avoided the dog by jumping into the passenger seat. She leaned over Gallo, twisting his fingers on the key and turning until it almost broke his wrist. Was then the Toronado rumbled to life.

"Why are you in here?" Gallo said.

The kid was struggling to get the dog off Breau while yelling at Gallo. He hammered at the window with his fist. Darling sat back, strapped in, letting the vibrations of the big engine rumble beneath her.

"Oh, baby," she said. "It's been almost a week. But mama's here."

"Get out," Gallo said.

"Don't yell." Soothed, and breathing deeply, she sank into the seat. "Just drive. We can sort this out later."

***

Darling told him she'd catch a bus back to Nashville from Odyssey. They argued like a married couple along the way. But she said he could keep the car. He said the Toronado wasn't his to keep, that he was taking it to its new owner. She said *okay, whatever, I'm off to Nashville.* They ate Cuban sandwiches at a gas station. A typical Florida monsoon fell and drenched the afternoon. He got a room at a cheap motel next to a Mexican place. Darling had seven tequila shots, and three margaritas and danced on the bar top until they were kicked out. Then they stumbled back to the room at 3am.

Here they were.

"How'd you get that wooden leg?" she said, lying on the bed. Going on two days wearing the same clothes.

Gallo looked at her from where he sat on the corner of the bed.

"It's not wood," he said. He lifted the metal, anatomically challenged extremity, and showed it to her. He rubbed lotion on his stump after drying off from the shower, then put on fresh jeans, having tossed out the pair that the dog had torn.

"Oh, sorry. You got that fighting a war?" she was slurring.

"Yeah."

"I've fought lots of wars before. Not like you, but they sure left wounds."

She yawned and turned over, facing the nightstand and lamp, coiled like a fetus. He stretched out on the bed. Watched TV, then stared at the ceiling. He turned to his side and reached for her. Caressed her smooth arm, her warm neck. Ran his fingers through her bushel of red hair. She hummed with approval. He urged closer, wrapping his arm around her waist, gently kissing her cheek. She spasmed and jerked. He sat up and she vomited across the room. Over the nightstand, on the wall, and the floor.

They cleaned it the best they could using up all the room towels. Afterward they slept as far from each other as they could. He dreamt of being under his cars. The satisfaction of the smell of oil, the grease on his hands, the tightening of bolts, the heat of the engines. The rumble, the roar.

Darling dreamed she lived in a cotton candy house and had to eat her way out of it.

When the sun came up, he jolted awake. The sun shined its brightest when leaking into the room through slivers in the curtains. He hadn't slept like that in weeks. Must have been the tequila. But he hadn't had nearly as many as...

He looked over and she was gone. His eyes shot toward the bathroom. Empty. Light off. The scent of dried vomit still lingered. He jumped out of bed, rubbed his eyes, and pulled the blinds open.

The front door opened into the parking lot, with all the cars facing the rooms. All except the Toronado, which was not in the spot where he'd parked it last night.

OUTLAW COUNTRY
BY J.D. O'BRIEN

What Ladd really wants is a meat-and-three at Arnold's Country Kitchen. Fried catfish, turnip greens, mac and cheese, corn pudding. Everything homemade. Served with a smile.

Instead, he and Esteves are idling in the drive-thru line at the Krystal on Charlotte Avenue. Sitting there like a couple of jerks. Hoping the kid working the heat lamps doesn't spit in their little cheeseburgers.

Before it closed in January, Arnold's Country Kitchen was the last place in Nashville a cop could get a decent meal on the house. You couldn't go snouting around for it every night, but if you dropped in occasionally, walked up to the counter in uniform, your money was no good.

When he became a Field Training Officer, Ladd made Arnold's a tradition with the rookies in his charge. Mostly to show them how cops used to be treated in this town. These days you rarely even get a free cup of coffee. And never at the places with the good coffee.

May as well be in San Francisco. Portland.

The Acura in front of them pulls ahead and Ladd rolls the patrol car up alongside the window. The sodas come right out. Just waiting on the bag.

Esteves sucks at his straw and looks at his phone. He's a decent kid. Barely twenty-five. Horizontal hairline over a round face with a thin strip of beard on it. Heavy for a young cop, though. Ladd didn't let himself go like that until he was past forty.

Another two minutes sitting there. Ladd gooses the siren and a guy with a manager tag comes to the window, says he's just waiting on the fries. Asks Ladd if he minds pulling around front to keep the line moving. "We'll run it right out to you."

"Not happening," Ladd says. "I'm sitting here until you figure it out."

By the time they get the rest of the order, a call has come in. A break-in at the George Jones Museum & Gift Shop, down on 2nd Avenue.

Ladd and Esteves arrive to find Marvin Milton, the building's owner, in a state of agitation. The ordeal has brought him straight from bed. He's in pajamas under his windbreaker and Ladd thinks he smells brandy on his breath. E&J. Like his old man used to drink. Milton looks to be in his early eighties, around the same age Senior would be if he was still careening around.

"Money missing?" Ladd says.

"No cash on the premises. We went out of business last month. Currently in the process of transferring items to the Country Music Hall of Fame. We've got the famous John Deere tractor here. Several guitars used on legendary recordings. But the only thing's gone missing is Possum's yellow Nudie suit."

Milton leads them to a shattered display case, a naked mannequin torso.

"Who's Possum?" says Esteves.

Milton looks rankled by the question.

"Possum's George Jones," Ladd says to Esteves. "Country-western singer."

"The Rolls Royce Silver Cloud of country-western singers," Milton says. "And the suit was a Nudie Cohn original. Custom made. Bright yellow with a constellation of rhinestone stars. Stunning embroidery patterns. The man was an artist."

"What would you say it's worth?" Ladd says, flipping a page on his pocket notebook.

"Jesus Christ," Milton says. "You think I could put a price tag on an item like that?"

Under the glow of the Second Fiddle marquee, strutting like a coyote in a bright yellow Nudie suit, Billy Dee feels like he's finally arrived in Nashville. Four months in Music City and it's been nothing but bad luck. Gutterballs on every roll.

He weaves through the sidewalk traffic outside the bars on Lower Broad. Nights when he's far gone, the honkytonk neon fogs together and he can picture what it was like in the seventies. When outlaws were rambling around down here.

Now he's still sober enough to make out the names in the lights.

Blake Shelton. Jason Aldean. John Rich. Fucking Kid Rock.

Tonight is about turning that around. Introducing Nashville to Billy Dee.

He's still breaking in the new name. His full name is William Drzewiecki. Rhymes with jet ski. Picture that in lights at the Opry. Even he can barely spell it, let alone pronounce it.

At one time he considered leaning into it. The first great Polish-American country singer. Get an accordion player, mix in some polka. Do a conjunto kind of thing. Didn't take. Better to keep it country. Break his name clean at the D, lop off the ugly mash-up of letters at the end.

Billy Dee. Like the Kristofferson song.

He ducks into Robert's Western World and has a shot of Wild Turkey at the bar.

The bartender compliments his suit.

"Used to belong to George Jones," Billy Dee says.

He orders another, double this time, to get his courage up.

On stage, a band of session pros runs through a Bob Wills number. See, that's the kind of sound Billy Dee needs behind him. The rolling piano, the weeping steel. The fiddle keeping everything on its feet.

Maybe after tonight. Not tomorrow exactly. A year probably.

When he gets out of prison.

He's got a backpack full of fireworks. That alone is enough to get him into trouble in Davidson County. But what he plans to do with them will land him on the eleven o'clock news. On the internet. And ideally on the radar of serious country music fans everywhere.

The key is to do something high-profile. Something unusual but not too serious. Should get him more than a week in county jail but doesn't need to be a ten-year stretch. Just enough to write a record and emerge an outlaw. Set himself apart from the bros who swapped their Stetsons for baseball caps. The skinny guys with Amish beards singing crybaby songs.

Other than David Allan Coe and Johnny Paycheck, none of the famous outlaw singers actually spent much time in prison. Merle Haggard was a small-time crook, but people only know the branded man out in the cold. The guy who turned twenty-one in prison, doing life without parole. People think Johnny Cash shot a man in Reno. The only time he did in Folsom and San Quentin was on stage.

There's an idea. When's the last time someone recorded a live prison album? Billy Dee could trash talk the guards, get the inmates riled up. Snake into his first song with them already cheering like it's over. The thought gets him so excited he almost jumps on stage with the band.

Not tonight. He grabs his bag and hits the street.

Outside, Billy Dee looks across Lower Broad at the spinning sign of the Ernest Tubb Record Shop. Home of the Midnite Jamboree. It closed right when he moved to town. Another fuck-you.

Walking south, he gets swept into a wave of bachelorette party girls. A dozen blondes in cowboy boots and tight dresses. All wearing pink sunglasses with big glitter dicks sticking up out of them.

Looks like they're going where's he's going.

After leaving the George Jones Museum, Ladd parks in a spot near Centennial Park so he and Esteves can finally eat.

They're a block up from Springwater, the oldest bar in Tennessee. Only a matter of time before it disappears like a short beer, Ladd figures. Put up another CVS, plant another Dollar Tree. That's the country now. We're sick and we're broke.

There he goes again.

He's trying to rein in the negativity. Especially on the job. Spare Esteves and everyone else the yesteryear act, the when-cops-were-kings bullshit.

A Field Training Officer is supposed to be a role model for new recruits. A beacon of morale and proper protocol. The fact that Ladd is an FTO at all is itself a sign of departmental decline.

Maybe Esteves and his group will turn things around. They're not wrestling the same demons. Ladd can't imagine tapping out a line on the dash with Esteves sitting there. The kid barely drinks. Smokes an electric cigarette. No side piece even. Just the live-in girlfriend, Penny. Baby son named Max. Saving for an engagement ring, he says.

Ladd takes it on home to an empty duplex near the reservoir. A soggy nightstand with a Las Vegas ashtray on it. He surrendered his wife and the house on Tanglewood seven years ago now. Playing the half-assed sugar daddy with Candace, a badge bunny dancer at the Hustler Club. He encouraged her to hang up the heels and set her up in a pad downtown. Then she wouldn't let him move in when his wife threw him out.

He remembers a run of weekly motel stays. Long sessions behind the glass-brick windows of a day-drinker bar, the seventh rail whiskey at a rolling boil in his gut, thinking severe thoughts. Candace has no idea how close he came to going O.J. on her ass. His ex-wife too.

So, good for Esteves. He won't be another chrome-dome at the cop bar. A divorced drunk with an axe to grind into somebody's head. Then again, criminals aren't getting any softer. Maybe the Esteves generation will get eaten alive. Have to call Ladd and his platoon of assholes out of retirement. Old guys kicking ass like in the Expendables movies.

"These burgers suck, man," Esteves says, unwrapping his third.

"Try again," Ladd says. "Maybe that one will be better."

He takes a sip of Sprite. Flat and watered down from sitting there.

A shot of Popov will breathe some life into it.

"Be right back," Ladd says. "Going to take a leak, have a smoke."

He gets out of the car, hoping Esteves didn't notice him palm the nip bottle when he grabbed the cigarettes out of his bag. Or wonder why he took his soda with him.

Ladd pisses in the park. Sits on a bench and lights an Old Gold. He pours the little plastic bottle into the big plastic cup. Swirls it around a little.

A slow night would be ideal. Leave here, take a twenty-five-minute shit somewhere, then cruise downtown until the bars close. Idle away the remaining hours in a speed trap by the overpass. Stretch a last vodka or two, sipping it in coffee. Zone out and watch the taillights blur on the Natchez Trace while Esteves dicks around on his phone. The museum robbery won't require much of a write-up.

When Ladd gets back to the car, Esteves tells him another call just came in. Like the radio read his mind.

An incident at the Wild Beaver Saloon.

"Sounds pretty serious," Esteves says.

The guy who sold Billy Dee the fireworks told him they were like M-80s, cherry bombs. The kind of thing a kid would put in a school toilet as a prank.

The idea was to go to the Wild Beaver Saloon, sing a rebel song at karaoke, and blow the ass off the mechanical bull. Strike a blow for authenticity. A middle finger to all that Nashvegas bullshit.

Billy Dee put in his song ticket and had two more Wild Turkeys at the bar while he waited. When he got called, he did "I'm The Only Hell (My Mama Ever Raised)" by Johnny Paycheck and announced the arrival of Billy Dee to all in attendance. He probably mentioned his name five times.

Something he regrets now.

The bar and karaoke was hopping, but there was no line for the mechanical bull, and no one paid attention to him when he got on. He thought it'd be more of a spectacle, but the thing just half-heartedly bucked around in front of a cheap barn backdrop.

With no one watching, it was easier than expected to open his bag and wrap the firecrackers around the saddle horn. Five or six tubes with Chinese letters on them. All strung together in a chain with a longer thread hanging off the end.

The fuse.

Billy Dee did a sideways flop off the bull and sparked his lighter while he rolled over on the safety mat. He made it through the gate and moved at a fast clip toward the door.

He got about halfway there before he had to duck.

Comets whistled in every direction. The giant antler chandelier came down in a rain of electric blue sparks. Bartenders were shelled by skyrockets, liquor bottles exploding on the wall behind them like they were being machine-gunned. These were clearly outdoor fireworks. Designed for Fourth of July spectaculars.

New fires were starting every second. He counted six before being tackled by a giant bouncer with a Taser in his hand. Somehow Billy Dee got hold of the Taser. Bit the bouncer in his fat neck with it before running out with the rest of the crowd.

Now he's back in his room at the Drake Motel.

Stay Where The Stars Stay, the sign says.

He takes off the suit and hangs it carefully in the closet. The theft of George Jones' Nudie suit was intended to be symbolic. The plan was always to keep it pristine and return it.

He wishes he'd gone through with his idea to steal the John Deere tractor instead. The one George drove to the liquor store when Tammy Wynette hid his car keys. Just pull out of the museum and turn onto Broadway. There's a liquor store right there. Walk in and buy a bottle of whiskey. Walk out and get arrested. Write a novelty song about it. He'd be in trouble but nothing like he is now.

He paces in front of the bathroom mirror, listening to the thump of bass from the room next door. Someone left electric clippers in the drawer and he gets an idea to shave his head. Eyebrows first, then work his way back. Just short of the crown, the clippers run out of juice. He can't go any further.

He turns on the news. Expecting to be there but still shocked by what he sees. A fleet of firetrucks. Gurneys rushing into ambulances. A reporter on the scene talking about terrorism.

The bass coming through the wall is deafening now. He can barely hear the TV. He stands on the bed and knocks hard on the wall above the headboard.

Time to get out of here. The cab driver will see the news and remember the suit. Remember where he dropped him. He puts on a dungaree jacket and grabs his bag.

The bass ramps up, even louder since he knocked. Billy Dee steps outside and sees a Ford F-150 parked outside the room next to him. Alabama plates.

He grabs the Taser out of his bag and walks up to the door.

"We're looking at six dead," Rodriguez, the lead investigator, tells the officers assembled outside the Wild Beaver Saloon. "Probably more. Too early to tell. We've got people who are severely burned. Someone had an epileptic fit."

He goes down the checklist of what's been established so far.

The suspect identified himself as Billy Dee. White, about five-eleven. One-seventy-five. Maybe late thirties. The bartender who served him was rushed out in an ambulance with glass in her eyes. The only other person who interacted with him was the bouncer, who went into cardiac arrest when the suspect used the bouncer's own Taser on him.

There was another tidbit. Several eyewitnesses mentioned a bright yellow rhinestone suit.

After the briefing, Ladd tells Rodriguez about the museum robbery. Describes the suit in more detail. Thinks maybe it will bring him and Esteves into the inner circle of the case.

Rodriguez is casual about it. Just takes down the information and tells Ladd and Esteves to join the officers out covering the airport.

"We need all access points locked up, Frank. Sounds like you have a good handle on what he's wearing. Keep an eagle eye out."

Ladd has always sensed Rodriguez doesn't respect him. The way he says his first name, Frank, always has some sarcasm behind it. At least to Ladd's ears. But he's in no position to elbow in on this.

Headed east on I-40 toward the airport, a report comes over the radio about an assault and vehicle theft at the Drake Motel.

"That's on Murfreesboro Pike," Ladd says. "Next exit."

"Aren't we supposed to go to the airport?" Esteves says.

"Fuck that," Ladd says.

He flashes the lights and radios in, telling dispatch he's in the vicinity.

There are two rookie officers on the scene when Ladd and Esteves arrive. Ladd takes command, instructing them to round up witnesses so he can start taking statements.

When Ladd checks the room, he finds a set of clippers and some hair on the bathroom floor. And bright yellow Nudie suit hanging in the closet.

He speaks to the motel manager who says the guy in Room 146, the guy who attacked the couple and stole the truck, was named William something. She shows him the register.

William Drzewiecki. Billy Dee.

The couple who were assaulted are still shaken up. Their room smells like crack smoke.

"We was playing Name That Tune when this guy bust in with a Taser," the heavy redhead woman says. "Then he run off in Edgar's truck."

Edgar looks embarrassed about it. Standing there with his head down, scratching the back of his neck.

"He come out of nowhere," Edgar says. "Weird looking. Only had hair on the back end of his head. No eyebrows even."

"He take anything else?" Ladd says.

"Just the truck."

Edgar gives him the make and model again, the plate number. Ladd calls it in. Along with the suspect's full name and the info about the suit. He wants it all on record. No one's going to swipe the credit this time.

"I should mention there's a gun in the truck," Edgar says. "AR-15. I got a license, and it's secured in the lockbox, but it's there."

"Where's the key?"

"It's on the ring with the rest of 'em," Edgar says. "That guy has it."

In a way, Billy Dee got what he wanted. He's all over Nashville radio.

Up to eleven dead now. Several more seriously injured.

This is worse than any country song scenario he's ever heard. He remembers the old joke about losing your wife, your dog, your job, your truck. Billy Dee never had those things to begin with.

Well, he does have a truck. For now, anyway.

The rear left tire is on rims by the time he hits McGavock Pike. He blew it out speeding away from the motel. All that shit in the road by the auto body shops. There was no spare, but he made a discovery in a lockbox.

The AR-15 that's now riding on the passenger seat beside him.

He holds it steady while the pick-up skids into the lot of a strip mall.

Billy Dee steps out and looks around, the gun down by his side. There are three establishments in the strip. The Nashville Palace, the Willie Nelson & Family General Store, and Cooter's Dukes Of Hazzard Museum.

He takes aim and lights up the entrance to Cooter's, the alarm already going as he kicks the door in.

He's actually been meaning to come here since he moved to town. He loved the Dukes of Hazzard as a kid. They've got all the vehicles from the show here. A bunch of original merchandise. Things he remembers like yesterday turned into memorabilia. The lunchbox he had, the toy cars, even the old General Lee bed he always wanted. The clothesline of Daisy Duke shorts brings back later childhood memories. He wonders what Catherine Bach looks like now. Must be in her sixties.

The Dukes theme was the first country song he ever loved. But there's a different Waylon tune running through his mind now.

This here outlaw bit has done got out of hand.

"We headed to the airport?" Esteves says.

"What does he need to go to the airport for?" Ladd says. "He's got a truck."

"Maybe he's driving the truck to the airport."

"I don't think so."

"So where's he going?" Esteves says.

"That's what I'm trying to figure out."

The business with the Nudie suit, broadcasting his name at karaoke, bombing the mechanical bull, the odd-duck haircut. This guy's not skipping town, Ladd thinks. He's trying to make himself seen. So what's next? Music Row? Country Music Hall of Fame?

Then he hits on it.

"The Grand Ole Opry," Ladd says.

"What about it?"

"That's where he's headed."

Ladd switches on the siren and hits the gas.

"Hot pursuit," Esteves says.

It's good to feel like a cop again. Ladd's been phoning it in for a few years. Dreaming about moving to Florida. A Catamaran Cruiser in Coconut Key, happy hours at Dolphin Tiki. Getting by on his pension, maybe working marina security part time.

Tonight will earn him some credence. One last win to go out on.

They're on McGavock, almost to Opry Mills, when Ladd sees an F-150 abandoned in a strip mall lot. Still running.

The country music blaring from the truck speakers mixes with the sound of the alarm from the Dukes of Hazzard shop at the end of the strip.

Ladd parks at an angle with the pick-up truck between the patrol car and the door. Esteves waits while Ladd checks the lockbox for the rifle.

"Box's empty," he says when he gets back. "So he's armed in there."

Ladd calls it in. Dispatch says backup is on the way.

"We waiting on them?" Esteves says.

"We can take the lead, but we need to play this right," Ladd says. "There'll be a million eyes on this. But we're first on the scene. We found the guy."

He and Esteves bump knuckles.

"I'm going to text Penny," Esteves says. "Tell her to turn on the news."

"Call her when it's over," Ladd says. "Play the hero."

Esteves nods his head, a little jumpy.

Then he shoves the passenger door open and vomits out the side of the car.

"You alright?" Ladd says.

"Just nervous, man." He hangs his head out there a little longer. "And I think it was those Krystal burgers too."

"Think about something else. Clear your mind."

Esteves closes the door and swishes some soda around in his mouth.

They sit there another second.

"You remember that question you asked the other night," Esteves says. "About whether I could name one example of something new that's better than what was there before?"

"Right."

"I forgot to tell you, I thought of one."

"What is it?"

"Recliner seats at the movies."

"The seats are better," Ladd says. "But now the movies are no good."

Sirens are approaching now. The cavalry is almost here.

"I'm ready," Esteves says, unstrapping his holster.

Ladd doubts Esteves spends much time at the range. But sometimes these kids surprise you. All the video games, probably.

"When it's time, I'll go ahead in front," Ladd says. "You just hang back and cover me."

That one cop car has been out there a while. Now the rest of them are descending. Billy Dee can hear the sirens.

He doesn't see any way out of this.

There will be no country music career. No tour bus with his name on it. No premium bourbon endorsement. No refusing a CMT award out of protest.

He's moved beyond all that fame shit. He's gunning for immortality now.

He goes out the rear exit of the museum into the alley. He considers hiding in the dumpster, opening fire on whoever opens the lid. But that's no way to go.

Maybe he should break into the Nashville Palace. As close to the Grand Ole Opry as he's going to get at this point. Walk out on stage holding the rifle like a guitar. Watch the room fill up with law. Biggest audience he'll ever have.

He's headed toward the back entrance to the venue when he's sees a ladder up to the roof. He remembers that tall wooden sign out front, like a saloon in an old western movie. Designed for an outlaw to hide behind.

He climbs up.

A matter of seconds at this point. Cop cars are thick on the ground, swarming from all directions. A helicopter closing in. The first two cops are out of the car now, guns up, one behind the other. Still ten feet from the building.

They have no idea he's up here.

Billy Dee gets into position. He's got a clear shot on the guy in back, but with this kind of artillery he ought to be able to get them both.

Just need to get off two quick shots before they look up.

Coconut Key, Florida. Three Years Later.

Ladd has told the story so many times, even he's sick of it now. But every time Billy Dee is in the news again, Ladd's picture comes up on the screen and suddenly he's the most interesting guy at Dolphin Tiki that night.

There's always at least one person at the bar who hasn't heard it. Some embellishments have been added in the retelling, but he's careful to balance the heroism with some self-deprecation.

Not that it was all that heroic. Billy Dee got off one shot, which drilled Esteves through the skull. The kick must have been something because the rifle slipped out of his hand and fell from the roof of the Nashville Palace. With Billy Dee right behind it. The rifle landed before he did, sending a round ricocheting around the lot.

Ladd caught a shot in the thigh, but the bullet came from somewhere behind him. From Esteves's gun, it was later determined. Either a death-flinch trigger squeeze or he fired too late and too low. The poor bastard. The department did their best to keep that part quiet, but it all came out eventually.

Ladd retired on a full pension after being shot in the line of duty. He's always felt there was an asterisk on that but fuck it. He's got a houseboat and a local bar within golf cart distance. No DUIs that way.

When he winds down the story, he always steps off his stool, pulls his Bobby Bermuda shorts up an inch and shows off the scar from the bullet wound. Says he's damn grateful it didn't go any higher.

Someone asks him if he's going to watch that new movie they're making about Billy Dee. The one they were talking about on TV.

"Not unless they go back in time and get Robert Mitchum to play me," Ladd says.

But that's bullshit. If they make a movie, even a lousy one, he'll dine out on it for the rest of his life.

Ladd tells Angie at the bar he'll have another Suffering Bastard.

He puts a twenty down but it's just to be polite. She slides it right back.

"Your money's no good here, Frank. You know that."

SUPPER'S READY
BY JEAN-PAUL L. GARNIER

You've heard of those no-light dinners, you know where you eat in the dark and can't see each other. It's supposed to be one of those great first date ideas where you don't judge each other on looks. As if judging each other by the noises you make while eating is better. So, I'd made the mistake of setting up something like that for diplomats visiting the space station. All being different species with different eating habits, I was worried when the brass sent down the tubes that I would have to host a dinner party for all of the emissaries visiting. I tried to tell them that my job wasn't to entertain, I had a station to run for God's sake. But they didn't care. If relations didn't stay good, then my job would be irrelevant anyway. No trade relations, no trade. I reluctantly agreed and silently cursed them. Someone up there must have it out for me.

As the guests arrived, I looked every one of them up and down, all those different physiologies, many of them clearly offensive to the other guests.

These kinds of meetups were uncommon. And now I knew why. It was one thing talking to an eight-foot slug, but watching one eat...that's how it dawned on me. There was a way to do this without everyone having to go through revulsion while dining.

Our tech department had out-shined all of the other departments recently by creating a pill that would temporarily make the one who swallowed it invisible. That thing would barely hit the stomach before kicking in, and oh boy was it weird to see someone disappear before your eyes. You could see right through them, but that wasn't really what was happening. Somehow it did something to the way cells interacted with light around them. Don't really get it myself, but I'm an administrator, not a science guy.

Anyway, I thought it might be a novel way to get around having to watch each other eat, and judging each other in whatever way that was going to happen. So, as the guests rolled into the mess and I did my best to pitch the idea.

"Welcome everyone. It's a great honor to have so many dignified guests with us tonight. As a special treat, I'd like to roll out one of our new developments, one we think you all will be interested in, and we hope to share the benefits with you."

The pitch went fairly well. I heard a few interested grumbles from the crowd. And no one seemed offended outright. At least as far as I could tell. Different species don't really have the same types of facial expressions, and some have no faces at all. It's definitely one of the many barriers to interspecies communication. Again, I wondered why they would put someone like me in charge of this gathering.

Everyone lined up and took their pill. A few absorbed it into their orifices, others ingested it in ways I didn't understand. The boys in the lab assured me that it would be safe for any physiology, and I sure hoped that they were right. It was no time for Guinea pigs, human or otherwise.

One by one they vanished. Typically, in the order that they had been lined up in. But it took longer with a few of them, which made me worry. I could hear everyone take their seats, and a few of them I could smell, but other than that the room appeared empty.

Polite conversation ensued. I was grateful that politics hadn't come up yet. And I had wisely made everyone wait before dinner, my hope was that the food would be more of a focus than talking shop. One by one, the waiters brought out all manner of dish. The meal was as varied as the company. For some of us eating, the guy next to your meal could be deadly. That wouldn't do for a diplomatic dinner, so the waiters had to announce every dish that arrived, further interfering with any forced small talk. So far, things were working out smoothly.

Until the meal started. I had intentionally not dimmed the lights, thinking that the novelty of not seeing each other sitting there might be interesting. Regret followed that decision. Customarily, I took the first bite. And as I looked down my mistake became crystal clear, much like my body. The food wasn't invisible. I couldn't see it being chewed up, would have needed a mirror for that. But I watched the smashed-up food slide down my esophagus and plop down into my stomach like shit working its way back up. And oh God, it would be worse later, if the pills didn't wear off before the whole digestion process.

Some of the guests seemed amused by this. But again, laughter and most vocal expressions vary pretty widely between species. They all started eating. It was gruesome. It was terrible. It was everything I had hoped it wouldn't be. Damn my stupid idea. Watching the inner working of various species was infinitely more horrorshow than whatever social faux-pas I thought I was avoiding.

And, of course, there was no muting the sounds. Most humans don't make the loveliest sounds while eating, and as for my alien companions, I could only guess what they thought. But the symphony of chewing and swallowing was enough to make the food come back up. And that was all *before* watching the food go down in so many different ways.

I rang for the waiter, desperately sweating and trying to stifle my nausea. Fortunately, or not, I wasn't the one to flash first. But once it got started, that purplish blue fountain of a jet that erupted out of the guy at the end of the table, it clearly wasn't going to stop. The sickness spread, and with it all the sounds became more grotesque, as well as the smells. The miasma was enough to cause nausea and a negative feedback loop began to develop. It was a complete disaster, but I couldn't think of anything to fix the situation while I was busy being sick. An empty room with vomit flying everywhere, it was surreal. And sick led to sick. Maybe I should have turned the lights off after all.

Next time, God forbid, I'll have to go with one of those dark dinners.

THEY LIGHT THEMSELVES ON FIRE

BY MEAGAN LUCAS

Olivia was so pissed off she didn't notice anything was wrong. She cursed at him under her breath, stripped off the platform stilettos that were stupid for the airport but necessary to keep Harrison's eyes on her, and started up the stairs. Her plane pill cocktail had long since worn off and she'd had nothing to take the edge off the ride home. It was her fault that she hadn't packed enough, she didn't know the trip was going to be that rough. But the rest, the rest was his fault. All she'd been thinking about for the last two hours was escaping into that orange bottle in her nightstand and forgetting.

"No one made you come," Harrison said, bourbon already in hand.

Barefoot, on the bottom step, she searched his face for even a sliver of regret. *Goddamn he was an asshole.* She gripped the spiked heel of her shoe and thought about standing on his chest wearing them. Stepping on his face. On his cock. *He'd probably like that though*, she thought, reminding herself of what she'd found on his computer. This trip was supposed to fix everything. Ever since he'd announced this book tour, and she'd announced she was coming too, she'd dreamed that seeing all those places together, fucking in all those hotel rooms, would reignite something. Take them back to when every story was about her. When her skin, her curves, were his muse. But she definitely wouldn't call coming back from the bathroom to find her husband in the airport lounge with another woman's hands down his pants, fixing the problem. Maybe it was the pounds that she'd put on, maybe it was the new lines on her face, maybe that's what kept him from meeting her eyes when she smiled at him, what kept his hands from ever finding her body. Or maybe it was all the bourbon, and the nudes in his DM's.

She threw a shoe at his head. He ducked. It landed with a hollow thunk on the marble floor. He took a sip of his drink. She realized he didn't even care enough to yell anymore.

It was Harrison who saw something first. Too distracted by the open basement door to bother about the shoe, "Why isn't this closed," he said, and then disappeared down the stairs.

She bit her lip. He did everything he could to put distance between them. She never went down there. *What did it matter that the door wouldn't stay shut? What was he doing down there?* She wondered if he even knew how long they'd been married. If he remembered that in only six more months she could divorce him and actually get paid. The prenup had been his mother's idea. Old money didn't trust young women in short skirts. Olivia hadn't even blinked. They were going to grow old together.

She felt her pills calling to her from the bedroom. She followed their song but when she opened her nightstand, she only found a variety of vibrators and the gun that Harrison didn't know she had. "We're Democrats," he'd say in that way that made her feel one inch tall. But he also didn't care if she felt scared in her own home, *so fuck him*, she thought. *Where are those pills?* "Where are my pills?" she screamed.

In the bathroom, she took off her jewelry, her lashes, and her makeup. Peeled off her Spanx. Breathed deeply for the first time all day. Slipped on a silk nightie. She opened the vanity drawer to get her second stash, but they were gone too. She opened the drawer below and then every drawer in their bathroom. Dumped everything on the floor. Lipsticks, eye pencils, cotton swabs, tiny jars of cream she spent too much money on, band aids and nail polish, and tweezers, it all skittered across the tile until she was standing in the middle of a disaster, sobbing. Olivia held her face in her hands. *Where were they?* "Fuck," she screamed, hoping that Harrison would come, but knowing that he wouldn't.

Then every drawer in their bedroom. She was sure there were more. She must have put them somewhere she thought was safer while they were away. She ripped everything apart until the floor was covered with bras and panties, t-shirts and socks. The tour had obviously turned her brain to mush. *Where had she left them? She'd never had this problem before. He must have moved them. Taken them? Thrown them away? Given them to one of his girlfriends?* She brushed and flossed and checked under her mattress just in case, before she climbed into bed to stew. She was exhausted. She'd clean up this mess tomorrow. Or wait for the cleaning lady to do it.

When eventually Harrison came to bed in just his boxers, her eyes followed his body, it's muscles and lines, the way his chest hair was getting a little bit grey at the top. She knew why the other woman couldn't keep their hands off him. She just didn't know what was wrong with her that he couldn't keep his to himself. She slipped one of her gown's spaghetti straps down her shoulder.

"Christ," he said, looking around at the mess.

"I can't find my pills," she said as he got under the covers.

"I'm tired," he said.

It wasn't just the rumors. Or even catching him herself. She remembered how the booksellers, and Harrison's agent, and the publicist, had looked at her with pity. Her cheeks burned with embarrassment knowing that they all knew exactly how little regard he had for her.

"Did you take them?" she asked.

"Really?" he snorted, scrolling his phone.

"They didn't walk away on their own."

"Christ, Olivia. You obviously took them. You were high as a fucking kite the whole tour," he said rolling on to his side, plugging in his phone. "It was embarrassing."

"I'm embarrassing?" she balked. "I should have cut your dick off."

He sighed deeply, grabbed his phone and left.

Olivia rolled over and tried not to cry. Tried not to think about the dreams she'd had for them before: babies, and a dog, and Christmas card photos. Tried not to think about how she thought marriage meant she wouldn't feel so alone and anxious. Tried to remember where she left her fucking pills. *They were here somewhere.*

Harrison was already downstairs when Olivia woke up. She felt like shit and needed her meds. She fixed her hair and face, but decided to keep the sexy nightie on, before heading to the kitchen. He was right about that basement door though; it was unsightly that it kept popping open.

"It's nearly noon," he said.

"That's your excuse?" she said nodding at the bottle of Larceny on the counter.

"Since we're home early, I've got to go to Atlanta today. Spend the night. Maybe two. Then I'll be back. I'm leaving in twenty minutes," he said taking a drink from his glass.

She looked at the clock, "I can't be ready in twenty minutes."

"Randy's coming with me, we're taking the Mustang."

"Then there's no room for me." A pressure built behind her nose, she pinched it and closed her eyes to hold it in.

"I can't take the Rover, you can't drive a stick," he said.

"If you took the Rover, I could come and wouldn't matter." She tried to keep her voice low and even, but it was betraying her.

He wasn't even looking at her, but at his scrolling screen.

She would wonder, later, if this was when everything changed? "If you weren't going there to fuck someone else, you could have woken me."

He finally looked up and sighed, "Baby, you need some time to relax. Is everything you own still on the floor upstairs? Take some time for yourself. Get some DoorDash from that place I hate. I opened a bottle of wine for you already," he said pointing at the bottle of red on the counter. "You can watch all those shows that have been piling up on Netflix. After all these weeks on top of each other, you can't tell me that you're not ready for a little quiet."

She couldn't remember the last time he'd called her baby.

"I need to do it for Randy," he continued, and there it was, she thought. He's losing the battle, so it wasn't about him, he was a martyr.

"He's your agent. He works for you." She opened the fridge. "Did you drink my protein shake?"

"Christ, Olivia, this again? We were gone for nearly a month. You obviously threw it away before we left. There's no way it wouldn't be rotten and stinking up this whole house after a month."

She slammed items around in the fridge, she knew she'd left one in there.

"I think you're just tired, baby. You're forgetting things."

God, she thought, *another 'baby.'* He must be exhausted from trying to trying to convince her not to believe her own memories or senses. She grabbed a water instead, noting that there were fewer of those than she remembered, too. Was he fucking with her? A chill ran over her; *had he let one of his girlfriends stay in their house while they were gone?*

She left Harrison working on his laptop and went back upstairs and smelled the sheets on the spare room bed, but they were clean and the bed was made exactly the way she did it. She looked underneath it, and in all the drawers. The guest bath looked the way that it did after her mother left six weeks ago. She went out to the pool, the gate was closed, and everything looked normal. She tried the back door to the garage, locked. Of course, she thought. Of course, no one had come in just to steal her protein shake and pills. When she came back in, Harrison was packing up his computer.

"Are you really going to leave me here like this?" she said. Once the sight of her nipples through the thin slip of silk would have kept them in bed for hours and inspired at least a short story.

"Two nights tops. I'll call you when I get to the hotel. You'll be fine." He still wouldn't look at her and she wanted to hit something, or cry.

"Get some vegetable curry and drink some wine," he said.

"I can't believe you're leaving me here."

He picked up his bag from the floor, "Wine!" he said. "I'll see you in a couple of days," and then he left without even a kiss.

Olivia turned the TV on. She dug through every drawer in the kitchen hoping to find a lost pill, a loner tucked in a corner. Tore apart all her purses. She took a shower and washed her hair, the level of her shampoo did look lower, but Harrison liked to use her shampoo, especially she thought, on days when he'd cheat. Her own shampoo cover for him smelling like a woman. She went through all of the pockets of his clothes, looking for condoms, or phone numbers, but only found an empty bottle of prescription sleeping pills. *I wish I'd had these last night*, she thought.

She decided: fuck the calories, and ordered a pizza.

She looked at his bottle of snooty wine and grabbed a beer from the fridge instead.

She called every doctor she could think of trying to get a refill on her prescriptions, but they all wanted her to make an appointment. Time for a check-in they all said. *Fuck.*

She watched happy shows about people falling in love without ever seeing each other on Netflix and ignored the pain in her chest. She switched to bourbon.

When her phone rang at ten thirty and the display said: FOUR SEASONS, she got scared that something had happened to Harrison, but he'd just let his phone die by accident, he said. And while she was pretty sure he'd let it die on purpose so he could ignore her, she felt some relief that he was calling from a quiet hotel room, but she struggled to calm down. Every little creak, every little bump made her jump, and her heart race. She needed her pills.

Ghosts of girlfriend's past, she thought. That's all. She'd hire someone to come smudge with sage and be done with it.

She took an edible she found in the back of a drawer to help her to get to sleep, but as she laid there, the scent of him on the sheets made her ache, so she stripped his pillowcases and put them in the whites hamper, but one of his black t-shirts was laying on top. She grabbed it, rolling her eyes at his laziness since the colors hamper was right next to it, when the smallest pair of red lace panties she'd ever seen fell on the floor.

Her vision swam. She landed on her knees. Her breath came hard and fast. *I already knew.* She told herself, but it didn't stop the ache.

Olivia dialed and redialed his room in Atlanta, but it just rang.

At two thirty she woke with a start on the floor in the closet. Heart racing. Her swollen face tight and aching. It was quiet in the house, but something had woken her. The panties still lay on the white carpet next to her; she felt nauseated. A soft thud from downstairs. She scrambled to her nightstand for the gun. She gripped the handle and pressed her back to the wall as she slowly descended the stairs. She wished that her heart would stop beating for just like two seconds so she could hear something other than her own blood. It was so dark she couldn't see shit. At the bottom of the stairs, she sensed more than saw, movement.

"Who's there?" she said.

The shadow went still.

"Who's there? I have a gun!" Olivia shouted. "I have a gun and I've already pressed the panic button!"

The shape didn't move away, but toward her.

"Don't move," she said, but it kept coming. Olivia closed her eyes, pointed the gun in the direction of the shape, and pulled the trigger.

***

At Jessamine's favorite diner, they let her sit all day nursing a cup of coffee and a plate of fries. There was also the day-old pie just happened to find its way to her table, with a wink from the waitress who looked like her grandma, if her grandma traded her pinch of snuff for frosted lavender lipstick. They called her "the poet laureate" unironically and it was pretty much the only place she felt safe.

Jessamine ordered, pulled out her notebook. Sage plopped down across from her. "Hey lady," they said. "You look rough."

"Just had to pull a Houdini."

Sage looked a little green, they always did when Jessamine talked about where she slept.

"The garage door opening woke me. I figured I had maybe two minutes to get out. You know heights make me a little dizzy, but I knew the trellis would hold me cause that's how I got in. But then like halfway down I remembered that I'd forgotten to close the window. Which shit, guess I can never go back there. And I really liked their tub." Jessamine said as the fries arrived, she squirted a puddle of mayo on the side of the plate. Sage mimed gagging.

"I don't know how you live like that," Sage said putting an unsullied fry in their mouth. "It would stress me out. I'd never be able to relax."

Jessamine had this conversation with her parents constantly. She couldn't afford her own place in the city, so she did something else. They thought Asheville was a den of iniquity anyway, and should come home. She was going to get murdered, or worse, they said. She wondered what was worse than getting murdered. "Bills are more stressful, dude. I have no bills."

"Some of us have regular folks have jobs though, you know? Write when you're not working. Have money in your bank account, and you don't have to squat in strangers' houses."

"Do you know what percentage of this town is third houses? They got their Atlanta house, and their beach house, that's one and two, and the mountain house is third. All these mansions sit empty most the year. I'm saving the fucking planet."

Sage traced their eyebrows with the pads of their fingers. Jessamine knew her friend worried. "It's gonna be okay," she said, pointing at a flyer advertising a local author's new book. "I've got an idea."

"Isn't he the one—" Sage started, shaking their head.

"He owes me." Jessamine said smiling. The plan really did tickle her.

Sage sighed. "Just don't do anything excessively stupid?"

She licked mayonnaise off her thumb. "I won't have to. If you wait long enough, they light themselves on fire."

Jessamine watched the lights turn on at exactly 7:00 p.m., timers, she guessed. They wouldn't want the house to look abandoned. Tours could last months. She knew his wife would go, too. His womanizing was too well known for her to let women throw themselves at him, unabated, all over the country. Jessamine swallowed her jealousy. What she wouldn't give to be on book tour. She wouldn't fuck it up by screwing everything that moved. He had another two weeks in the Northeast at festivals. She bet that there was food in his fridge. She slunk down the street, breath catching in her throat, until she could slip into the shadow of a magnolia tree by their fence. There was a keypad on the gate.

Shit, she thought. He'd brought her in through the garage. She googled his birthday, then his mom's, then his wife's, nothing worked. Then the year his first book was released. Then Cormac's birthday. Then Hemingway's. Nothing. Then Jessamine thought back to her first job in Asheville, it had been incomprehensible to her parents. That people would pay her to go into their house and walk their dog. *Who had that kind of money?* They'd give her the code to their garage or their front door, and she could not believe how often it was just the street number. So, she tried that and, bingo.

The code worked again on the back door, and she was in the house, and surprised again at the enormity of the space, everything was gleaming white and the ceiling was thirty feet high. She looked for a security panel and when she saw nothing, she took off her shoes and stepped further inside to find a place to nest. After the trellis situation she didn't want to be on a second floor. He'd had her in his office the last time. In the basement the walls were dark wood. A gleaming desk. Papers everywhere. White board covered in scribbles. She stashed her stuff behind his huge leather couch and went upstairs to find some food. Back downstairs with a protein shake, four bottles of water, a box of crackers, a wheel of brie, a bunch of grapes, three bottles of pills, a pair of gold earrings, and what looked like cashmere socks. She felt a tiny bit bad. But cashmere socks? Shit. Plus, this guy had sent her inappropriate DM's all summer, and cornered her at the bar showing her pictures of all the pussy that was being thrown at him. She'd wanted to tell him how gross women thought that was. That it didn't impress anyone, but she'd ended that night with his face between her legs draped over the very couch she was now sitting on, spilling her secrets. She justified it to herself by thinking about how she'd cleaned up a little. She'd found a black t-shirt, Harrison's signature, and a pair of red underwear on the floor under the couch and had put them in the hamper upstairs in the bathroom. Not to mention how he had stolen her life story for one of his bestsellers, and then ghosted. Being a muse paid poorly; she was gonna keep the socks.

She ate at the desk. Imagined writing there. Imagined that this was her house. Her friends from home would never believe it. Not someone whose daddy was a short order cook, and her mama cleaned hotel rooms and desperately wanted her to come home and quit messing around with the writer nonsense.

She tried sleeping on the couch but could not stop thinking about waking up to Harrison's wife's face looming over hers. She could never admit it to Sage, but it was creepy to be in someone else's house. What if what if they found her? Would they hurt her? Or just call the cops? She'd convinced herself that Asheville was too liberal for these people to have guns, but she knew what she'd seen in that nightstand. She collected all of her things and made a spot behind the couch. If they came home, and they came down here, she'd be trapped but not immediately visible. She wrapped her arms around herself and thought about how the kind of success that bought a house like this would feel. What she couldn't give for her own place, it didn't need to be fancy like this, just a steady roof over her head, sheets she'd picked out, maybe new towels. Just not having to carry everything she owned in her backpack would be enough.

Her phone said it was nearly midnight when she woke up and had to pee. She was sitting on the toilet with the bathroom door open in the dark when she heard someone coming down the stairs. *Shit.* She squeezed her thighs to stop the pee and pulled up her pants as fast as she could. She closed the door to the bathroom, but if anyone walked in, she was caught. Quiet talking came through the wooden door, but she would recognize his voice anywhere. He wasn't happy, he was whisper shouting about crazy people. She thought he must be talking about fans. Fear crawled over Jessamine, that's what he'd assume if he found her in there, that she was stalking him. Ice clicked in a glass. Then he started ranting about six months. "Less than six months!" he hissed. She couldn't hear anyone else. He must be on the phone. Jessamine coiled herself up ready to spring if he opened the bathroom door.

But he didn't. She heard shuffling and rustling but no other voices, then the sound of a body landing on the sofa. She prayed that he didn't go to sleep or look behind it. What came next was worse. "I'm being bad" he whispered, "what are you going to do about it?" She remembered exactly what he had wanted her to do. If he hadn't been on the phone, she might have been tempted to reveal herself. He'd be surprised but he'd let her stay if she put her hands on his throat while she rode him. Then a repetitive rubbing sound started, then grunting, and a moan and then a shuddering gasp, and she knew she was too late.

An eternity later, she heard footsteps go back upstairs. She jumped back behind the couch and curled up as small as she could. It was late, he would go to bed sometime. She counted the heartbeats in her ears until an hour had passed. She left her stuff behind the couch and tiptoed up the stairs, just to check. Thankfully, the automatic lamps were off. She was in the kitchen when she heard footsteps. She dove behind the kitchen island. Harrison came into the kitchen and opened the cupboard. She heard what sounded like a cork popping and a sloshing sound. *Shit, was he getting a drink?* It had been a mistake coming up here. But he was supposed to be asleep. There was a squeak as he recorked the bottle and then room was so quiet she could hear her heart beating, and she prayed that he would leave and go to bed, but instead he started talking. "I'm ready," he said. "It's done."

Jessamine froze. Was he talking to her? "Tomorrow. I'll leave noonish. Leather?" Once she realized that he was on the phone again her stomach turned. *What an asshole*, she thought. He just got home, he just got off, and already he's arranging something with another woman. She shook her head. Leather. Christ. At least he could say he knew what he liked. After he left, she stood and looked at the expensive bottle of wine on the counter. He's gotten so distracted by the other woman he'd forgotten to have some. Well, she thought, don't mind if I do, and took a few big slugs, and then a few more before heading back to the basement to get her stuff and get out.

When Jessamine awoke, she couldn't believe the time. It was late afternoon, and she was laying on the floor in the middle of the basement with her half-packed bag beside her. *What the fuck had happened?* Her head felt like it had been crushed by a sledgehammer. The last thing she remembered was putting her stuff in her backpack. *The wine,* she thought. *Fuck.*

She slowly made her way up the stairs, but at the top she heard talking, and her heart fell. The TV was on. If someone was watching it, and she came out that door she'd be face to face with them. She wondered if Harrison didn't leave? Or if his wife was still home? She crept back down the steps to what she was coming to think of as her prison, and played on her phone behind the couch for an hour, and then went back up the stairs to check. Still with the tv. She tried again and again, hour after hour. At 9:00 p.m. she wondered if maybe the TV was just on and maybe no one was actually watching, so she opened the door just a tiny bit more and peeked through the crack between the door and the jam she could see legs. Female legs. Harrison probably left and his wife had camped out on the couch all day. Jessamine wondered if maybe she could go out there and make friends? Maybe the wife was lonely? Or, Jessamine thought, she'll scream bloody murder and call the cops. Jessamine went back down the stairs, back behind the couch and decided as soon as she heard that TV go off, she was out of there. The squatting idea was shit.

Jessamine was sure it was a noise that woke her, but when she got to the top of the stairs the TV was off and the house was quiet and dark, and she nearly screamed she was so excited. She grabbed her stuff and was pushing open the basement door when she heard, "Who's there?"

Her heart sank. She was caught after all of this? She froze. "Who's there," the female voice said, "I pressed the panic button and I have a gun." Jessamine dropped to the floor as the shot rang and the bullet thunked into a wall.

"For fuck-sake, Olivia," Harrison said from the darkness. "What the hell are you doing?"

Jessamine's body went cold with surprise.

"It's you," Olivia said. "Why didn't you answer?"

Jessamine pressed her cheek to the cool floor, praying that the darkness was cover enough. The room felt like it was humming.

"I knew the panic button was a lie, so I thought the gun was too. Since when do you have a gun?" Harrison's voice was high with anger and surprise.

"Why are you home? Why didn't you answer the phone? Why are there panties—."

A long pause filled the dark and Jessamine wondered what they were doing? *Why had no one turned on the light? Why was Harrison home?* Her whole body was clammy and the hum in the air had turned into a buzzing.

"You didn't drink that bottle of wine I left you?"

"I had a beer instead. Tell me whose fucking panties?"

Jessamine's eyes were searching the darkness for a way out. This was bad, and getting worse rapidly.

"The panties, Harrison! The fucking panties. After everything I've given up for you?"

"You were supposed to be asleep," he said.

Jessamine swallowed hard at the mention of the panties. *Shit.* She decided that it was now or never, she would use the cover of darkness, and their obvious distraction to get out. She stood and moved away from the safety of the door, and out into the hall.

"Why are you home? Why are you sneaking around in the night? Why are my things all missing or moved? Red panties! Which of your girlfriends was here while we were gone? Which of them kicked you out tonight and sent you back home to your wife?"

Then there was a click and the room was full of light and Olivia was holding a gun with one hand and the other was on the light switch, and Harrison had his hands up, and he had leather gloves on, but they were both looking at Jessamine.

Olivia looked between Harrison and Jessamine and back. "In my own fucking house," she said, and then two impossibly loud bangs tore through the room. Harrison fell to the ground. Jessamine did, too.

Olivia sat down on the stairs and sobbed.

Jessamine opened her eyes, slowly got to her knees. A red puddle was spreading on the floor beneath Harrison's body. She was shaking. "It's not what you think," she said. "I'm not—"

Olivia looked at her blankly. Blinked rapidly. "Do you have my pills?" she asked.

THE SWEET SCIENCE BLUES
(A SONNY HAYNES JOINT)
BY BRIAN TOWNSLEY

Palm Springs, 1952.

The desert sunset hung in horizontal hues of orange and purple in the rearview mirror as Sonny Haynes cruised the 111 east in his black Mercury, the palm trees leaning that same direction in deference to the winds that drove down from the San Jacinto Mountains. Katie, his adopted daughter, sat next to him, while her newest boyfriend sat in the back seat, looking as comfortable as a hamster in a snake cage.

"Been to a fight before?" Sonny asked, looking at the kid in the mirror.

"No, sir. Looking forward to it though," he said, and nodded in recognition. He was a handsome lad, with lots of hair parted in one general direction, though it didn't seem to take orders.

"So we're seeing this guy, Boomer Johnson, and man can that fucker punch. Pardon my Scottish. A right hook from the gods," Sonny said, and shook his head at the thought of it. "Saw him finish a fight in less than a minute at the Olympic. Absolutely pummeled the guy."

"That's in LA," Katie added, "downtown." She turned at looked at the kid, scrunching her nose and the freckles there, as they made eyes at each other.

"And I did a favor for the guy," Sonny said. "Got him out of a little jam. Nothing big. But he owes me, so I'll see if we can meet him after he smashes this guy up."

"Never been to LA," the kid said. "I'd love to go sometime."

Sonny nodded at this, pursing his lips together. "Thing is," he said, "there's lots of LA's. There's Hollywood, skid row, the Ravine, the beach, Beverly Hills, the Valley, and corpses everywhere you look."

Katie reached over and smacked him on the shoulder. "Don't listen to him, Johnny. He worked homicide for too long."

The kid looked at Sonny and they locked eyes in the rearview mirror. "What was your favorite part of working homicide?" he asked. Truth be told, there was something he was missing in all of this. This guy? A homicide detective? Sure, he was built like a brick shithouse, but he had tattoos on his hands, his neck, even a teardrop below his eye. Katie had told him it was for his dead wife, but still. Something didn't add up. Not that he was going to say that. Like, ever.

Without breaking eye contact, Sonny said, "beating the absolute living shit out of fuckers that deserved it." Then he smiled, and added: "and sometimes a few that didn't," with a shrug, and he winked at the kid then, and turned the radio up. It was 'The Wild Side of Life' by Hank Thompson, and the orange had dissipated from the sunset and darkness had begun to take root.

***

They passed the city limits riding east, as Palm Springs had publicly led people to believe that they wouldn't stoop to the level of hosting a prizefight (*City Council Votes Prizefight Down!* screamed The Desert Sun headline), but Sonny knew that was as much bullshit as everything else a politician said—it had simply meant that certain palms had not been sufficiently greased by the promoters, and so they turned where everybody else did who wanted entertainment in the Coachella Valley and didn't want to lose their wallet for it: Cathedral City.

The event was being held in a gymnasium, so the ring had been constructed, and seats had been brought in from a rental company. It was all first-class in a very second-rate kind of way, and Sonny found comfort in that. They sat in the third row and caught the tail end of the preliminary fight, one that featured two Hispanic boxers in the flyweight division, each of whom Sonny could have picked up with one arm and hoisted about like a trophy, and

97

then the decision had come down. An arm was raised, and with it, the short echo of history. The man in the ring with the microphone started introducing the main event, when Katie leaned into him.

"Why do the announcer guys wear tuxes?" She asked.

Sonny nodded at the question, knowing he was going to answer it but not really knowing the answer. "Well," he said, "boxing is an *event*."

She looked at him sidelong, knowing bullshit as it came and went. "It's two guys beating each other up. I saw a fight outside the library, about a month ago. These guys got into it over a parking space. Yeah," she said, and they made eye contact, "a *parking* space. Like it's hard to park in Palm Springs. Anyways, they went at it. One guy looked like he knew what he was doing, the other didn't." The announcer continued to speak and one of the boxers, a gent named Jimmy Castrovince, aka Jimmy the Kid, walked to the ring in a recognizable but particular gait so many boxers used.

"Did you?" Sonny asked. "I'd like to hear about that," he said, earnestly. Then he jutted his chin towards the ring and looked over at the kid as well. "Here comes," he said, shortly before the announcer, a dapper blonde man wearing the forementioned tux, introduced Boomer Johnson, who bounced down the aisle towards the ring, shadowboxing as he went.

The gym was full, and it was fight time.

***

Boomer dominated the first three rounds, peppering Jimmy with combinations and body shots. Sonny was impressed with Jimmy's footwork and defense, as he made Boomer work for everything he got. He was equally unimpressed with Jimmy's punch, which he doubted could knock Katie down. And she weighed 110 pounds.

Round four, however, seemed a different script entire, as Boomer was tired, or, Sonny found himself thinking, *seemed* tired, while Jimmy hammered away at the midsection. Both Katie and the kid, he couldn't remember his name right now, seemed into it, but Sonny's internal alarm had gone off. This wasn't a round off, this was a surrender.

The bell rang and echoed in the small gym and the crowd buzz was all around them and Katie leaned into him and said, "what's up with your guy?"

Sonny looked at her, scrunched his face up, and said: "he's going down. Either this round or the next."

She drew back, looking at him squarely the whole time. "And you know this how?" she asked.

Sonny nodded his chin towards the ring. "Watch."

The fifth was another barrage of body shots that Sonny felt Janice, the desk clerk at the Starlite Hotel & Resort where he worked as house dick, could have weathered easily. She'd have had a wisecrack after it as well. As for Boomer, well, he went down and stayed down.

Sonny looked at his company and Katie was looking at him with a confused face, while the kid was smiling, and said, "your guy is down, Mr. Haynes!"

Sonny thought briefly of flooring the kid right there but didn't think it would sit right.

Half an hour later in the dressing room, Sonny sat with Boomer. He had been let in after Sonny flashed a badge and told his trainer he knew Boomer from the deal with the escort in Los Angeles. The trainer moved aside.

Sonny went a legit 230, maybe 235, now. He hadn't been on a scale in a while. Avoided them, actually. Boomer was 211 on the dot, and sat with a towel around his shoulders, looking decidedly not tired. Sonny had been around fights, and he knew tired. Boomer wasn't.

"Remember me?" Sonny asked.

"Course," Boomer responded. "Never forget ya. You did me a solid."

"You just cost me two grand," Sonny said.

Boomer looked at him then, a combination of concern and anger writ across his face. Then it passed, and moved his gaze to the floor. "I lost," he said.

Neither man said anything for a spell. Sonny nodded to the trainer to leave, and, to his surprise, the old guy did just that.

"Whatcha gettin' out if it?" Sonny asked.

Boomer shook his head.

"You're pissing on the gods of war, man. That never ends well," Sonny said.

Boomer picked his head up, and nodded. He had tears in his eyes, and he pinched them with his still taped hands.

Sonny stood and walked towards the door.

"You really lost two large, Mr. Haynes?" Boomer asked.

Sonny smiled widely and shook his head. "Boomer, if I had lost two on that shitshow I just watched, I'd kill you myself. I was a homicide dick, and patrol before that. Bribes are *everywhere.* Just gotta learn how to spot 'em." He opened the door and walked out.

***

It was two days later when Sonny walked from his office to the busy front desk of the Starlite and got his mail from Janice. She smiled and popped her gum at him, then nodded towards the lobby.

"Guy's been here all morning," she said.

Sonny looked out into the lobby, knowing immediately to whom she referred, but chose to play the game anyways. "Which guy?" he asked.

Janice popped her gum and looked at him, trying to decipher the amount of bullshit he was shoveling.

"Well, let's see here," she said, her New York accent making vowels disappear on the regular, and used the pen in her hand to point her way around the lobby, "we've got the family of four over there," she nodded in their direction and popped her gum, "we've got the two old ladies chatting up a storm in the corner," she pursed her lips here, as if considering, "and then there's the guy sitting by himself who looks like a lug if they had a picture next to 'lug' in the dictionary." She scrunched her brow and looked at Sonny over the top of her glasses, "so, I'm gonna go out on a big limb here and say the guy who wants to see you looks *exactly* like you'd imagine a guy looked who was waiting to talk to you." She popped her gum again and used the pen she had been pointing with to bop Sonny on the nose.

"You're a master detective, Janice," Sonny said.

"That's what we love about you, Sonny. You bring such quality clientele into the establishment," she said, and winked.

Sonny walked over and touched the big lug on the shoulder. The shoulder belonged to Boomer Johnson, so it was about as soft as a sandbag. "Boomer," Sonny said, "I understand you're here to see me." With that he nodded his head in the direction of his office.

Spartan did not begin to describe Sonny's workplace. There was a hatrack, a desk, and two chairs. Two books and *The Desert Sun* sat on the desk. One window high up on the wall that looked out onto the palm trees lining the street. Sonny lit a cigarette and sat down, motioning for Boomer to take the seat opposite. The man did, wearing an expression that Sonny would have described as 'sheepish.'

"What's the haps, Boomer?" Sonny asked, picking a piece of tobacco from his teeth and putting it on the edge of the glass ashtray with his finger.

"I'm in a bit of a fix, Mr. Haynes," he said, rubbing his formidable hands together.

"No pun intended, I assume," Sonny clapped back.

Boomer looked at him for a long time, comprehension never quite arriving.

"Alright, kid," Sonny said, and exhaled towards the ceiling. "First you're throwing fights, now you're in a fix," Sonny rubbed his face with this free hand. "So, let me guess, it's one of two things here: first, you got a visit from somebody not in on the smart play and they lost big, either that, or you threw a damn fight and now the weasel you made it with ain't coming through with the cash. Which is it?"

Boomer nodded his head, looking between his feet, and said: "It's like you said, Mr. Haynes, I was kinda forced into taking the fight and throwing it, and now this guy—Delgado, he arranged it all—he says he don't owe me jack." He looked at Sonny, and, despite him being a young, athletic, bull of a man whose right cross would kill most civilians, his expression was hopeless.

"Don't fuckin' cry on me, kid," Sonny said, and lit another smoke with the burning tip of the first. "Delgado, Delgado...sounds familiar. And not in the good way. How'd you get involved?"

"I mean, you know," Boomer said, and waved a hand at it all, "I knew a guy who knew a guy, and they wanted to get a fight out here, but there was a catch." He shrugged. "It was supposed to be easy money, big payday, and just a...glitch in my career, you know? That's what they said, *glitch*. I lose to this guy, pick up some money, boost this guy's name, then after the glitch I go right back on the road to the championship." He said it as if it sounded just as stupid to his own ears.

"That's what they said, huh? Well, kid, I don't know what to tell you," Sonny said, and sat smoking and looking at Boomer as he did.

Boomer said nothing in return. They both sat there, the exhaled smoke in the room the only thing moving.

Finally, Sonny said: "Look, kid. You gotta square with me here. What do you want from me? You made a deal. It went south. That's life." He laughed then, as if his own words held a poignancy only recognized once he heard them himself. "Literally, that's life, most of the time."

Boomer looked up at the ceiling and said, "yeah. Bennie, my trainer, that's what he said you'd say." The words were forlorn and embarrassed and contained a sadness in them Sonny didn't like.

"Boomer—look, I don't know what you're asking me here: you don't have the money, of course there is no contract," he looked at Boomer here for confirmation, to which he got a head shake, "and it's your word against his. So, either go kick the guy's ass and get your vig, or don't be so fucking naïve next time, but..."

"Oh, I can't go after him, Mr. Haynes," Boomer said.

Sonny stopped talking and tilted his head and looked at the boxer. Nodded, as if to say, go on, and scratched at the inked teardrop below his right eye.

"Delgado's the guy who set it all up, but he's fronting for Guisseppe Enzo. It's five grand"

It was involuntary, but Sonny grinned at this. "Really?" he said, and stretched the word out to far more than its two syllables.

Boomer nodded, quickly, seeing Sonny's interest.

Sonny stood and walked towards the window in his office, the palm trees leaning and swaying like drunkards on a Friday night. "So, let me get this right," Sonny said, and nodded in Boomer's direction, "you know that Delgado is fronting for Enzo how?"

"He told me, when we first met. In LA."

Sonny nodded at this. "Okay," he said. "Guiseppe and I go back, maybe I can talk to him."

"You know Guiseppe Enzo? The mob boss?"

Sonny waved his hand at this. "Yeah, we're old pals. And I do love fucking with the greaseballs," he said, more to himself than Boomer.

Sonny, of course, was not old pals with Guiseppe Enzo. He doubted there was such a thing. He had, however, done a job for they guy, one that benefited the both of them. He and his sometime partner, Melvin Easley, had managed to save the girl involved, albeit sans her tongue, but the mark himself had proved more elusive, and was presently in hiding. Either way, he found himself driving south on the 111 to one of the swankier neighborhoods in the Palm Springs foothills.

It was a white stucco, red-tile roof affair on a cul-de-sac. The foothills were often windy in this area, the gusts blowing down the eastern face of the San Jacinto Mountains, and this day was no different. Sonny's cigarette nearly blew out of his mouth as he parked and exited the Merc. He scrunched the snapcap on his head down further and made his way to the front of the house. The twin palm trees that sat sentry as he approached swayed like they were underwater, and he heard the fibers in the elongated trunks creak like the laughter of the unhinged.

He knocked on the front door. He heard it echo inside the house. He knocked again. The door opened, and Sonny saw a small Italian man looking up at him. He held a .357 in his right hand as comfortably as an author holds a pen. There were piano notes coming from somewhere in the house.

"Mr. Sonny Haynes," the man said, smoothly. Sonny didn't like to admit it, but everything this guy did was smooth. The last time he had been here the guy had been sitting in a lawn chair with a sawed-off in his lap as he and Melvin approached. He was one of the little ones, and, when it came to Italians, those were the ones to worry about. The ones his size, and often much bigger, were meatheads that had to ask permission to think. They were cake. But the little guys, the ones who looked like they had just gotten off the plane from Sicily or Napoli, and had names like Giovanni or Alessandro, they were the ones who cut you up and walked away before you even realized the limb was gone.

"Got a permit for that?" Sonny asked.

The guy looked down at the gun like he hadn't noticed it was there. "You a cop?" he asked.

Sonny smiled. "Used to be."

"Yeah, funny thing about used to be," the man said. "I used to live in Italy. Now I don't. See how that works?" The man looked Sonny up and down. "I see you left the spade at home this time," he said.

Sonny had ten remarks jump into his head, everything from defending Melvin, his black friend and sometime partner, to wisecracking about the Moors in Italy just to offend, and in the end, settled on none of them. Now was not the time. Sonny half-smiled, and said, "Enzo in?"

"He is," the man said. "Upstairs. Now, whether he wants to meet with you, we'll have to see on that." He nodded to a man Sonny couldn't see, and Sonny heard footsteps going up a staircase, the leather footfalls echoing on the tiles in juxtaposition to the piano playing.

"So," the man said. "Here to kill or maim any more Italian-American citizens just going about their business, making a living?"

"That depends on you, I suppose," Sonny said, and smirked.

"You cut Big Vinnie up the front like he needed a zipper, you smashed Gio's knee up with those brass knuckles of yours so he can't walk right, you smashed Anthony's face into a car door. His nose still ain't right."

"That doesn't sound like me," Sonny said. While there were certainly qualifiers to each of those situations, that didn't make them inaccurate. "Is there a point here?" Sonny asked.

"Yeah, you're a fuckin' walking caution sign, that's what. And you come here, to this house, and worry about the gun in my—" he stopped as if he heard something, looked in the direction of the staircase, and said something to the man in Italian. Nodded.

"Enzo will see you," he said.

"I'm honored," Sonny said.

"You should be," the man said. "You know the drill. Empty your pockets," the man said.

***

Enzo's office seemed slanted with the filtered light from the sunlit window blinds, and he sat behind a large mahogany desk. He wore black hair, silver at his temples, and a scowl that seemed given at birth. A giant Italian man, currently serving as gargoyle, Sonny figured, stood off to the side in a suit about the size of a circus tent. Enzo did not stand to greet Sonny.

"Here you are, Sonny Haynes," Enzo said, and gestured to one of the chairs in front of the desk, "I'd like to say you are always welcome, but," and he motioned with his chin towards the window as if he didn't quite know how to finish the sentence.

"Mr. Enzo," Sonny said, "I've come seeking guidance."

Guisseppe Enzo smiled at that, but there was no mirth in it.

"I have a gentleman with whom I have a business relationship, a boxer, I imagine you've heard of him, he recently lost a fight right here in our own little valley." Sonny lit a Chesterfield then, shook the match out and tossed it in the crystal ashtray on the desk. "He was offered a sum of money to lose the fight. He did his job. Badly, I might add," and he rolled his eyes a bit here, "but I'm now of the understanding that while this was a significant burden to his career, he took the fix," Sonny exhaled here, towards the ceiling, "and hasn't been paid his due." He held his hand out here, as if to stop Enzo from speaking. "I know, spare me the innocence, 'what has this got to do with me, you have no proof I'm involved', yada yada."

Enzo reached into a box on his desk and grabbed a cigar. Struck a match and lit it, turning it clockwise as he did. "I like how I don't have to involve myself in this conversation you're having with yourself," he said.

"Normally," Sonny continued, and shrugged his shoulders, "I couldn't give a shit. Life sucks. But, well," and he stuck his left hand out and started counting out fingers, "the kid he lost to was Italian," he tipped his first finger, "he couldn't have knocked out a twelve-year old," he tipped his index finger, "and the guy who owes the money swears he's fronting for you," he tipped his ring finger. Sonny smiled with the cigarette between his lips.

Enzo nodded, not in agreement so much as that he had heard the demonstration. He puffed his cigar. Sonny smoked. And they looked at each other, neither saying anything.

Finally, Sonny leaned forward and stubbed out his cigarette. "Look," he said, "I think we both know I'm a square guy. You leave me alone, I leave you alone."

Enzo snorted at that.

"We both exist here, and, *most* of the time, we're good. But here," Sonny said, and scrunched his face, looking towards the blinds, "my guy needs his money. His career is currently circling the toilet bowl like a floating turd, and a deal is a deal. And," he pointed towards Enzo with his cigarette here for emphasis, "whoever made the deal, I imagine, had no idea I was on one side of it. So, I just wanted to let you know. To provide some...*clarity*," Sonny said.

"I know of no such deal," Enzo said, and spread his arms wide. His voice was soft but had presence. "But even if I did, how does this involve me? I'm a businessman. Lots of guys out there have my name on their lips. Means nothing," he said, and Sonny saw some of the famed temper just beneath the calm veneer.

"Of course you don't," Sonny said. "I expected as much. I just wanted to bring it to your attention." He lit another Chesterfield and smiled. "You gotta watch that though, guys using your name on the streets. Could bring trouble," he said, "and nobody wants that."

Enzo nodded, as if in thought.

"I'll show myself out," Sonny said, and knocked once on the desk while he stood up.

***

Sonny was at his desk on Friday morning when there was a knock at the door.

"Yup," Sonny said. Zeus, Katie's German Shepherd, was curled up in the corner today, and his tail wagged.

Janice opened the door and stuck her head in. "It smells like a tobacco factory in here, open a window for chrissakes," she said. She looked at the window and so did Sonny but neither made a move for it.

"Is this a social visit?" Sonny asked.

Janice made a face at him and said, "somebody dropped something off for you. Here," and walked two paces into the room and handed him a sheet embossed with the Starlite Hotel & Resort logo, and below was a hand written address. Then she walked to the window, and, reaching up, cracked it. The palm fronds rustled in the breeze. "Get some fresh air in here," she said.

"Who gave you this?" Sonny asked.

"Some guy," she said. "Kinda little, kinda cute. Italian, maybe?" and she cocked her head to the side in possibility.

The Merc cruised southeast towards The Cove, an artsy community in the Cathedral City foothills. Katie was working at the library, so he had thought about bringing Zeus, and had thought again about stopping by Mel's liquor store to see if he wanted in. By the time he had finished dropping his brass knuckles into his pocket, checking his .45, putting the piece of shit, drop .22 in his ankle holster, and chosen the tweed snapcap, he had decided: he was going solo.

The address was quite a way up into the foothills, and houses up there had some space, featuring pools and large yards and discreet neighbors where there were neighbors at all. 'Wheel of Fortune' by Kay Starr was blaring on the radio. The windows were down—with the sun beginning to descend behind the mountains to the west, and the shadows in contrast against the shafts of celestial beams shooting through the peaks, the scene was one that has launched a thousand tourism ads for Southern California. The events of the next few minutes would not be included in them.

***

The house had a large empty lot on one side and the nearest neighbor on the other was half a block away. It had pink and yellow desert flowers blooming in the cacti out front, and it was a wood and brick structure unlike most of the newer desert architecture a few miles west in Palm Springs. Sonny drove by the address once, stopped at the corner to make sure the particulars—his guns and

112

brassies—were at the ready, and drove back down the street and parked behind a Cadillac in the driveway, lest the occupants here get the urge to leave.

He lit a Chesterfield, pocketed the keys, and made his way to the front door with an unhurried purpose. He knocked twice, loudly, and waited, slipping his fingers through the brass knuckles in his pocket.

A young man answered, obviously drunk or quite stupid, with a lopsided grin on his face and his hair unkempt. He was olive-skinned and clean shaven. He looked at Sonny, eyes focusing up after seeing the tattoos on the visitor's neck and the teardrop that hung pendant from his eye. "You here to sell us something?" he asked.

"I'm here to see Mr. Delgado," Sonny said, and blew smoke in the open doorframe.

"*I'm* Mr. Delgado," the man said, and chuckled. He looked back into the room, Sonny assumed at whatever company he had in the living area, to let them into the joke. "Guy looks like he belongs in a carnival, tattoos all over," he said to his company. He smiled the lopsided grin again and Sonny realized all at once, the final piece a wafting skunkiness, that this cat was stoned out of his head.

Sonny punched the door back with his open left hand, a pistoning motion that saw the door connect with the left side of the man's face and send him sprawling backwards. Sonny walked into the living room and closed the door behind him. The man's nose was broken and had already begun streaming blood from both nostrils and he looked up at Sonny, some combination of surprise and fear and anger etched across his face. There were two men and a woman on a couch in the living room, with a bevy of drug paraphernalia—pipes and tinfoil and such—on the glass coffee table in front of them. There was also a revolver.

"So, you're Delgado," Sonny said. It wasn't a question.

"N-no, man!" the guy on the floor said, and put his hand out in front of him, while the other gingerly held his nose. He scooted backwards on his ass to create some space between them.

Sonny looked at the three people sitting on the couch. One of the men had raised his head at the commotion but had put it back down again, either far too high or tired to care. The young woman, maybe not yet out of her teens, covered her mouth with a hand and her eyes were wide as saucers. She seemed unable to move. The man on her right was surprised as well, but seemed more functional than the others, which was a low bar. Sonny saw him eye the gun on the table.

"Son, you reach for that and your day becomes very bad, very quickly. Right now, all I want is to leave you a message. You pick that gun up, that all changes," Sonny said, with a sober clarity.

The man quickly licked his lips and leaned back into the couch. His eyes darted about like a hummingbird. Sonny pointed at the bleeding man on the floor. "Is this Delgado?" he asked.

A chorus of voices, all three of them in disparate timing, gave a negative in some form or another. "Well," the functional man on the couch said, "kinda.

That's not the one you're probably looking for. That's his younger brother. He just came out here last week, man."

Sonny looked down at the young man on the floor, who nodded, still holding his bloody nose. Sonny took a step forward and kicked the man in the ribs, a brutal shot that caused him to curl up into a fetal position and deliver an elongated grunt that turned into sobbing.

"Jesus Christ," Sonny said. "Don't cry." He reached into his sportcoat pocket and retrieved the handkerchief there and threw it down at the man. "Clean yourself up and have some fucking dignity," he said.

"So," Sonny raised his head and said to the man on the couch, "since you seem to be the fount of information," and he looked about the room here, "and the only one sober enough to be of any use, where is Delgado? The, uhhh, older one."

The younger Delgado, on the floor, sobbing, bleeding, and making noises so absurd that Sonny was embarrassed for him, still managed to blurt: "Don't say nothin,' Henry—" although it sounded more like a question than a declaration, and had far too many syllables, it still made its way out there, seemingly the only thing in the room. Like a balloon everyone was watching float about. Or a fart in an elevator.

Sonny looked down at the man who immediately covered up and starting sobbing again.

"Jesus," Sonny said. "You can't simultaneously hold out on information and be fucking terrified, kid. You gotta make a decision. Tell me what I want, and I leave, or don't, and I burst your head like a fuckin' pumpkin. Makes no difference to me, I'm gonna get it anyways." He leaned down and knelt on one knee, smacking the kid on the cheek softly, with an almost kind expression on his face. "Ya gotta decide," he said.

The man on the couch decided he had had enough at this point and burst from his seated position towards the sliding glass door that Sonny could see led to the back yard, and the swimming pool there. In his panicked and inebriated state, however, the man did not realize the glass slider was closed, and ran full speed into the door, making a large clatter than vibrated about the room for some seconds. He fell backwards, his nose bleeding as well now.

"Holy shit," Sonny said. "I think you guys may end up killing yourselves without me even raising a finger," and shook his head. He took three steps towards the couch, grabbed the revolver on the coffee table, winked at the woman who still sat frozen on the center cushion, and walked over to the most recently fallen man, who was now writhing in pain. Henry, right? He thought. He tucked the gun into the back of his pants, reached down and grabbed the man by the shirt collar and the belt, and, with one backward arc for momentum, threw the man at the sliding door. The whole thing shattered and collapsed, a waterfall of glass, and the man landed half in and half out the doorframe, surrounded by jagged shards. It had broken very evenly, in small pieces. Interesting, Sonny thought. The man began to crawl then, his face bloody and his forearms peppered with small cuts.

Sonny took a look back in the room, he certainly had time, he realized, and saw that Young Delgado was still holding his nose and staring at the chaos the scene had devolved into, and the woman on the couch, whom he was pretty sure had shrieked once when the glass door shattered, continued to sit frozen in place. The other man, well, he hadn't moved. He was comatose. Or dead. Or just way too high.

He turned his attention back to the crawling man, who would soon make the swimming pool. Odd choice, Sonny found himself thinking, but most things don't make sense.

Sonny walked outside, shoes crunching on the broken glass, and got to the pool as the man rolled over the edge and into the water. Sonny stood there at the lip and waited for him to surface.

When Henry finally did, he brushed his wet hair from his face and said simply: "Don't hurt me no more. Please"

Sonny scrunched his brow and pulled a cigarette from the pack and lit it, exhaling into the dusky evening. He realized he had no idea what had happened to the one he was smoking when he punched the front door open. "I have a message for Delgado," he said.

"You're not going to hurt me?" The man asked.

"I will if you don't shut up," Sonny said. "Are you sober enough to pass this on? Or do I need to carve it into your forehead so you'll remember?" He exhaled into the near dark, where the stream dissipated into the easterly wind from the foothills that had kicked up.

"Jesus, man!" The guy said. He was standing in four feet of water and looked hopeless and blood streaked, the crimson drops disappearing like smoke upon contact with the water.

"Okay," Sonny said. "Delgado owes me money. He fixed a fight—you guys may know something about that—and he didn't pay up. He owed Boomer. Now he owes me, 'cause he fucked up." Sonny flicked the end of the smoke into the pool. Both men watched its arc, sailing end over end.

"He's got 24 hours to bring me the money. He doesn't, and I'm gonna paint the walls with him. It was five grand, now it's ten. *Ten grand.* You got that?" Sonny asked.

The guy nodded, blood from his nose continuing to drip into the pool.

"Name is Sonny Haynes. Ask around, he'll find me." He turned then, before circling back. "Twenty-four hours, that's it."

"I got it," the man said. He continued to stand there, hiding in the middle of the kid's side of the pool. Sonny realized he was going to continue standing there until he left, so he walked back into the house. Young Delgado had gotten up and sat on the couch, next to the woman. They both looked at Sonny like he was the big, bad wolf.

"Where's Delgado's room?" Sonny asked.

The woman pointed in the direction of a hallway. The younger brother said nothing.

Sonny walked into the bedroom. It had Spanish tile floors and a large bed. He checked under the mattress, then the frame. Nothing. Then he walked to the closet and found a bag practically bursting with cash on the shelf above

some shirts and jackets on hangers.

"Fucking amateurs," he said.

"You folks have a nice day," Sonny said, and smirked, as he walked

through the living room with the leather satchel in his hand. "Don't be an

asshole next time, and save yourself some pain."

"Can I have the gun back?" The younger Delgado asked in a nasal tone.

Sonny wondered then at the stupidity involved here, and shuddered to

think that this was Katie's generation. He started to walk out, then stopped.

He couldn't help himself. "The gun? Seriously?" He said, as he turned. He

stared at the kid. "Son, your brother has put the name of Guiseppe Enzo on the

street, in the wrong way. You don't make a deal with the devil and stab him in

the back." He looked at all of them—the younger brother, acting like his femur

was broken rather than his nose, the young lady who seemed incapable of

movement, the comatose man, and, interestingly, Henry, who was now looking

in from the doorframe, dripping onto the glass shards—and said: "look, I'm not

sure you guys are really up to date here, but the guy who owns the house you're

getting high in got the dime dropped on him by a *mob boss.* Think about what

that means for you." He scanned the faces in the room. "Be honest, I'm sure

he'd like it if I got rid of y'all. And it'd be *easy.* But I'm not giving him that.

Consider yourselves lucky." Sonny picked up the bag and turned to go. Before he closed the door, he said, "and, as a quick word of advice, if you're not a big fan of greaseballs with guns, I'd get the fuck out of here by morning."

***

When he returned to the hotel, he called Boomer and Melvin and told them what time to meet in his office the next morning.

Katie was home from work and together they watched an episode of I Love Lucy on the tube, then some talent show that Katie found interesting. Sonny took a shower, put the .45 under his pillow, and fell asleep almost immediately reading *Cassidy's Girl* by David Goodis with the side lamp still on.

Delgado had two choices at this point, the way Sonny figured: He could get the fuck outta Dodge, which was probably the smart play, or he could try to save face and get the money back. It made no sense whatever to go to Enzo, because Enzo would, within a day or two, be forced to rid the Palm Springs area of Delgado for sullying his reputation. Simply a business necessity. There was no coming back from that. So, it was bolt or try to get the money back, and then bolt. Sonny assumed the latter.

Katie had a day trip planned with Anna, Sonny's sometime girlfriend and Katie's librarian boss, to visit the Salton Sea and the resorts there. He gave Katie two hundred bucks and told her to make it a weekend, just in case. So, no worries on that end. He planted Melvin in his suite with Zeus, although, because Mel was black, they needed to carry on a charade of Mel wearing a Starlite Resort maintenance jacket lest the delicate sensibilities of the guests be offended by thinking a black man might be on the premises for anything other than service. It was a maneuver they had carried out many times before, but neither man felt any less ridiculous each time, some small measure of dignity lost, meted out in teaspoon portions.

He put Boomer in his office, and gave him some magazines and the Goodis book in the hopes it would hold him over. Sonny, then, sat in the furthest corner of the lobby, mostly hidden from view by a planter and a stand of tourist guides.

It was nearly four hours later when events began to unfold. There was a line maybe six deep at the lobby counter, with two kids running in circles around their parents. Two men entered a side door from the garage and headed for the House Investigator's office. Sonny was impressed, after what he had witnessed the night prior. They were dressed in garage mechanic or maintenance coveralls, and looked the part. Henry was there, which was a surprise, along with another, older man—obviously Delgado, who carried a case at his side that generally held tools, although Sonny was willing to bet the ten grand that today it held more dangerous cargo. Henry's nose was swollen and discolored and carried white tape atop it, but otherwise he looked no worse for wear, with the long sleeves covering any cuts from the glass. Neither looked his way in the busy lobby, and Sonny knew they couldn't afford to openly carry weapons in that crowded a room.

Sonny stood and made his way towards them, as quickly as he could while remaining discreet. A few things happened simultaneously then: Delgado knocked on the office door while Sonny was maybe ten feet away, and Henry looked back and saw Sonny approaching—as Boomer opened the office door, Sonny reached Henry and pushed him into Delgado and the four of them awkwardly shoehorned into the office and Sonny locked the door behind them.

Boomer had taken hold of Delgado by the collar as the man awkwardly reached to open the case he held in the crowded space. Boomer threw one short right cross and Delgado fell like a puppet with its strings cut. He hit the ground fast and without grace, one leg tucked helter-skelter under the other. Sonny looked at Henry and the man held both hands out, fingers splayed, and he wore the fear of the hunted in his eyes. Sonny smiled and said, "Henry. Nice to see you again."

***

In the next few hours, the details of the day began to take shape. He paid Melvin for his time; had Boomer gag and tape up Delgado; bid Henry farewell with the promise to never see him again; confirmed the dropoff point with a phone call, and paid Boomer his money, provided he did one last thing.

Sonny drove the Merc northwest towards the outskirts of Desert Hot Springs, which, while being an area known for the healing properties of its namesake, was also one of the many places to go in this area when you wanted to rid yourself of something unneeded. Like someone in your trunk.

This particular visit was to an abandoned building, from which there were plenty to choose. The flatlands throughout were dotted with such structures, generally wood shacks or brick shells that had once been someone's idea of escape. Now simply a part of the desert landscape, as much an enduring symbol as the tumbleweeds spinning restlessly across the hardpack.

Boomer was in the passenger seat, and it was clear he was uncomfortable with the events of the day. Sonny didn't blame him, but wouldn't give him a pass either. This was his mess—Sonny wasn't going to clean the whole thing up and not allow the kid to see the inner workings. He was a part of it, and, Sonny hoped, his discomfort would keep him from dealing with men like this again. He wasn't a get-out-of-jail-free card.

The windows were down and they were too far into the hinterlands for the radio thus the exhaling of smoke and lack of conversation would serve as both company and entertainment. The dust cloud blossomed behind the Merc as Sonny drove, managing the dips adequately, and the wind blowing east, along with the thuds and muffled bumps from the trunk, acted as soundtrack for the late afternoon.

He saw the structure as they approached it, not unlike so many others they had passed, and he put the car in park, the dust whipping about chaotically. He ordered his hair and smashed the snapcap on his head and closed the door behind him. His .45 was in his right hand and he motioned for Boomer to follow and the two of them approached the structure. It was no larger than a studio, a single room with a cement floor and mostly intact brick walls. The window frames had lost whatever glass they once contained years before and thus the wind whipped through the structure as well. In the center of the room was a metal chair, bolted into the concrete. The arms and front legs had metal cuffs. Sonny looked at Boomer, who wore an expression of a man realizing he was in a much darker situation than he originally imagined. Sonny felt for him, but also didn't. "Yup," he said, and nodded. "It's a dirty game, kiddo."

Boomer put his hands on his knees like he was going to be sick. "Quit it," Sonny said.

"Mr. Haynes," Boomer said, and gagged once as if he was going to blow. "I—I wanted the money, but...," he stopped there. Sonny didn't need a narrator for the rest.

He said nothing in return and motioned with the .45 towards the Merc and said, "get him outta the trunk and bring him here," and handed Boomer the keys with his free hand. As he saw the boxer walk towards the car, leaning into the wind, Sonny smirked as he considered the possibility of the kid getting into the car and just driving away. That would be a wrinkle in the day. He'd hardly even blame the kid. He lit a cigarette, cupping it from the wind, and scratched at the teardrop that hung from his right eye for a long-dead wife. When he looked up, Boomer had the restrained man slung over his shoulder like a GI bag, the man's muffled cries lost to the wind.

DOG EAT DOG

BY GREG MOLLIN

Arthur howled in pain. Mason had to clench his teeth to avoid doing the same. Every blow he landed on the man's ribcage felt like it was shattering his hands. Every shot caused an explosion of agony from knuckle to wrist. He worked the gut hoping for some relief. The soft tissue there offered little resistance. Arthur gagged and sobbed. He threw up on the filthy tile underneath him. Mason stepped back and rubbed his fists. The vomit had an acid stench. He could see chunks of undigested food pooling in the grout.

Mason said, "You're lucky that didn't get on my shoes," and gave him a hard kick to the shin. Another howl echoed in the little bathroom. Mason wondered how well the sound carried into the other room.

He needed a smoke. He left Arthur tied to the chair and went out to the kitchen for his cigarettes. The pack and lighter were there on the table next to a hammer and pliers, just in case. He lit one and exhaled up at the ceiling.

Muffled whimpering emanated from the living room. It sounded like a dog begging to be let in. He tucked the pack into his pocket and walked out there.

The place was a wreck. Dirty clothes, fast food containers, garbage piled shin high. It smelled like urine, rot, and something worse. He moved across the room in semi-darkness. A thin line of light peeked around the edge of a sarape blanket covering the lone window.

Lycanthropes were scumbags. They lived more like pigs than wolves. They wallowed in their own filth. This place was worse than most. These two were junkies strung out on Wolvesbane. The synthetic opioid blended with their animal cravings and drove them half-mad with hunger when they came down. They gorged themselves to the verge of sickness before being satiated. He kicked a pizza box out of his way. A half-dozen cockroaches scurried for cover.

The couple had been in the living room when he broke in, both still in their skin, dazed and incoherent, minds wasted on that chemical dope. He held them at gunpoint and forced Arthur to tie up his wife, Maryanne. Afterward, he took him into the bathroom and fastened him to the chair before going to work. He wanted her to hear and not see.

Now she lay tied up on the cluttered couch. A table lamp with a dim bulb cast an orange glow over her. She looked ready to pop. Her eyes danced in their sockets. She was shaking and sweating, the fear and drugs in her system probably sending her redlining toward cardiac arrest.

He knocked a pile of dirty clothes onto the floor and sat down next to her. She tried to wiggle away from him. He reached over and pulled her up by the knot of cord behind her back. The tape over her mouth turned her screams into kazoo honks.

Mason took a deep drag from the cigarette. The cherry glowed red in her frightened face. Smoke billowed out as he said, "Shhhhh."

He took a last pull from the smoke and dropped it into one of the soda cans on the grimy coffee table. He put a finger to his lips with one hand and tore the tape from her face with the other. She turned crimson. She bit her lip and fought back a scream.

"Good girl," he said. "You ready to tell me where the money is, or do I need to go back to work on Arthur?" His throbbing hands warned him it was an empty threat. They both felt broken, but he would do whatever he had to do to get the job done.

Tears ran. She said, "Yes." She choked back the tears, cleared her throat. "It's in little Jamie's room. There's a cash box hidden under a panel in the top dresser drawer." She looked toward the hallway.

Yuri had mentioned nothing about a kid, and Mason hadn't run a thorough check on the place before he started in on Arthur. He felt a jolt of panic, but didn't let it manifest. He said, "She in there? Jamie?"

The woman nodded. She looked waxen; her skin was almost translucent over the malleable skull it covered. Mason could see scars in the pale flesh of her neck. Lover's bites. A fine dusting of blonde fur covered her exposed cleavage.

"We aren't bad people," she said.

Mason looked into her eyes. Her fear intensified.

He gave her a reassuring smile. She returned it. He viewed a mouth full of sharp and jagged teeth. He picked the piece of silver tape off of the coffee table, said "Shhh," and pressed it back over her face.

The unexpected sound of laughter came from the bathroom. Mason left the woman on the couch and went to the bathroom door. He could hear Arthur struggling as he guffawed.

Mason opened the door. The laughter stopped. Arthur was mid-transformation. Blood and vomit stained his pants and shirt. Coarse black hair had sprouted all over his face. A wet red smile spread under his partial snout. Arthur said, "You know I'm gonna kill you, right? I've got your fucking scent now. You can run, but I'll find you. I'm gonna tear off your cock and eat it while you watch, you piece of shit."

Mason smiled. He pulled a pouch from his pocket and poured some of the contents into his palm. He held his hand in front of Arthur's face and blew the silver dust into his mouth and eyes. The man/wolf howled and thrashed in the chair. Mason said, "Shut the fuck up, Arthur," and slammed the door. He headed down the garbage strewn hall toward Jamie's room while Arthur screamed in pain.

Yuri had hired him to collect ten grand that Arthur and Maryanne Miller owed him for a half pound of Wolvesbane he'd fronted the couple a month earlier. After the transaction, the two lycanthropes had fucked him off and disappeared with his dope. None of Yuri's regular people could find them. He gave Mason a call and offered him half of whatever he recovered. Mason didn't trust Yuri. One too many sketchy gigs had soured their relationship, but times were tough and he needed the cash. He took the job and tracked them down to this shithole apartment in Norwegian Gardens. He might be old, but he could do the work better than guys half his age.

He stood in front of the door and cursed Yuri. Still the same old shit. He knew Mason had a strict no children policy, but here he was. He put his ear to the wood and listened. Throbbing bass thumped from somewhere else in the complex. Nothing from inside. He grabbed the handle and turned.

The room was dark. A sliver of light cut through a part in the curtains. It smelled like body odor and wet dog in there. He stood back in the hallway, holding his breath to avoid the stench. Mason waited for his eyes to adjust to the darkness. There was a guttural sound, like a low growl. His hand went to the gun in his shoulder rig. He popped the retention strap and held it there. He said, "Jamie? Are you in there?" Another low growl came from beyond the doorway. He took a step inside.

On the other side of the cluttered room was a thin, bare mattress. There, amidst a pile of filthy blankets, was a lycanthrope girl who looked to be only eighteen or nineteen years old, held down with wrist and ankle restraints. She growled as Mason stepped toward her, the light from the hallway glinting off of her frightened eyes.

She struggled against the shackles, muscles working all over her naked and fur covered body. A black leather muzzle kept her jaw locked tight.

Quivering red lips pulled back, revealing a mouth of spiked canines and razor incisors.

His boots squeaked underneath him. Bile rose in his throat as he looked down to see he was treading on discarded condoms.

Mason stomped back into the living room. Maryanne saw the gun. She read the look on his face. She flopped over on the couch and tried to squirm away again. He stood over her and pressed the barrel to her head. Kazoo honks ensued.

"What the fuck was that about, Maryanne?" he said. "Who's the goddamn wolf girl chained up in there?" Maryanne honked. She struggled to pull away. Mason flipped her over, ripped the tape from her mouth again.

"It's no big deal," she sputtered. "It's just Jamie."

Mason was straddling her. He said, "No big deal?" and pressed the gun against the greasy blonde hair at her temple. "I should kill you right now."

"We don't let them hurt her," she said. "I swear."

"Fuck you, asshole," Arthur yelled from the bathroom.

"You pimp your daughter out to your drug addict friends? What the fuck is wrong with you?" Mason yelled at Maryanne. He holstered the gun, lit a cigarette with shaking hands. He paced in front of the couch, taking big drags from the smoke. Maryanne looked up at him like a scared animal.

More yelling from Arthur: "Don't tell him shit, Mary." Mason pulled the gun and quick stepped to the bathroom. He kicked the door open and pointed the .40 caliber at Arthur. The man squirmed in the chair. He squinted and scrunched up his damaged face like he'd tasted something horrible.

Mason spoke slowly. "Arthur, I swear to God, if you don't shut your fucking mouth, I'm going to put a bullet in you." Arthur rocked the chair back and forth. Mason wondered if he could even see the gun.

Mason wished for more duct tape. He scanned the bathroom, dropped his cigarette into the grimy toilet.

"Jamie sounds upset. Probably hungry too." Arthur said. He had a smirk on his half animal face. Mason didn't like it. He stood over him, looking down in anger.

"That girl isn't our daughter, dipshit, just some junkie that owes us money. Now she's working it off. She had her chance. We didn't force the dope on her." Arthur smiled. "Some of you single-breeds will pay a pretty penny to stick it in a little wolf girl. We're making good money off that little bitch. Yuri sure didn't have a problem with it when he was still getting his cut."

Mason shook his head. He thought of the girl in the room. Her ribs showing through the fur on her sides, the desperate look of hunger and fear in her half-human eyes. He felt his temper building; the fury rising in him like mercury in a thermometer. There was a time when he could separate work and emotion. Seemed he'd gotten sentimental in his old age.

Mason pulled a mildewed rag off of the towel rod and shoved it into Arthur's mouth. He pressed the barrel of the gun so hard into the plugged-up hole the chair legs squealed on the tile. He squeezed the trigger and painted the wall in a crimson bloom of blood, bone, and brain matter.

He could hear Maryanne screaming from the living room over the ringing in his ears. "Nooowooooh!" she howled.

Mason picked up the discharged shell casing and put it in his pocket. He used the filthy shower curtain to wipe the blowback off of his hand and leather jacket and draped it over the mess that used to be Arthur. The rag had muffled the shot, but he still needed to get moving fast. He went to check on Jamie.

The wolf girl was in a feral rage. The smell of blood in the air no doubt working her into a frenzy.

He stood in the doorway and watched in awe. Jamie was almost fully animal now. She thrashed on the bed, foam spewing from her restrained maw. Her eyes were red and furious.

"Let me go," came her snarling words, more bark than actual speech. "Let me have her," she growled.

He kept the gun trained on her as he crossed the room. He stood over the mattress and looked down at her. Her eyes pleaded to let her loose.

He tried not to think about what she'd gone through. The evidence wouldn't allow him blinders. He holstered the gun and pulled his pocket knife. He clicked the blade open with his thumb and leaned over.

"It's okay," he said. He fought the urge to pet her, to calm her like the scared animal she seemed.

Her body shivered as he put the blade under the restraints and worked through the thick leather, releasing her arms and legs. She sat up on her haunches. He hesitated a moment before cutting through the muzzle harness.

The mask dropped, and Mason stepped back. The girl rose onto her hind legs, nothing to her but fur and muscle. She sniffed the air and let out a howl more fearsome than anything Arthur had mustered. Mason watched her tear out of the room like a born hunter.

Fearsome growls and howls sounded from the living room. Bestial screams and wet tearing noises. Mason found the box hidden in the dresser where Maryanne said it would be. It was almost twice what they owed. He pocketed a few grand and left the rest for the girl to find when she finished with Maryanne.

Mason glimpsed the carnage in the living room. It was as gruesome as it was justified. The girl watched him warily out of the corner of her eye as she ripped and tore at her fresh kill. He collected his gear and exited the apartment to the tune of Jamie's rabid feasting.

Yuri had wanted the couple alive. He'd been very specific about that point. He wouldn't be happy, probably call a hitter for Mason.

Fuck Yuri, he thought, lighting a cigarette and closing the door behind him. Maybe Mason would just pay him a visit first.

GENIUS IN A BOTTLE:
A TOM BOYLE MYSTERY
BY ALEC CIZAK

I'd checked in with my personal pharmacist, Huey, to see if he'd front me a few days' worth. He said, "My man Willy Floyd's looking at time. He's collecting every day to make sure he's got money for a lawyer. You know how it is."

I said, "Let me call home, see if some work's come in." I used a cordless phone near a television on the floor of Huey's house, one side of a duplex on College Avenue. One of those Amityville Horror Dutch-Colonial joints with a chimney splitting a pair of mournful eyes. I dialed my office and entered the code to send the answering machine to PLAY mode. Some chump from a collection agency yip-yapped empty threats about a credit card debt I'd abandoned in 1985. A Puritan from the local Republican party wanted to take my pulse on the president. Did it bother me that he dodged Vietnam but had no qualms carpet bombing the Middle East? Did I have a problem with his pecker landing in every soft spot not named Hillary? About six messages in, a young woman's voice said she needed someone to look into something. Very vague. Could mean money. Could be a grift. I hung up and called her. "Is this Molly..." Took a moment to remember the last name. "Molly *Beckett?*"

"Who's this?"

"Tom Boyle."

"How soon can we talk in person?"

"Where's good for you?"

She told me to meet her at the German bakery on Pendelton Pike. A cramped building surrounded by lawn gnomes. Sold the best cake in the universe. Before the habit took over, I ate wurst and potato salad there once a week.

" *Voila,*" I said to Huey. "Now that I got work, how about some sympathy?"

"No can do."

"I should just quit."

"Not a bad idea." He lit an unfiltered Camel. "Let's see how sobriety looks on you. Then maybe I'll give it a go."

"How about you rot in hell?"

"The idea is to escape, isn't it?" He pointed his cigarette's cherry at a community of mustard-colored bruises splotched across his arm.

***

A mural depicting a Bavarian village in the Black Forest covered the side of the bakery. I chipped paint off it as I glided my '84 Buick into an angled parking spot. The brakes needed work. I'd have to rent a garage to fix them.

A host of vulgar German souvenirs greeted me inside as I wound through a constellation of wrought iron patio tables. Plastic gnomes coupled missionary style. Beer steins shaped like a woman's torso. Naked male and female salt and pepper shakers. Indicators of a culture drowning a guilt complex in kitschy perversion. Beer Garden oompah music pulsated speakers mounted in the ceiling. A tuba and accordion mating in a bounce house. Oddly comforting. I'd have to chat with a shrink to figure out why. A woman in a blue and white-checkered dirndl said hello. She'd contained her wild, scarlet hair in mini-lightning bolt pigtails. She told me she'd be with me as soon as she finished ringing out customers at the register. I said, "I'm good for now." Down a narrow corridor toward the bathrooms, I spotted a woman seated in the café's only private room. "Miss Beckett?"

She pointed to a picnic bench running alongside a wooden table. Glass covered the table's surface. Shielded a collage of photographs taken during the bakery's twenty years of existence. "Call me Molly." Faint eyeliner complimented by shaded lids matched her violet, form-fitting dress. The skirt stopped midthigh. She'd tied her long, auburn hair into a sloppy bun. Ignited a montage of Marian Librarian fantasies dormant since adolescence.

"What can I do for you?" I rested my elbows on the table. Folded my jittery hands together. How long since I'd felt the need to keep cool around a woman? Maybe Felicia, the last full-time affair I engaged in before letting the needle extinguish healthier appetites.

She leaned toward me. Her mango scented perfume brightened the room's stale air. Clashed with the ambience created by antlers and other hunting trophies mounted on the walls. "My father, Melvin, Mel, most people called him, maybe you heard of him? Mel Beckett?"

Oh, how I wanted to lie and say I knew the man. "I apologize, Molly."

"It's okay." She wrapped her fingers around a glass of water in front of an empty plate. A slice of lemon floated amidst thin ice cubes. Flaking polish on her nails suggested she fussed over her looks every now and then. "My father invented Seraphim. Have we heard of it?"

An anti-depressant. One of several legal drugs designed to alleviate mortality's grim forecast. Daisy Chemical, a pharmaceutical company based in Indianapolis, led the charge in the late 1980s with Seraphim. A doctor from which I expected better advice once suggested I replace heroin with it—*Seraphim will alter your brain's chemistry so you no longer feel the need to escape reality.* What an idiot. Say what you want about dope, at least it didn't rewire the mind. "I've heard of it."

"Daisy owns the patent," she said. "I suspect my dad, who was a very stubborn man, decided to complain. Maybe he threatened legal action. Daisy's making all kinds of money off his work. Can we blame him?"

"So far," I said, "I can't see one good reason to think the man brought anything but good to this world."

Her eyelids dropped. The corners of her lips tightened. "Mr. Boyle..."

"Call me Tom."

"Mr. Boyle," she said, "I can't afford someone...*bigger* than you. Not at the moment."

I straightened my shoulders. "Please, continue."

"Official story, the one they printed in the back of the *Star*, is he was under the influence." She stared at the table. Traced a circle near her glass of water with her pinky. "Dad had a problem, it's true. And he was probably drinking that night. But he'd never get behind the wheel if he, you know, if he was so far gone..."

"Your father was probably a genius," I said. "Smart folks throughout time have needed something to quiet their thoughts."

"That's kind of you." She asked what I charged. Normally, I'd dodge a gig like this. Daisy Chemical *owned* Indianapolis. Sniffing around their porch could invite all species of trouble. But that wouldn't bode well for my wallet or my interest in a carnal conversation with Molly Beckett. I gave her the usual numbers. "Act fast," she said. "Find out what happened to my father. I'll pay you double when it's over." Her thick, glossy lips drifted into a smile.

***

By the time I returned to my office that night, the yearn had graduated to anxiety. Sweat. Chattering teeth. The entire body a whack-a-mole game starting fires a thousand mallets couldn't quell. Before the madness of withdrawal started, I'd have to solve Molly Beckett's case. I hopped into my Buick and drove north, for Broad Ripple. The woman told me her father fed his habit at The Outback, a restaurant/bar combo on the corner of Westfield and Winthrop.

The patrons, or the management, or both, must have considered darkness necessary for consumption of the nation's favorite dope. Neon lights behind the counter colored a fog of cigarette smoke so thick I copped a nicotine rush before I could sit down. Early 1980s Southern California punk rock battered a pair of speakers doubling as bookends for bottles on a glass shelf mounted in front of a wall-sized mirror. Odd hangout for a chemist of Mel Beckett's stature. Then again, what genius didn't have quirks? Molly had shown me a picture of her father taken at Christmas, the previous year. A bean-shaped man with an unruly mop of salt and pepper hair. Horn-rimmed glasses more appropriate for a 1960s NASA scientist. A frumpy short-sleeved button-down shirt, half of it tucked in baggy, beige dress pants. He seemed a tad too old for The Outback. Again, how could I judge the man? I didn't agree with his solution to the miseries of existence, but if he helped the bungled and botched get through the night, well, good for him.

The bartender shouted over the music. Asked what I needed. Alcohol never did a thing for junk sickness. I ordered a Jack and Coke anyway. Coming off as a customer might facilitate the interrogation. I didn't want to flash my license to snoop. Spook the guy into silence. He retreated to the ledge at the bottom of the mirror behind him. Popped the top off a prescription pill bottle. I pondered what poison fed his blood. Resisted my mind's prompt to ask whether the bottle contained a synthetic opiate. He took his medicine. Then he set to the burden of making my drink.

He placed a sweating, diamond-patterned rocks glass on a napkin and slid it to me. Faded tattoos covered his arms. He'd cut the sleeves off his jeans jacket. Patches advertising various bands—The Cramps, Big Black, The Damned, etc.—had been sewn to the jacket without mind paid to symmetry. The anti-aesthetic of punk, a trend I'd hoped would die when Nirvana commercialized it a few years earlier. He introduced himself as Glenn. He hadn't bothered to dye his Mohawk. His gray hair promised a rational, adult conversation. He said, "Starting a tab?"

I slid a Lincoln across the counter and told him to keep the change. "I wondered if I might ask you a few questions?" He held up the five-dollar bill. Looked at it as though he'd never seen anything so offensive. I fished a twenty from a wad of cash in my pocket. Some of the dough Molly'd given me as a retainer. Every instinct, every vessel of desire in my body insisted I forget the whole thing, ask Glenn what species of drug he'd just taken and, should it be Vicodin or Demoral or something equally benevolent, might he be willing to sell me half a dozen? My hand shook as I flopped the bill onto the counter.

The bartender scooped it up. His expression barely altered. "What's going on?"

"I wonder if you knew Melvin Beckett?"

Glenn leaned forward. "Who?"

I repeated the name.

Fast, confident nods. "Yes, yes," he said. "Mel. Used to come in here every night."

"Are you aware he drove his car into the canal a few weeks ago?"

"Yeah, dude," said Glenn. "Gnarly way to go. Nice car, too. Fifty-nine Chevy, I think. Cherry red. Sweet ride. I just nabbed a seventy-four Dodge Dart, myself. Cost a pretty penny. I can't begin to imagine what Mel's car is worth."

"Dodge Dart," I said. "Impressive. Let me ask you, did Mel drink here that night?"

The bartender grabbed a rag from a bucket near the cash register and wiped the counter on both sides of my Jack and Coke. "Already told the pigs he only had one, you know? Strange for him, I guess. He usually got blotto and walked home when I'd cut him off. He lives just over...*lived* just over on Broadway."

"Anybody else here tonight saw him that night?"

"Nah, dude. It was a Tuesday. Unless it's summer, when the Butler yuppies invade Broad Ripple with mommy and daddy's credit cards, we're slow on Tuesdays."

***

I didn't fall asleep until four in the morning. I curled up on the floor beneath my desk. Listened to classical music on the UIndy station. My usual diet of whale songs on the tape deck would only have reminded me of the absent medicine. My bones protested when I unfolded myself with the rising sun, used the edge of the desk to hoist myself to a standing position. Lack of sleep. Lack of dope. I felt a thousand years older. Dry mouth. Foggy brain. The elders gods of withdrawal, closing in.

When dealing with fresh worm cuisine, I usually checked in with my old girlfriend Felicia Hill. She studied the dead in the morgue on Market Street. The basement of the city-county building. A twenty-eight-story warehouse for bureaucrats, lawyers, and cops. Too many knew my name. I used to spill dirt on local dealers. Scored some scratch and confiscated dope in the process. The paperwork and courtroom dramatics required to remain copacetic interfered with my desire to stay wasted and stare into the abyss. Must have showed in my work. They gathered what few nick-nacks I had on my desk—a framed picture of Felicia and I at Kings Island, a crayon drawing of my mother I made in kindergarten, and a ticket stub from a Lou Reed concert I saw in Merrillville in 1984—threw them in a box, and escorted me to the rotating front door. Can't say I blamed them for firing me. They wanted Huey and his supplier, Willy Floyd. I pretended I'd never met them. I fed the habit for six months off the unemployment checks. Snagged my license to snoop in my waking hours. Now, I had to sneak down a set of concrete steps in the back to avoid running into anybody with a score to settle.

The temperature dropped lower than the frigid October air outside. Camphor barely masked the unnerving stench of other chemicals used in the preservation of the recently expired. Felicia stood hunched over the corpse of a naked woman. The woman, while still alive, I assumed, had shaved her pubic hair. A bizarre new trend egged on by *Playboy* and porno flicks. Felicia peeled back the dead woman's scalp. Sawed off the top of her skull. Her eyes peered over a pair of work goggles positioned halfway down her nose. "Well, well," she said. "The invisible man."

"We're cool, right?"

"*Shit.*" She stepped away from the slab. Retrieved a clipboard from a hook on the wall. "What do you need?"

"You say that like I'm a leech or something."

"You are."

"You know anything about a guy named Mel Beckett?"

She returned to the slab. Refused to look at me.

"What's the story?"

"I didn't do the work on that one." She dug her gloved hands into the dead woman's skull and extracted the brain. Let the blood drip into a pan next to the dead woman's head. She plopped the organ onto a hanging scale.

"Who did?"

"Private party." She held up the dead woman's brain. Pointed to several gaping cavities in it. "That's from smoking crack," she said. "Daily use. I'd say three, four years in a row. Like Swiss cheese, don't you think?"

"Good thing that's not my kick."

"No." She made notes on the clipboard. "Your brain's just dull and grey."

"Kind of like my life..." I angled toward the slab. "Since we busted up."

"Whose fault was that?" She carried the brain to a metal cart with saws, drills, and a microscope resting on it.

"I'm going to eighty-six, if that makes a difference." I shoved my hands into my pockets. Shuffled my left foot back and forth like a windshield wiper. Felt stupid. A twelve-year-old asking a girl to the autumn dance.

As she set the brain on a tray and picked up a Gigli saw, she said, "To whom? Me?"

"What say you tell me what those private folks discovered when they did the autopsy on Melvin Beckett. This time, next week, we'll have dinner. I bet you we pick up right where we left off."

"What makes you think I haven't moved on?"

"I fully expect to have to win you all over again. Whether there's immediate competition or not."

She let out a 'pfft' noise. "I'd have to break some rules." Her focus left the dead woman's brain. "I do an awful lot for you, Tom Boyle. When the hell are you going to do something for me?"

"I just told you..."

"I've heard this story before. You give sobriety a try, panic the first night, and wham bam, you're right back on the needle."

I couldn't tell her *she* had competition. "You could try to be encouraging."

"Once, maybe once," she said, "you could share some of the loot you make off these suckers. I'm the one who tells you how these chumps cashed in."

I studied the tiles on the floor. Caked blood stained the thin paths between them. "Okay," I said. "Thirty percent."

"Fifty."

"Thirty."

"Forty-five."

"Thirty."

"Forty, and that's as low as I go. For now."

"Thirty."

"Son of a..." A gust of air escaped her lungs. Her shoulders collapsed. A proud woman, defeated. "Meet me at the old spot, tonight. Seven."

***

If I returned to my office, the sickness would win. I'd double over, load the industrial trash can by my desk with vomit. Before my appointment with Felicia, I'd end up stopping off at Huey's. Plug my blood with junk. I'd risk losing Felicia's help, her trust. Again. I'd place myself back in the bubble preventing enjoyment of natural relationships with other human beings. Normality, according to those unafflicted. No, I decided, I'd fill those hours with productivity. I sounded like my angry old father, a working man who talked responsibility and discipline while scratching his bloated belly and dissolving his liver with beer and tequila. He'd worked at Klein Transmissions. Inhaled asbestos every day on the assembly line until it summoned cancer in his lungs and killed him.

Daisy Chemical's main offices sat on a fat strip of land between Market and Ohio, south of the city-county building. I ducked into Shapiro's, a deli nearly as old as the city itself. Nibbled on a pastrami sandwich. Eavesdropped on an argument between college students the next table over. They couldn't agree on whether *The Myth of Sisyphus* constituted blind optimism or cynical nihilism.

The sun set. I trekked east on foot. Used nervous energy storming my veins to climb a fence bordering a near-empty parking lot. Negotiated barbed wire looped across the top. As for the slim man in uniform in the booth at the gate, he must not have shared Daisy's concern for security. He slept with his hands folded across his stomach. Feet raised, poking from the sliding window I assumed he'd examine the identification of anyone driving up. I found a service entrance near the right. Generally, businesses in Indianapolis kept these doors unlocked. Not so with Daisy. I paced until it opened and a man in a grey jumper emerged. He pushed a rubber trash barrel on wheels. I crept inside the building before the door closed on its own. Fluorescents flickered and buzzed as I snuck down a corridor toward the main lobby. A directory board hung at the far end of an elevator bank. Management had yet to remove Melvin Beckett's information. Three-twenty-three. I pressed the UP button on the nearest elevator and waited.

Navy carpeting covered the floor of the hallways on the third story. Black and white photographs of scientists and business squares dotted the walls. I rounded a corner and found Mel Beckett's office. Lights out. Door unlocked. The office reflected Mel Beckett's dressing habits. Sloppy. Papers all over a teacher's desk in the corner next to a window with no shades or slats. The files spilled onto the floor, as though someone had knocked them off a pile as they exited. Or maybe someone had rifled through the man's documents to find something. Or hide something. I tried the drawers on a wooden filing cabinet. Someone had jimmied the lock on the top drawer. No surprise finding all the drawers empty.

I left the office. As I shut the door, the man who'd inadvertently let me into the building approached. He dragged a vacuum cleaner behind him. Stopped and said, "Could I help you?"

"Friend of Melvin Beckett," I said. "I was just seeing if he was still working tonight."

"Nobody else is here."

"You familiar with Mr. Beckett?" I pointed to the name stenciled on the door's smudged window.

The man let the vacuum cleaner stand upright. Ran his hand across his bald scalp. "I am new here." He picked at the ends of his handlebar mustache. "Diego," he said. "Diego cleaned the place before."

"Before what?"

"Before last Thursday. Before somebody put him in the hospital."

***

The days Felicia and I spent blue hours coiled at my old apartment in Broad Ripple, we'd meet up first at the Red Key Lounge. A small joint on College Avenue. Russ, the owner, prohibited foul language. Played Big Band music at a volume unable to compete with conversation. As the name promised, a scarlet glow animated the neon sign outside and continued inside, thanks to track lighting along the walls. The nuance, the quiet, all factors preventing babies in their early twenties from taking interest in the place and ruining it with drunken stupidity. When I arrived, Felicia waved from our booth. How many hours had we killed on those vinyl seats? We talked sex, religion, and politics. Never blushed at each other's opinions. The occasional gawker might give us static, Indianapolis still not used to seeing people with different skin tones getting down in the 1980s. Felicia, like all women, would insist I ignore it. Like all men untamed by offspring and a mortgage, I didn't listen. I'd invite the bigots to step outside. Like all bigots, they proved themselves cowards and attempted to laugh off the episode as a misunderstanding.

Felicia nursed an Irish coffee, steam rising off the rim of her cup and curling around her. She nodded at a checkered rocks glass filled with booze resting on a coaster. "If you're not shooting dope," she said, "I hope you're at least drinking." She sipped her coffee. The pleasant scent of Irish crème lingered between us. "You got to do something, right?"

I thanked her and took a swig. With my natural senses making a comeback, the Jack and Coke warmed the belly a bit better than the night before. "So," I said, "what do you know?"

Her lips curled inward. "No foreplay?"

"The clock is ticking."

"Yeah, it is," she said. "Melvin Beckett drifted off Westfield, into the canal three weeks ago. They planted him at Crown Hill two days later. Awful fast turnaround. He was driving his car, a nice one, apparently, one of those old models with fins, in the wrong lane. Police assume a car approached from the opposite direction. The man probably whipped the steering wheel to the right, thinking the guard rail would catch him. Thing is, they're repairing those rails right now, so it wasn't there. Car goes into the drink. Sinks. Beckett must have had his window up, must have had his seat belt on, something. He couldn't get out in time. Official cause of death? Drowning."

"And the contents of his system?" I said. "I mean, besides the crappy canal water and a goldfish or two."

"A smidge of booze."

"He wasn't drunk?"

"The man had Ativan in his blood." She sipped her coffee. "You mix Ativan with even a tiny bit of alcohol..."

"Yeah," I said, "Weeble-Wobble City. I've been there."

"Yeah," she said, "I drove you home that night. Watched you projectile vomit all the next morning."

"Memories." I tapped the table three times and stood.

"Where you going?" she said.

"I need to see someone in Methodist."

"You feeling sick?"

"Not quite," I said. "Not yet."

Russ chastised her for cussing at me as I walked out the door.

***

The lights in Methodist Hospital's windows lit up I-65 and the main roads surrounding it. Lazy clouds loitered overhead, illuminated by a golden half-moon. A sleepy eye guarding the night. I parked the Buick in the visitor's lot. Shuffled through the rotating front door. Clutched my belly. Cramps. Aches. Muscles tightening. I struggled to conduct myself like a civilized human being.

While inquiring as to the condition of Diego Sosa, Bonnie, according to the nametag pinned to the receptionist's mint green scrubs, asked if I needed to see a doctor. "Honey..." She spoke in a perfect Hoosier accent. Country, without the bullshit. "You look like someone dug you up from Crown Hill and flopped a ten-cent suit on your bones. Pale as a ghost, I tell you. I seen my Papaw stumble to his bedroom for the last time, Easter, 1981. Same ghastly Sammy Terry face you got." She handed me a clipboard, as though she'd settled the matter. "You fill in the vitals, we'll get you with a doctor in a jiff."

I gently pushed the clipboard back in her direction. "Long day is all." I asked again for information on Diego Sosa. She let some of that old Indiana bias leak from her lips:

"You mean the Mexican?"

153

"Naptown's got more than one," I said. "This guy's name is Sosa. Diego Sosa." I drummed my fingers on the top of a computer monitor to the right of Bonnie's thinning, curled hair. "Bet you two dimes you can type on that there keyboard and gather up everything I'm looking to learn." I couldn't help slipping into my own Hoosier habits. Talking like a poet who earned his bread harvesting wheat. Truth be told, yammering on like that distracted me from the urge to grind my teeth into nubs.

The woman probably dismissed me as one of these pesky progressives who believed in basic decency. She said, "He's recovering. Fifth floor." She gave me the room number. "You got thirty minutes before they give you the boot."

A ride up the elevator and a short walk to room five-ten. No less than three women in scrubs asking me my business. I showed them my license to snoop. Prayed my hand didn't shake every which way while I held out the laminated card. Diego Sosa rested in a bed hosting a tangle of IVs traveling from his arms to a forest of metal trees sprouting bags of fluid from their branches. A diminutive woman in a cobalt dress, dark hose, and large, clumsy work boots sat in a folding chair next to the bed. She held the man's right hand in both of hers. I explained why I'd come to see Diego.

"He barely speaks." She introduced herself: Marisol Martinez. Diego's wife. Wide, suspicious eyes framed by smudged eyeliner. "The police have all the information."

"I'm not the police."

Her head pivoted on her neck. A crane sensing danger in the water.

I couldn't waste minutes negotiating with her. I stepped around to the other side of the bed. Somebody had worked over Diego Sosa with brass knuckles or perhaps a lead pipe. His face must have resembled the Elephant Man when he arrived at Methodist. Purple welts zig-zagged up and down his skull. "Diego?"

"Please," said his wife.

"Diego," I said again. "You are familiar with Melvin Beckett? He worked at Daisy..."

The man's swollen eyelids separated. He groaned as he turned toward me. Studied me for a moment. "You are no police...."

"That's correct." I showed him my license. As though it would mean anything to anyone in his condition.

His chest rose. A wheeze worked its way through his lungs, his throat, and out his nostrils. "I can tell you one thing." He adjusted his curled fingers so a single digit extended beyond the others. He stared at the ceiling and said, so hushed I barely heard it, "*1959.*" The utterance apparently taxed him. He sank into the bed, shifted his gaze to his wife.

***

The UIndy station played two hours of music by Ligeti. The psychotic shrieks of violins enhanced the sensation of hooks attached to strings attached to my flesh controlled by unseen hands, threatening to tear off my skin. I fidgeted on my desk, humored myself into thinking I'd fall asleep. The night's pleasant shades of

155

blue did nothing to quell the rage of withdrawal. At one point, I tried to wrap the desktop around me like a blanket and fell over the side. The pain of slapping my bones against the concrete floor felt wonderful. The senses alive and bickering. A brief victory in the war that takes place when the mind has accepted it's time to leave a destructive lover, but the body doesn't agree. I stayed on the floor. Watched reels of my life play out in the dark until the memories became dreams and my worn-out brain granted sleep.

I held my stomach as I woke up. Throat dry. The horrid stench of vomit and other fluids surrounded me. I'd thrown up. Lucky to be on my side. My body released other things. Stifled things that should have been ejected long ago. My belly rumbled. Begged for nutrition. My favorite suit, soiled and rank, required a date with the laundromat on 64th Street. I changed into an older black number I'd worn to court during the days I lied for the city.

I grabbed breakfast at Perkins near Castleton. Sunlight baked my booth while I ordered. I savored my stomach's renewed interest in tasty, destructive American cuisine. A stack of pancakes smothered in the blood of a maple. Eggs over easy. Buttered toast to sop up the eggs' yellow souls as they meandered across the plate. I used a payphone near the restroom to call Phil Hack, a technician at the city impound. Phil worshipped the same chemical god I did. Unlike me, he'd managed to keep his job with the police department. He told me to meet him at the Delaware Street entrance. I finished my breakfast. The best I'd had in years. Tried, with no success, to snag the waitress's phone number when she handed me the bill. Her strawberry blonde hair bounced around as she explained all the ways her boyfriend would kill us both. "He used to be a skinhead," she said. "He's reformed, you know, from being a Nazi and all. But he still likes to hurt people. Says it makes him feel all tingly in the knuckles."

I thanked her for the detailed rejection and drove south. I'd had enough run-ins with neo-Nazis both current and rehabilitated. They never fought fair. Always required a mob of their own to take on a lone enemy. Most threw punches lighter than air. Every now and then, however, you'd run into a lunatic who worshipped violence.

The impound inhabited six blocks between Delaware and Penn. Rumor slated the land for development. A bigger venue for the Pacers. Because the city's youth getting dumber, the poor getting poorer, the corrupt getting richer, none of these things mattered in the face of entertainment. The basketball team had made the playoffs. This warranted shelling out millions of tax dollars to build a gaudier, more impressive arena befitting national heroes like Reggie Miller and Rik Smits. Even the vital work of containing cars confiscated by IPD played second fiddle to grown men chasing orange rubber balls across a hardwood floor. I told myself to calm down. Harsh cynicism always accompanied sobriety. Who the hell was I to judge how other people got their kicks? Felicia once lectured me about culture, how it donned multiple masks. People cheering on overpaid athletes, she'd said, qualified.

Phil Hack stood by a gate fashioned from tall white pickets. Dressed in an oil-stained diesel coverall. Dying cigarette drooping from the side of his mouth.

He stared at the rocks covering the parking lot outside the fence. Barely hoisted his attention upward as I approached. "Hey…"

"What do you know?"

He spit his cigarette onto the ground. Crushed it underneath his combat boots. "Walk this way, brother." I followed him through the gate. We navigated a labyrinth of parked cars. Many species. Many conditions. An alarming number decorated with bullet holes. High grass sprouted through the interiors of vehicles long abandoned and deemed unworthy at police auction. He said, "I'm surprised the Beckett Chevy ain't been smooshed yet."

"Oh?"

"They stashed it in transition." He led me to an elongated building. Grey bricks. A dozen bays. Some open. Some closed. He rolled up a garage door near the middle. A cherry Chevy Impala with cream-colored trim stretching from the front to the fins glowed in the morning sun. Remnants of growth from the canal dangled along the bottom. Taupe strands of vegetation stretched across the hood and the roof. "Damn shame," said Phil. "That was one wicked whip."

"A little work," I said, "she'll roll again."

A slow, deliberate movement of his head from side to side. "Don't think so, brother. This honey's scheduled for block city. They just ain't got to it yet."

I strolled around the Chevy. Peeked into the windows. Mel Beckett treated his car better than his office. No trash on the seats. Nothing on the floor. An unpleasant mildew aroma surrounded it. Another souvenir from the canal. I tried the handle on the driver's side door. A slight squeal from the hinges. I reached into the folds between the seat cushions and backs. Impeccable. I leaned in and opened the glovebox. Mel Beckett had kept the original owner's manual. No webs on the spine. On top of the book, he'd placed the registration and what appeared to be a check stub. The man made good money. More in a week than I made in a month. Flipping it over, I found a note scribbled in blue ink:

They're nixing the 59. Gonna make it vanish for good. I were you? I'd let it go.

-Hank

Hank?

I couldn't figure out how the car, beyond diving into the canal and drowning Mel Beckett, represented any kind of threat. I shut the door and stepped away from it. Surveyed it once more, sought anything out of place. "What's so special about a 1959 Chevy, Phil?"

"Beats me." He seized a pack of Pall Mall cigarettes poking from his coverall's breast pocket. Knocked one out and lit it. "Don't see what any of that's got to do with this car." He pointed at the Chevy with the cigarette. "This here's a '61."

***

Molly Beckett worked in the reptile booth at the Children's Museum. They'd recently covered the square, red-brick building with a giant yellow and green arch. Tried to make it look jollier than the other ten-thousand red-brick buildings in the city. Five floors of entertainment for kids, including a massive model train display on the top level, across from an old-time carousel. Like most museums in Naptown, no entry fee. Benevolence supported by donations and charity. A fleeting glimpse of the kinder iterations of human nature.

I found Molly Beckett on the first level. The Critter Corral, a miniature zoo of lizards and rodents in glass tanks. Kids fidgeted in an unorganized line to pet a boa constrictor coiled around Molly's waist. She explained to more than one anxious tyke they needed to calm down and gently stroke the beast. "If we anger him," she said, "he'll suffocate me. We don't want that, do we?" Some of the boys nodded and assured her they wanted *precisely* that. She acknowledged me and used her forehead to point at a clay bench outside the front doors. I waited a half hour under grey, autumn Indiana clouds. A thin chill lurked, announced itself in sporadic gusts. The cold needled me, taunted me. *Wouldn't a rocket full of heroin obliterate this frigid atmosphere?* Just a short drive north to Huey's place. Molly arrived in time to interrupt the debate. Her work uniform, apparently, a pair of khakis and a collared T-shirt with the museum's logo stitched over her left breast. Gorgeous, auburn hair in a ponytail. No makeup. None needed. She said, "God, I hate this job."

"I wonder if you know anything about the year 1959?"

"How old do I look?" She laughed before I made the mistake of taking her seriously. "I mean, no. I don't know anything about it."

"Your dad never mentioned anything about 1959?"

"If he did, I missed it."

"How about somebody named Hank? Your dad have a friend named Hank?"

"His boss's name is Henry Till, if that helps."

I spoke without thinking—"Want to go to dinner when things are all wrapped up? Maybe Steak 'n Shake. I'll pay for the skinny fries."

"I think we'd better get back to work." She swayed toward the Museum's entrance. Glanced back at me twice.

***

Despite the barbed wire atop the fence surrounding Daisy Chemical, they didn't seem too bothered by the idea of someone casually traipsing through the front gate during business hours. I parked at a strip club called The Magic Carpet Lounge. Neon silhouettes of dancers kicking their legs doused the asphalt with colorful lights. I greeted several ladies dressed in sweatpants and jeans jackets as they entered the club. The scent of Pink Lemonade sat on the air long after they disappeared. I dodged cars on Market Street. Strolled past the guard house in front of Daisy's lot without having to say hello to a thin, uniformed geezer seated in front of a black and white television set. I ducked my head to avoid making eye contact with cameras wedged in the ceiling over the main entrance. Checked the directory near the elevators for Henry Till's information. Third floor, same as Melvin Beckett. Employees, some in suits, some in white lab coats, scuttled about. Bosses at Daisy must have ruled with an iron beaker. Their wage slaves hustled like drones. Or maybe that's how workers behaved when they brought home paychecks like Mel Beckett's.

Henry Till's door stood half open. I nudged it with my foot until it creaked out of the way. A round man torturing a wobbly office chair tore his attention from a clump of dot-matrix printed files in his hands. "May I help you?" Ah, the old yuppie standard. Sounded polite. Blanketed an army of thorns intended to communicate how much the existence of another irritated him.

I produced Mel Beckett's pay stub from my pants pocket. Uncrumpled it and pointed at the note on the back. "You Hank?" My hand didn't shake as much as it had the previous two days.

The man placed the papers he'd been examining on his otherwise spotless desk. He took the stub from me. Elicited a concerto of tisk tisk tones. "Mel always was a slob." He gave it back to me. "He leave that on the street? In a public toilet?"

"What's the problem with 1959?"

Color evacuated the man's cheeks. His eyes, previously tiny behind his thick, rectangular glasses, doubled in size. "Are you crazy?" He jumped to his feet, pulled me into the office, checked the hallway for marauding ninjas or something equally upsetting, and shut the door. "Lord," he said. "That man is causing ulcers from beyond the grave."

"I'd think anybody working in a joint like this has ulcers." I stuffed the pay stub into my pocket.

"This is serious, ah, what'd you say your name was?" He stepped to a grey file cabinet five drawers high. He lifted a set of keys attached to a chain on his belt and inserted one into the lock on the top of the cabinet. He pulled out the fourth drawer. Scrunched a row of brown file folders toward him and grabbed a metal box with a combination lock on it. "Substance 1959, to be precise." He set it on his desk. "I have the only remaining sample." I looked away, gave him an opportunity to dial the combination. The lock clicked. Removing a clear, plastic container with a corked test tube inside it he said, "You're familiar with HIV?"

"Shouldn't we be wearing protective gear?"

"This isn't the virus." The man raised the clear container closer to the fluorescent light humming overhead. The dull glare illuminated an amber substance inside the test tube. "This is Substance 1959. One dose of this acts like a magnet. Like an ant trap, if you're familiar with the concept. The virus is induced to visit the injection site. Once there, Substance 1959 eradicates it and teaches the immune system to do the same to any future invasions."

"I haven't heard..."

"Nobody has." He placed the container back into the lockbox. "Nobody other than Mel, myself, and Leo Black, the man who makes executive decisions for Daisy." He locked the box and slid it behind the files in the drawer.

"People are dying," I said.

He secured the file cabinet. Let the zip line on his key chain return the flock to the side of his belt. "You ever wonder why there isn't a cure for cancer?"

"I was told we hadn't created one."

"There's multiple," said Hank. "But think of all the people put out of work if cancer is cured with a simple shot or pill."

I needed heroin. Right then, right there. Who did I think I'd fool, trying to tackle the wicked world without dope? A fresh ache twisted through my stomach. "This isn't available to the public because of...*profit?*"

"Welcome to capitalism, Mr., ah, what was your name?"

"Mr. Till," I said, "you have an ethical responsibility. People I know are in the graveyard because of AIDS." I stopped short of telling him what a nuisance bleaching needles had become. "Keeping this quiet is a crime against the entire species."

"You sound like Mel Beckett." The man assaulted his office chair once more. Ignored the crackling vinyl as he leaned backward. "You see where his optimism landed him?"

"Who did it? Leo Black?"

Hank Till peered over his glasses. "Why do you insist on pretending you're some kind of innocent, ah...what did you say your name was?"

"I didn't."

*****

I hid my face a whole lot more on the way out. Ducked as I returned to the strip club. I'd forgotten how easy it is to feel no guilt if you've snuffed somebody without having to put your hands around his throat. Mel Beckett's killer, at least the one who did the deed, had enjoyed that luxury. Traffic up Meridian moved slow. The yearn for junk in my blood graduated from physical terror to a simple debate: If I plugged my veins one time, I'd collapse into the daily hunt all over again. It only took one time. The rational circuits in my head insisted such a backslide represented a lack of discipline. Hell, a lack of intelligence. The opposition, however, hinted at its defense. The same rationale that drove every rocket into my skin:

What's the fucking point?

I pulled into the lot at the McDonald's on the edge of Broad Ripple. Used their pay phone to call Molly Beckett. She suggested we rendezvous at the Steak 'n Shake on Keystone. Said she'd pay for the skinny fries.

After hanging up, I sat by a window in the McDonald's facing Winthrop. Watched the parking lot behind the Outback bar. A few beat up cars moseyed in over the next thirty minutes. Finally, a black Dodge Dart, gleaming in the red haze of the setting sun, rolled into a corner away from the other cars. The driver positioned it at an angle, communicating his disdain for anyone heartless enough to devalue the sight of the muscle machine by placing an inferior vehicle next to it. Glenn the bartender stepped out. Same drab, dated punk rock wardrobe he'd worn the night I spoke with him. The night I should have given in to the yearn and asked what pills his doctor had prescribed him.

I crossed the street and used the employee entrance to sneak into the Outback. Three cooks worked on prepping vegetables and meat for the evening.

They noticed me, let their eyebrows communicate their concern—*Who the hell are you?*

Glenn stood behind the bar examining a row of booze bottles on the counter. He started to speak as I snaked around him and grabbed the pills on the ledge under the mirror. They belonged to him, according to the name on the label. Glenn, it appeared, suffered from anxiety. Hey, I could relate. He clearly didn't belong in Indianapolis. Neither did I. Indy catered to conformists. People content to grow a family and run the same cycle of life, over and over again. Oh, sure, the Phoenix Theater ran plays business types would call edgy, meaning, one or two gay characters and a live goat for shock value. The yuppies, the locals who'd landed jobs paying more than a nickel, they referred to this as culture, and assured each other it granted Indianapolis major metropolitan status. The truth being, however, the dominant forms of art in the entire state revolved around basket weaving and banjo music. Frankly, I had no problem with any of it as long as the yuppies and yipjacks left me alone.

Glenn asked what the hell I thought I was doing.

"Ativan?" I dumped the pills onto the counter. They made tiny white islands around a whiskey bottle at the end of the line.

The bartender knew I knew. He hesitated before offering a snotty, half-hearted, "So? I get panic attacks."

"I don't blame you," I said. "Life is rough." I grabbed a fifth of Jack Daniel's. Took a swig. "I gather you didn't come up with the idea to drop one in Mel Beckett's drink on your own."

If Glenn thought he'd mastered anxiety, he learned better in that moment. I heard him swallow his fear as he stumbled backward. Caught himself on the lip of the bar. "I don't..."

"It's not me you have to worry about," I said. "Or even the cops." I helped him regain his balance. "My math says Leo Black, or someone associated with him, someone who looked like maybe they could crush your skull between their palms, slid you some cash. Enough to buy that sweet Dodge out there in the parking lot. Maybe they told you it was a gag? Let's see how Mel Beckett walks once he's committed one of the biggest no-no's in the wild world of inebriation. I mixed Ativan with tequila once. Suffered enough the next day to know I'd never make that mistake again."

"I..."

"I don't need an explanation, Glenn. If I were you, I'd use whatever money you got left from that gig to load up your belongings and drive as far away from Indianapolis as you can. If you think they're going to let you walk around with knowledge about what happened to Melvin Beckett, well, you haven't listened to enough Dead Kennedys or Circle Jerks, right? Power protects itself. Always."

"I don't know what I was thinking." He promised he'd do as I suggested. "I got family in..."

"Don't tell me," I said. "I don't want to know any more than I already do."

***

Molly Beckett stood near one of the large, plate glass windows in the Steak 'n Shake facing Keystone. A wonder she hadn't caused an accident. She'd squeezed herself into a turquoise one-piece tight enough to communicate her disdain for panties and a bra. I'd have to give her a mini lecture about not calling attention to herself at the moment. She might have to leave town, the same as Glenn, once she knew the truth. I parked and entered the side of the building. Molly beckoned me to join her in a booth in the corner. "You look terrible, Mr. Boyle."

"Call me Tom, please."

"I brought the rest of your salary, Mr. Boyle," she said. "I'm hoping we have a little more information today than we did yesterday."

"Your instincts are correct," I said. "Your father was killed."

Her lower lip curled inward. Her eyes followed her pinky, tracing a circle on the table between us. "Do we know why?"

"He developed something incredible, something that would prevent Daisy or any other pharmaceutical company from making lifelong customers out of HIV patients."

"I'm not sure..."

So, I told her. Pops found a cure for AIDS. In an upside-down world, this had been a problem. People in charge didn't consider it a lucrative discovery. She said, "You know this...for a fact?"

"I've seen the last remaining bit of it, in a glass tube in your father's boss's office."

"What's he holding on to it for?"

"Insurance, I suppose." I grabbed a menu wedged between a metal napkin dispenser and a bottle of ketchup. "If he didn't keep it, the same man who ordered the hit on your father would probably snuff him next."

A different gleam inhabited her eyes. I saw the vapid hunger before I heard it: "We could rake them," she said. "You tell them we know what they have, tell them we'll tell the world, or they pay us, monthly. I wouldn't have to work at the stupid Children's Museum anymore and..." Her thin, newly manicured fingernails nudged the sleeve of my sports jacket up my arm. Trailed across a mishmash of fading injection bruises. "And you, Tom Boyle, could feed your ugly habit for, well, as long as it takes before you do what all junkies eventually do..."

"Was this what you were actually looking for?" I don't know why I even asked.

"Are we scared?" She rested one hand over the other.

I demanded my salary. Double. And the skinny fries she'd promised.

***

The fantasy of living clean dissipated as the Steak 'n Shake's neon-soaked exterior diminished in the rearview mirror. Can't say conscious thought directed my hands to steer the Buick in the direction of College Avenue. Unconscious knowledge of myself, perhaps. An acceptance that the world didn't deserve the effort required to negotiate it sober. I parked down the street from Huey's and

169

hiked through the alley behind his house to avoid any possible cop eyes lurking on the main road.

A peek in the kitchen window and I saw the glow of Huey's television casting strobing light in the living room. I knocked on the aluminum outer door. Knocked several times, assuming he'd fixed up already and required persistence, nagging, to get him to his feet. He wandered into the kitchen. Eyes barely open. Annoyance glued to his face. "Thought you were finished?"

"I'm not looking for charity, old friend." I turned so I could slide past him and ignore the horrid mess in his kitchen on the way to the living room. I removed a clump of twenty-dollar bills from the fold Molly Beckett handed me under the table at the Steak 'n Shake. She vowed to follow through with her blackmail plan. I'm not into necrophilia. Making love to the woman before Leo Black and Daisy Chemical cured her the way they cured her father would have been just as futile as anything else in this world. The only reliable lover rested snug inside a plastic baggie corner. Black tar. Cooked in a spoon. Or maybe a modified bottle cap. Absorbed into a fresh cotton ball. Drawn into a clean syringe and mixed with the blood of the faithful. "Let me get ten squares of the good stuff."

Huey prepared the order. He handed me a needle with the orange cap still attached. "Welcome back," he said. Junkies trusted each other in such circumstances, trusted the rocket hadn't been used, didn't require a round of bleach, and harbored no virus capable of turning the immune system inside out and laying waste to a human being for doing nothing more than seeking reprieve

from the manmade bullshit spinning the world on a crooked axis.

THE STOWAWAY

BY ALEX SLUSAR

1886

While the *Virginia May* churned its great paddlewheel through the muddy Mississippi River and the revelers aboard it laughed into the starless night, Gideon Hall lay boxed up in a crate aboard, listening to water slap against the hull.

He'd worried the idea was simple — not simple like easy, but like a hoof had stove his head in. It came to him in Natchez while he waited under the eaves watching the river dock, thinking he'd get Auguste Lancaster when the stately steamboat stopped on its journey to New Orleans and the thieving bastard disembarked to avail himself of local game tables and whores. But the *Virginia May* had tables, liquor, and its own soiled doves — if Lancaster stayed on the boat, seeing him dead meant boarding the *Virginia May*. She would arrive in the morning and leave before sunset, making a scramble aboard impossible. Hall hadn't enough money for a ticket, nor for the finery necessary to blend in with the revelers aboard — that was Lancaster's fault, and partly why he had to die. Seeing bulky crates lugged along the dock and loaded into passing watercraft prompted inspiration. The paddle-wheeler would stop for provisions.

With his scant coin Hall bribed a dockhand to see the manifests. In fog-choked early morning he broke into the storage warehouse, found the stacked crates of replenishments for the *Virginia May* and selected a long crate about his size and shape which was packed with potatoes. He removed enough spuds to fit himself, two .44 Remington Frontier Army pistols, a Bowie knife, and a skin of water. Then he lay down and shut himself inside, like a man in a casket sent off with his meager possessions.

In the crate Hall nibbled on raccoon jerky and sipped water, keeping hunger, thirst and the need to piss at bay. Before long a shifting and jostling told him he was being carried outside by the dockhands. If there was any question about the cargo's weight, he didn't hear it — only grunts of exertion, muttered curses, and clattering as the dockhands set him down. Hall sipped dusty air through a slit between two pine slats which he'd pried open slightly with his knife and waited for the loading

to stop. He prayed they wouldn't pile cargo atop, preventing his exit. He

said something to himself like *Lord I've got this far.* When the footsteps

and scraping of shifting cargo finished and he wagered he was alone he

pressed gingerly against the lid. It gave well.

The belly of the *Virginia May* rumbled and sloshed as its massive

stern paddlewheel turned. It sounded close, telling him he'd been placed

somewhere near the stern. When the noise built to a sustained cacophony

and they were well underway he grinned and allowed himself a low,

hoarse, guttural laugh.

Now he lit a match to check his battered silver pocket watch —

could fairly taste the burning sliver. It was nearly midnight. He'd been in

the box fifteen hours. For four months he'd tracked Lancaster. Five

months since he'd got the news. What was fifteen hours?

Briefly Hall wondered if he'd been wrong somewhere. If Lancaster

had disembarked in Natchez for good or had given him the slip entirely

and was on a train halfway to San Francisco, instead of steaming down

the Mississippi to rumrunner friends who'd spirit him to Mexico. Perhaps

Lancaster had double the protection he anticipated. Back in Memphis

Hall had counted four detectives, hard-looking men in long black coats

with Stetsons slouched low. They'd shadowed Lancaster while he strutted the street like a bantam rooster. Hall had watched silently from a narrow alley with a rag tied over half his face, appearing a destitute workhouse casualty instead of an avatar of vengeance. Watching had tested every scrap of nerve he had left.

Hall grit his teeth. Knew he wasn't wrong. Knew the time was now.

Lord, I've got this far.

He pushed the lid up. Pine slats snapped and swung awkwardly on bent nails as he came out as though from a grave. He emerged sweat-drenched and stale into humid darkness. The air was a warm syrup redolent with pine and grease. Briefly Hall worried about kerosene vapor. He chanced it, struck another match, held it up. Its faint glow showed he was in the *Virginia May's* hold, which was stacked with crates and draped with heavy cordage. Against the far wall was the outline of a door.

Hall extinguished the match, tasted its smoke. Touched the Remingtons holstered at his sides and the Bowie knife in its sheath at his back. Fingered six .44 rounds studding his gun belt — the only extra ammunition he could afford. Went to the wall crouched low, cracked open the door. The night air came in, cool and heavy with scents of loam, water and cut ivy.

The stern deck was empty. Hall saw white walls, pillars garnished with beveled accents, a row of curtained windows glowing with amber light. From within the ship came sparkling piano music, something like "Camptown Races" above the din of low conversation and the occasional peal of laughter. To his right, starboard way, was a large bollard and two crates covered with a flap of canvas — good cover if he bolted out of the hold.

He heard footsteps approaching. Through the jamb he saw a gangly man in coattails and a rotund woman in a plumed dress, her arm in his, come down the starboard side. The man whispered something to the woman. She giggled with an affected pitch. They glanced furtively around, then stole behind the canvassed crates. The woman hiked her dress up.

"Chrissake," Hall whispered to himself. "Ain't got a berth on this tub?"

They strained and gasped for a minute before a third appeared — an angular, hawk-nosed man in a long dark coat and a Stetson. The woman yelped in surprise. The man in the Stetson muttered something angrily, jerked his thumb over his shoulder and scowled as the couple scurried sheepishly past him and down the port walkway. Hall recognized him as one of the detectives he'd seen in Memphis.

When the detective turned away Hall crawled out and scuttled low along the deck, his footsteps muffled by the wet *chunk-chunk-chunk* of the paddlewheel. The sound harmonized with blood pounding in his ears. He got behind the crates and peered over them. The detective sauntered along the starboard deck, lit a cigarette and stopped with his elbows set on the railing.

Hall unsheathed his Bowie knife. He crept over to the wall. He crouched under the windows and glanced around the corner. The detective smoked and stared at the purple-black banks coursing past. Hall stalked closer, heard the detective sigh. When the cigarette stub was pitched into the river he came up from behind, locked his arm around the detective's throat, and brought the curved point of the big gleaming knife under his chin.

"Where's Lancaster," he said.

"Who?" the detective grunted.

"The man you're protecting."

The detective made a strangled chuckle. "You the one got him worried. Don't matter. You ain't gonna reach him nohow."

"Worth asking," Hall said. He sent the knife up through the soft part of the detective's chin and into the brain. Blood spilled hot and slick over his hand. The man shuddered and spasmed, tried to break free, tried screaming something unintelligible past the cold hard blade in his mouth before he loosened and went slack. Hall yanked the blade out, wiped it against the longcoat, then heaved the detective's body over the railing. It went in with a muted splash and was battered under the wheel.

Hall sheathed the knife. Something came over him, triggered by the wet blood and frothing water below. Adrenaline stayed the empty pit in his stomach where salted raccoon bits gurgled around but did nothing for his swollen bladder. It was like a heavy stone pushing against his guts.

"Goddamn it," Hall said, fumbling the buttons of his jeans with his non-dominant hand, since it was free of blood. He got unhooked, saw nobody around — *Lord, I've got this far* — and pissed over the railing after the detective's corpse.

When he was finished he skulked toward the bow, grateful for one fewer between him and his quarry. Under tall black columnal chimneys belching woodsmoke into the night a narrow stairway went up to the second deck, and Hall reckoned going up made sense. In Natchez he'd learned the main deck was for cargo, staff and entertainment, built around the central bar, stage and gaming tables within. The second and third decks had guest cabins, rooms for sporting, a smoking parlor, a library. The more opulent guest cabins were on the third deck, under the wheelhouse. Lancaster would have one of those, with berths for his guardians nearby. And should Lancaster be indisposed at the tables or with evening company, going up higher might provide an advantage — perhaps allow a view above from which he could send a bullet down like a divine bolt of lightning. Hall alighted the stairs as a starboard-side door behind him opened. He glimpsed a steward in a white jacket and coat, emerging from the riverboat's heart and walking toward the stern unaware of Hall or of the violence that had recently transpired.

The second deck was clear. He scooted close to the wall. He cursed himself for not taking the detective's coat and hat, disguised himself better. Why hadn't he done that? Caught up in the thrill of the kill, perhaps. The hunt, the manic desire to carve his way to his enemy and blow him away with a volcanic fusillade, the knowledge of finally being *this close* to doing it — these replaced thoughts of How with those of Now. And Now he slunk along the second deck in his filthy tattered union suit and dirt-slaked jeans like some primordial bog creature reeking of blood, grease and potato skins, leering through cabin windows for sign of his prey, seeking a surreptitious way inside this great white river monster of the Mississippi. Hall thought of Jonah, freshly vomited, wanting back into the whale — *let me in, let me in* — and nearly laughed. The way and the prey would appear, he figured. He had faith. At the least, he could kill another detective for the proper camouflage.

Something primal flickered in his mind. Perhaps it wasn't necessary. Going further up, he could reach the wheelhouse. Wrest control of the *Virginia May*. Run the paddle-wheeler at full speed onto the bank. Perhaps it would ignite the steam boiler as well. All those aboard would flee. They'd swim for the banks. In burning splashing chaos of his design he'd spy Lancaster and fill him with enough lead he'd sink to the bottom.

Hall shook his head. Snuffed the thought. Such an act could kill others without part in his vendetta. He wanted to avoid that. He'd only killed thrice in his life. The detective tonight, the loafer whose challenge on an Arkansas whisky boat had showed him how easy killing was, and the swindler and fence named Rigby, who'd told him everything he knew about Auguste Lancaster before Hall ended the interrogation by dashing his brains out with a farrier's rasp. Hall figured only one more needed to die. Those in his employ were acceptable. And if his own life would serve as toll for ferrying Lancaster to Hell, he was ready to pay it.

Soon Hall saw the next set of stairs ahead of him, further up the bow. He passed a starboard side door. The door opened. He pressed his back to the wall and held his breath. Two grey-haired men in dinner jackets walked out trailing plumes of cigar smoke. They kept their backs to Hall, ambled over to the railing and looked out at the banks.

"— nearly had it with those tens, I thought."

"Doesn't mean you lack skill none, George."

"Kind of you. I should've known better. Damn those kings."

"Next play."

"Next boat, maybe. Fair night, uh?"

"Innit?"

Hall crept past them and went up the stairs to the third deck low and crablike. The deck was bereft of any presence. The cabin windows were mostly dark, with ruffled curtains drawn shut on passengers unaware of the phantom outside. Hall grinned, hoped to keep it that way.

The *Virginia May* sounded a low, mournful whistle as he found a door and entered the steamboat. Dim electric lamps illuminated green paisley carpet and egg-white rows of cabin doors. The sounds of the night outside vanished.

Got this far, Hall thought. But where was Lancaster?

He chastised himself again, for not trying the windows outside. He might have seen Lancaster through one, reading by lamplight with the window cracked open to allow fresh night air, and could have snuck in. Instead he'd hurried inside, attracted by the inviting shadows.

Jonah in the whale.

Hall scoffed, cursed himself for cursing himself. The odds of finding his prey as envisioned were slim to none. He went down the hallway, figured he needed a way to walk the floors unobtrusively, needed a better strategy than trying each doorknob until he found what he was looking for.

From far behind him came the creaking of footsteps. Hall stopped, turned and saw a shadow down there at the far end — the shape of a man in a hat and coat. It rounded the corner and started toward him.

Hall tried the door to his right, figuring it for a closet. The knob gave. He darted inside and shut the door quickly. He pressed his ear to the door and waited until clomping reverberations approached, passed, and kept going.

Hall exhaled, turned and saw he wasn't in a closet, but a cabin lit by a single oil lamp. In a double bed in the center of the room sat a girl, awake and staring at him with eyes like saucers of milk. She was about twenty, with river-black hair cascading around her shoulders and skin like burnt walnut. The sheets were pulled up under her neck, though one exposed shoulder displayed a strap of white taffeta. She stared, unsure whether to scream. Hall stared back.

"Help you?" she said.

"I, uh..." he said quietly. "Don't scream, please. I won't hurt you."

"You don't hurt me, I won't scream," she said. "I ain't got money or jewels, 'n if you touch me, I'll holler."

"I ain't interested in any of that."

"But you're in my room when you shouldn't be."

Hall smiled wryly. "That's so. Not what I intended."

"You lost?" she said. "You ain't a guest. Don't work the boat." She eyed him up and down, then frowned. "Lord, you swim here?"

"No."

"You look like a drowned rat. And you're bleeding."

Hall followed her gaze to his shirtsleeve. It was stained in the detective's blood.

"Ain't nothin'."

The girl frowned. "You ain't here for Mr. Weatherby, are you?"

"Who's that?"

"Mr. Horace Weatherby. The man got the mousetrap factory up in Memphis."

"Oh. No, I ain't here for him." Hall glanced around the cabin. "You his maid?"

"I ain't his maid. More his woman."

"You expect him soon?"

"Maybe. He was in a fit over losing money in five-card to that catfish from Biloxi. I told him losing or no, I was gettin' my sleep. He said he was gonna have a drink with that man Wells, drown his sorrow a little. Reckon that was an hour ago."

"What catfish from Biloxi?"

"Said his name was Lancer. Got big fat sucker lips he tried putting on me other night. Tried to pull me into his cabin, 'fore I slipped away on account of he sweats like a greased hog." The girl shuddered. "Don't understand, Mr. Weatherby treats me better'n any other man ever could."

"This Lancer got silver hair and dark eyes?"

"That's right."

"Have some men with him?"

"Four or five. They walk around the boat at night. There's always one outside his room."

Hall felt a twinge of fire in his belly. "Sounds like who I'm lookin' for."

"Lookin' for him why?"

"He did me wrong. I'm gonna make it right."

The girl eyed his guns. "I never seen none of those make nothing right," she said. "Don't stop fools from tryin'."

Hall grinned. "What's your name?"

"Millie."

"Millie what?"

"Millie Doucette. What's yours?"

"Gideon." He realized it had been some time since he'd said it. It felt foreign.

"That's a nice name," Millie said. "It's Biblical."

"Yeah."

"Gideon's a judge and a warrior."

"He was."

"You know the Bible?"

"Indeed."

"Then you know what it says about killin'."

"Yeah." Hall opened his palms up. "Says somethin' about an eye for an eye, too."

"You still got both eyes, from where I'm sittin'."

Hall snorted.

"He fleece you, like he did Mr. Weatherby?" Millie asked.

Hall swallowed dry. His voice was hoarse. "Yes. Worse. Others too."

"How much he take?"

"Everything."

Millie pulled the sheets up tighter. "Then maybe you see to it, and I go back to sleep. Call this a dream."

"Maybe." Hall scratched the stubble along his chin. "Was he still playing, last you saw?"

"He was. In the salon. Two others at the table."

"He tried to get you into his cabin. Where'd that be?"

"Other side of the boat."

"All right. Mr. Weatherby have a spare coat and hat in here?"

Millie's eyes narrowed. "Now you gonna steal?"

"Just goin' down the hallway. I'll bring 'em back. How much Mr. Weatherby lose?"

Millie licked her lips. "Think he said three."

"If I can, I'll bring that back, too."

She rustled under the sheet and nodded toward a standing cabinet in the corner.

Hall opened the cabinet. Among hanging clothes he found a brown duster and a black creased homburg hat.

"Still some water in the basin," Millie said. "Clean you up some."

"Thank you," Hall said. He went to a washing stand where a smear of lukewarm water rested in a basin. He splashed it on his face, rubbed his bleary eyes, caught himself in the shaving-glass. The wet face staring back was wild and narrow, with curly black hair gone wiry and beady eyes like a starved fox.

"Some stink on you," Millie said.

"Potatoes. Other things," Hall said. He wiped his face with a linen cloth, then threw on the duster and the hat.

"This was just a dream, remember," he said. "My thanks to you are real, though."

Millie nodded.

Hall left the cabin, closing the door gingerly on his Samaritan. The hallway was empty.

He figured Lancaster's cabin was his best bet. He went past the stern cabins and approached the port-side wing. At the corner he stopped, peered around the edge of the wall, eyed down the port side. Outside a cabin door stood two men in black coats and Stetsons. One leaned against the wall closest to the door, smoking a cheroot. The other was thickly bearded and had his arms crossed over his barrel chest while he growled something.

"— that peach. Wouldn't mind some myself, but not after *he's* done with it."

"If'n you want we could trade places. You can listen in."

"Go to hell, Burl."

The cabin door opened. The men straightened. Hall saw a woman emerge — petite and lithe in a yellow satin dress, with her hair in a pile of auburn curls.

"Gentlemen," she said sedately. She walked past them toward the bow cabins. Hall heard the smoking man mutter something like "No such compunction" and follow her down the carpet and out onto the deck. The other detective scoffed and shook his head.

When the detective turned around Hall was there, pointing a cocked Remington and holding a finger to his lips.

"Yell and die first," Hall whispered.

The detective raised his hands. "Shoot and bring everyone down on you."

"I'd take my chances. And you'd be dead."

"All right. You ain't got to use that."

"Where's Lancer?"

"Inside."

"He pay you well?"

"Not well enough to get killed."

"Got some sense in you." Hall twitched the Remington toward the door. "Call him."

The detective turned away, rapped sharply on the cabin door and said "Mr. Lancer? It's Marwayne. Somethin' for you."

Hall got the Bowie knife in his free hand and closed in. He ran the wide blade fast under Marwayne's beard and across his neck. An artery threw an arc of blood over the cabin door. The detective's hands flew to his throat and he gasped as the door opened. Lancaster stood there, his belly straining a burgundy velvet smoker's jacket, his silver hair pasted down with sweat. His black eyes shone with annoyance, then confusion, then shock as another gout from Marwayne's neck spurted out, splashing across his face.

Lancaster yelped. Hall drove the Bowie knife into Marwayne's back up to the hilt and shoved him into Lancaster, sending them tumbling to the cabin floor. Hall followed, shut the door behind them and shunted the deadbolt. He rolled the gurgling detective off Lancaster, clamped his hand over a blood-slicked mouth so Lancaster couldn't scream, then stuck the Remington's barrel along Lancaster's nose, threatening to drive it into his left eye. Hall kneeled on Lancaster's chest. Beside them the detective heaved, seeking breath that wouldn't come. Blood bubbled out of his gaping neck wound before his head lolled over and he went still.

"He let me in easy," Hall said. "Get what you pay for."

Lancaster strained under his hand.

"You know who I am?"

Lancaster tried shaking his head.

"You know who you are?" Hall grinned. "Albert Lawrence?"

Lancaster's eyes bugged. His caterpillar eyebrows worked.

"That's right," Hall said. "Arthur Lattimore. Dr. Anthony Lambert. Reverend Allan Lawson. Auguste Lancaster. Now you're Mr. Lancer. I been busy learnin' all about you. I know most every name you've used in your crimes. Only one I don't is whichever one's real."

Lancaster groaned underneath.

"I'm gonna take my hand away, so I can hear your confession."

Hall stood. He trained the Remington between Lancaster's eyes. The portly man skittered back on his elbows, away from the detective's body, then propped himself up trembling against the foot of the bed.

"I-I don't know what you're talking about."

"Yes, you do."

"You're blathering names I have no knowledge of. You're accusing me of something when I'm innocent."

"We both know that ain't true," Hall said. "Maybe you can't do nothin' anymore but lie. Maybe there's too many lies to keep track of. But you know you're lying."

Lancaster's eyes danced.

"I'm Gideon Hall. Ransom Hall was my father."

Lancaster said nothing.

"Must've figured you cleaned him out easy," Hall said. "A poor farmer that wasn't gonna make it anyway. An easy mark, like the others. Hardly nobody knows about them, so you probably reckoned you'd get away with it, like always. Except my father wrote it all out."

Something flared behind Lancaster's bloodstained face.

"You took him for a simple man, couldn't read well and all. But he could write, sorta, if you know how to parse it. He wrote how this land man Auguste Lancaster talked him into buying a mining stake to settle his debts, got him to put up his farm for an investment. But Lancaster took the money for himself. The mine wasn't even for sale in the first place. He wrote how the bank took the farm from him, because his signature was on papers he didn't remember signing, which gave Lancaster power to take out more loans with the farm as a guarantee. All that he wrote, in his way, on five parchment scraps, then hanged himself in the barn."

Hall leaned forward. Lancaster shrunk away, pushed himself against the bed.

"If I'd been there, I'd have never let something like that — like *you* — happen," Hall said. "But Ransom insisted I go away, get educated at the seminary, become something more than a sodbuster. He ponied up what little he'd saved for me to go learn. I listened. I went. When the priests told me what happened, I figured he wouldn't have gone for it if he hadn't given up everything for me. Thought it was my fault. You...you know what that's like, to think it's all at your feet, for doin' your best?"

The Remington quivered in Hall's hand. He lowered it slightly, trained it on Lancaster's chest. Saw that Lancaster was sweating heavily, breathing apprehensively.

"I near hung myself. In the seminary chapel. Two initiates restrained me. When I came to my senses I rode for home. Read his note and went looking for you. Took some work, but I'm good with records and newspapers. Found you've pulled games over ten years in three states. Found people you swindled. Found people who knew you, knew if you were hunted you'd make for New Orleans. You've got money stashed there and old Biloxi buddies who'd ship you to Mexico. And I thought, well, you stole so much and killed my father, I couldn't let that happen."

Lancaster exhaled loudly. He hissed and spat.

"You can't prove anything," he said.

"Don't have to. We know it's true."

Lancaster glared. "You're insane. Describing a fantasy hinged on the fact that your father made a bad business decision."

"Nothing business about it. You're a swindler. A charlatan. Confess."

"I confess nothing. You kill me, all anyone will know is some lunatic killed a known businessman." Lancaster smiled faintly. "Your daddy'll go down a failure. You'll go down a lowlife murderer. That how you want this to end, son?"

"I already know how it ends. You can unburden yourself or take it all with you."

Lancaster's eyes narrowed. His lip quivered. "What's to unburden," he said. "I do what I do, and if someone else don't know it could go wrong for them, that's their fault."

"Worth askin'," Hall said. He looked around the cabin. "Where's your billfold?"

Lancaster said nothing, but Hall saw him briefly glance toward a cabinet like the one in Weatherby's cabin. Hall held his gun on Lancaster, went over and opened it. He dug a leather portfolio out from a set of hanging trousers and opened it up. Inside was just over four hundred in bills — three plus some for the trouble, he figured as he took them out.

"This what you won tonight, from Weatherby?"

Lancaster sputtered. "Fair and square."

"I don't care," Hall said and pocketed them.

"Lowlife murderer *and* a common thief," Lancaster said.

"I'm kinda glad you ain't repentant." Hall aimed the Remington squarely between Lancaster's black eyes. "Makes this easier."

There came the muted scuffling of footsteps outside the cabin door. Hall whirled around and drew his second Remington as it blew in. Splinters flew from the split jamb. The shadowy outline of one of Lancaster's guards stood in the open space, a bull of a man with something in his hand drawing a bead.

Hall fired. His Remingtons thundered in the small space of the cabin. He saw a flash of white lightning, felt the heat of a bullet along his right, heard the *snap* as it passed an inch from his head. The detective jerked and spasmed as Hall's .44 rounds painted the hallway wall behind him with a crimson spray. He crumpled to the floor like a broken doll.

Something shattered, high-pitched and crystalline. Hall spun back. Lancaster was stumbling over the window ledge, where the glass was jagged where he'd sent the shaving-glass from a washing stand and followed it. Cold night air poured in through the ragged hole Lancaster scrambled through. Hall heard glass crack and Lancaster howled as he cut himself rolling out onto the deck.

Hall fired after him fruitlessly as Lancaster fell away below the window. Hall dashed over and window and looked out to see Lancaster crawling frantically on hand and knee toward the bow, where a set of stairs went to the lower deck. Lancaster put his hand up on the railing to hoist himself up. He screamed, bellowed for help, tracked bloody hand- and footprints on the deck that shimmered faintly in the moonlight.

Hall leapt through the broken window. He heard a *skrrrrit* as Weatherby's duster coat tore on a glass spike. He darted forward, took aim at the round figure down the deck and fired both Remingtons. Two rounds caught Lancaster in the back as he reached the stairway, their explosive rapport choking out his screams as the bullets blew out his lungs into the night. He arched back, pitched forward, and disappeared.

Hall ran for the stairs. He heard shouts, the murmur of voices. He saw the port-side door to the third deck cabins open and the dark lanky figure of the detective that Marwayne had called Burl come out, a slender Colt Buntline Special firing in his hand. Hall felt a round punch in his gut, low on the left side. It nearly spun him, but he kept moving forward as warmth spread from the wound. He surged and fired. His bullet caught Burl in the eye — a chunk of skull flaked away. Burl pitched limp to the deck.

Hall reached the stairs and looked down. Lancaster lay below, a twisted and broken mess of blood and velvet. Hall eased himself down the steps, leaning against the railing, careful not to collapse and fall after his kill, while the wound in his lower belly burned and spilled and drenched his jeans. He reached the bottom and stood over the broken corpse. Lancaster bled out freely from two gaping chest wounds, and his head was turned nearly all the way around with an expression between fear and surprise fixed on his face.

Didn't seem right, Hall thought. After all the hunting and tracking. All he'd learned. How far he'd got. The man who'd done so much damage, taken everything from him, seemed so small now. A blotch on the deck, an insignificant smear in the Mississippi night.

A man's voice said, "Hold it."

Hall looked up. A young mustached man in a plaid wool suit and a bowler hat stood on the deck, aiming a silver revolver. Hall grinned. He'd wondered if the *Virginia May* had its own detectives, the ones who watched the gaming tables. He briefly considered whether taking one of them out was the same as one of Lancaster's. He realized he'd lost count of how many rounds he'd sent, whether he'd fire on empty chambers. Wondered if he should try.

"Lay down your guns," the man said.

Hall dropped his Remingtons. They clattered hard to the deck.

"Kick 'em over."

He did.

"Turn around slow."

"Wait," Hall said. "I've gotta get somethin' out my pocket."

"Slow."

Hall nodded. His wound throbbed as he brought out the bills he'd taken. In the morning, he figured, Weatherby would thumb through the blood-garnished cash with surprise and confusion, with Millie at his side. Hall doffed the homburg hat and tucked the bills inside the crown. "I'm gonna take this coat off now," he said.

The steamboat detective watched Hall warily. Hall set the duster and the hat with the bills inside down, grunting in pain as he placed them. He stood back up with his hands raised. "Those belong to a man aboard, named Weatherby," he said. Slowly he backed away from Lancaster's body, until his lower back touched the railing.

"I meant to return all that," Hall said. "Think I tore the coat some, got blood on it too. Didn't mean to. You'll see Weatherby gets everything back?"

The man's brows creased. "Sure," he said. "But you listen, now. You're gonna turn around and come with me. We're gonna keep you in the hold 'til this boat gets to New Orleans, sort it out there. Understand?"

Hall shook his head. He grinned.

"No thank you," he said. "I just came up from the hold."

Then he laughed. He laughed as he arched himself backwards, heaving himself over the railing. He laughed as the steamboat detective's pistol spat fire and a bullet found home deep in his chest, reverberating throughout his body. He laughed as he plunged from the second deck of the *Virginia May* into the obsidian water of the Mississippi, the river flooding his wounds to baptize him and welcome him into its cold dark depths. The paddlewheel chopped the water above as it passed over him, propelling the steamboat past where he went in, taking her further along two thousand plus miles of black ribbon as he sank. The cold took over as he felt the embrace of the river bottom, the soft touch of silty mud at his back.

Got that far, Hall thought.

MARKED
BY
MICHAEL BRACKEN

"Women mark their territory," Brad explained. "The first thing you have to do after a date leaves your place is look for anything she left behind. Usually it's something she left 'accidentally,' like the earrings she took off when you were kissing or the sweater she removed because it was too warm in your apartment."

"Sometimes it's not so subtle," Charlie added. "A few months ago, one of my dates left her thong on my nightstand. How do you forget to put on your underwear?"

"Why do they do it?" I asked. The three of us were sitting around a high-top table at a sports bar named Snuffy's, drinking beer and discussing my re-entry into the dating scene after a rancorous divorce ended several years of marriage. Most of the televisions were tuned to sports channels, but the one behind me was tuned to a local station.

"It's an excuse to talk to you again," Brad said. "If you don't call them a day or two after the date, they'll call you to ask about their stuff. The conversation will start innocently enough—'I think I left my earrings at your place. Have you seen them?'—and by the end of the conversation you'll have arranged another date."

"Or she's trying to warn off other women. What do you think will happen if you bring home a date and she finds another woman's earrings on your nightstand?" Charlie shook his head. "There's no way to turn that conversation into a win-win situation."

"I found a toothbrush once," Brad continued, "and another time—and this is the worst of all—I found a box of feminine products under my bathroom sink. If a woman leaves feminine products at your place, you know you're in deep. She thinks you have a relationship."

"So what do you do?" I asked.

"Depends," Brad said. "Do you want to see her again or not? If not, call her before she gets home and leave a message on her machine. Tell her you found her earrings or whatever and that you'll return them right away, but don't imply that returning them is anything more than common courtesy."

"But if you do want to see her again, wait a day or so before you call. Tell her you just found her earrings and that they reminded you of how much you enjoyed your evening together. Tell her that you thought of sending them back, but wouldn't it be so much better to give them to her in person, over dinner, perhaps, and set up another date."

I finished my beer and looked at my two friends. They were my age, but neither one had ever been married. I knew they had more experience on the dating scene than I had, so that's why I'd asked the question that had started the conversation. I said, "I met a woman last night."

"So, what'd she leave behind?" Brad asked. He lifted his beer to his lips to take a swallow.

"A revolver."

Brad spit beer all over Charlie.

Charlie wasn't fazed by the beer bath. He leaned forward and lowered his voice. "Where'd you find it?"

"In a ziplock bag in my toilet tank."

Brad motioned for the waitress.

"How'd you think to look in there?"

"The toilet wouldn't stop running. When I lifted the lid, I saw the gun. The barrel was interfering with the flapper."

Brad caught the waitress's attention and told her he needed a towel.

"What'd you do?"

"I took the .38 out of the tank and examined it closely. Two shots had been fired and the empty shells were still chambered. The serial number had been filed off."

The waitress returned with a bar towel. Brad dried Charlie's arm and most of the table before returning the towel to the waitress. Then he ordered another pitcher.

"So, do I call her? What do I say?"

"You have her number?" Charlie asked.

She'd written it on the back of one of my business cards. I took it from my pocket and pushed it across the tabletop to him.

Brad looked over his shoulder. "That's not her real number."

When Charlie and I looked at him, Brad pulled out his cell phone. "Look at the numbers. Those spell EAT-SHIT."

I stared at him.

"It could be worse," Brad said, "she could have told you her number was—"

I cleared my throat, interrupting him before he could finish.

"Did the two of you do anything?" Charlie asked.

I nodded. "And I woke up alone. The sound of the running toilet woke me."

"She leave anything else behind?"

"Not that I could find."

While Brad and Charlie stared at me, the waitress returned with a fresh pitcher of beer. As she placed it on the table, a bit sloshed onto my business card, rendering it a soggy mess.

"Sorry," she said as she peeled it from the tabletop, wadded it into a ball, and shoved it into the pocket of her apron.

Brad refilled our mugs as he said, "So tell us what happened. What'd she look like? Where'd you meet her? How'd you get her to go back to your place?"

"That was her idea," I said, and then I told them how I had met the woman who identified herself as Candy Mann.

***

I'd worked late Friday evening and, on my way home, I stopped at Caruso's, an up-scale watering hole half a dozen blocks from my apartment building. The place catered to the youngish singles and the older divorced men occupying all the high-rises in the neighborhood. So, despite the threads of gray taking residence at my temples, I didn't stand out.

Most of other drinkers packing the place were dressed in business attire like me, having also stopped on their way home. I loosed my tie as I settled onto one of two empty bar stools near the back, and I ordered a boilermaker. I had just dropped my whiskey shot into my beer when a good-looking brunette appeared from behind me and settled onto the stool next to mine. I didn't know if she'd come from the ladies' room or through the rear entrance.

She asked, "What're you drinking?"

I told her.

"Why would anyone ruin a perfectly good whiskey by diluting it with cheap beer?"

I didn't have an answer.

She smiled. "Buy me a drink," she said. "A whiskey shot."

I caught the bartender's attention and ordered two. While we were waiting, she introduced herself and I did the same.

"You married, Kevin?

I showed her my left hand where the indention around my ring finger had nearly disappeared. "Divorced."

"Tell me about her."

"My ex?" I knew better than to discuss my ex with other women. Brad and Charlie had made it clear that nothing I might say about her would appeal to any woman in which I was interested. If I praised my ex, the woman I was with might think I was still in love, and if I trashed her, the woman I was with would worry about what I might say about her if things didn't work out. Even so, I couldn't stop myself. "She left me," I said, "for a woman."

"You ever meet the other woman, see pictures of her, know anything about her?"

I shook my head. "I thought my ex made her up. Sheryl was like that, always saying the most hurtful things."

"Her leaving you for a woman was hurtful?"

I hated to admit it, but it was.

"I dated someone like that once," Candy said. "Kept throwing the ex in my face."

We were both silent for a moment before Candy placed a hand on my forearm and asked, "Think she was as pretty as me?"

"Who?"

"Your wife's imaginary lover."

"Don't see how she could be."

Candy smiled.

Our shots arrived. Candy lifted hers and made a toast. "Here's to us, Kevin," she said. "Here's to a night we never forget."

***

"One thing led to another," I said, wrapping up my story, "and she suggested we go back to my place."

"And what happened when you got there?" Brad asked.

"What do you think happened?"

"Did you fix her a drink? Was there any small talk? Did you—" Charlie asked.

I shook my head. "She wasn't interested in any of that. We went right to the bedroom."

"Small talk after?"

Sheepishly, I admitted, "She wore me out. I fell asleep."

"And when you woke up, she was gone?" Brad asked.

"And the toilet was running."

"Where's the .38 now?" Charlie asked.

"On my kitchen sink."

"You didn't get rid of it?"

I shook my head.

"Don't you think you should?" Charlie asked. "There must be a reason she left it at your place."

Brad was staring over my shoulder, and he pointed at the television behind me. "You'll want to see this."

The ten o'clock news had just started, and I turned in time to see a photograph of my ex-wife filling the television screen. We couldn't hear what the news anchor was saying but a chyron across the bottom of the screen informed viewers that Sheryl had been found dead in the house where we'd lived, and that she'd been shot twice.

When I turned back, I found Brad and Charlie staring at me.

"I didn't do it," I protested.

"But the .38—"

Brad didn't need to finish his thought. I had thrown the ziplock bag down the trash chute that morning when I'd gone to the laundry to wash my sheets, and I'd left the .38 on my kitchen counter, my fingerprints all over the revolver and the shells. Ex-spouses were always persons of interest, so I had to get home and get rid of it before the police paid a visit.

I finished my beer, tossed a twenty on the table to pay for my share of the beer, and hurried home.

I wasn't fast enough.

The police were waiting.

I'd been marked.

STARLITE PULP
MAMA TRIED
LOS ANGELES, CA

DEAD MAN'S MUSE
BY DANIEL PYNE

Icy AC fouls the black Escalade with a grim funk. It's a hearse for the living, the left behind, the remainder bin. Emily rolls down the window to let the unfiltered smoky hot night blow in on her. She can taste the grit of cinders.

"Crom save us from mopey loser wannabes," Chemo is grumbling, hipster hat bowled in his lap. Does he mean the grieving fans they've just left outside the Club Pandemonium? Or Vike (Mucho) Maas?

Poor Vike.

Her eyes are leaking again. She digs in her bag, finds a pill bottle. Her anchor. Her forever friend.

"Are these Ativan?""

Chemo glances, shrugs. Disinterested in her self-medication.

"They don't look familiar," she says.

"What does it say on the label?"

She squints through the tears. Her eyes ache from too much brushfire brume. "Zovrax." A prescription Mickey got for herpes, use-by date of oh-nineteen.

"I suspect those are the putative Demerol I purchased yesterday from a cable grip backstage, during sound check," Chemo sniffs. "I put them in a rando bottle I found in Mickey's kit." Chemo says he thinks he left them in the hotel suite, did Emily pick them up?

They don't look familiar.

"What does the label say?"

Acyclovir. She tries to remember when he got it -- when she passed to him (surprise!) the cankerous gift that keeps on giving. She shakes out little white buttons and thinks: no, acyclovir doesn't look at all like this.

Oxy? Mickey didn't do Oxycontin. Fear of interloping fentynal hijinks by middlemen unknown. "Toe tag dope," he would say. "Death's shortcut. Only white-assed lowlife losers and luckless first timers buy street 80s anymore. Not this soldier. Buyer beware. Dance me to the end of love."

Well, death found another way to him.

Rank soot clouds scud under tarnished twilight, clipping sawtooth skyscrapers downtown. Sirens bleed from the falling darkness like coyotes, calling from the smoldering canyons of *El Pueblo de la Reina de Los Angeles*.

The Aerosmith earworm is back banging around her head.

Dum dum dum.

Hell on earth.

She pops a pill in her mouth and washes it down with bougie water courtesy of the cupholder in the seat's center console. Vike's face has burned itself onto the back of her eyelids, a perverse gender nonconforming Virgin of Guadalupe candle glow to soften Steven Perry's peripatetic keening.

But, surprise, she's feeling blissful. What's up with that?

Optimistic, even.

Could Emily Hooper and Vike Maas still have a future? Did they ever? She can't answer; she can't keep her eyes open. A sweet exhaustion overtakes her. She'll sleep, won't dream. Ativan, must be. And when she wakes up, she'll feel convinced somehow, it will be a new start. Right? Sleeping Beauty, Snow White – a Disney princess ⁓ growing up, sure, she had all those crazy little girl fantasies.

"I hate California," Chemo is murmuring, staring out at it with a look of disgust. "Counterfeit paradise." Chemo hates everywhere. He claims it's crucial to his brand.

Translucent searchlight columns sweep the heavens above L.A. Live, probing for answers to questions she's too tired to ask. Mickey once turned down a chance to open for Imagine Dragons at the Novo. He'll never get asked again. "They should be opening for me," he had sniffed, and then got bent and did another stint in residential rehab instead.

The Uber Black is nearly at the four level interchange of the 101 and 110 when Emily dimly realizes she's made a mistake.
The world is tilting. She has to remind herself to breathe.

Dizzy. Nauseous. *Here we go.*

Uh-oh.

Breathe.

She wants to tell Chemo but her mouth won't cooperate, her arms are too heavy to lift, and she even isn't sure what it was she wanted to tell him.

Oh shit.

Breeeeeeeathe, Em. *Breathe.*

Her sleepy lungs bunch and sag. In and out, twist and shout, something something, woulda coulda shoulda put a *Cinderella dressed in yella went upstairs to kiss a fella made a mistake and kissed a snake how many doctors did it take? One, two, three one four one five nine* out --

-- A vacuum sucks her inward. No tunnel, no light, no highlight reel of her too short life.

Black hole.

***

Dum dum dum.

Got a gun.

Perfect. An *Aerosmith* fucking earworm had crawled into her brain, and she'd be suffering it for who knew how long. Awesome. Add it to the list.

Run away.

No. C'mon, girl, get a grip.

Run away pain.

Stop. *Just stop.* She had nothing against Aerosmith.

But there were limits. Even for her.

***

Dusk in the underworld. Sawtooth flames leapt and roared on the ridge-lines. Wanton brush fires gyred and danced.

Nothing good ever blew in on Santa Ana winds.

Devil's work, a fresh Santanic inferno. Panicked city, angels calling it quits, canyon hillsides ablaze and her boyfriend cruelly cut down by some crazed gunman at yesterday's Pandemonium gig. Emily Hooper's whole life had exploded into fiery bits and shards that surely would prove impossible to gather and repair.

What sucked most was how she couldn't stop crying. And couldn't decide if it was from sadness or relief. Or was it just the Zoloft? In the fog of her grieving she may have taken an extra dose.

She was grieving, wasn't she?

Never one to trust big emotions, and ever since she got the shocking news, Emily had been trying to convince herself that her tears were chiefly a reaction to the foul air from the fires. She didn't love him. She had never loved him, Mickey was another useless habit she'd acquired and couldn't shake. Both users, they used each other. She guessed that was fair. But the shock of seeing Vike Maas last night among the crowd outside the club in the immediate aftermath of the shooting, had sent her reeling sideways like a boat blown off course. And seeing him again, here, one day later, up on the parking lot stage of the open mic tribute to the late, great Mickey Madrid had her unglued and sobbing again.

Even worse, she hadn't even seen the shooting go down. Imagining that moment, over and over in a TikTok loop ~ Mickey extinguished, the cataclysmic journey of the bullet through his chest and heart and scapula badly informed by every violent movie or TV show she's ever seen, a Hollywood technicolor lie ~ horrified her more than witnessing it ever could.

No, they weren't married. She lived off his fame. A remora, he once teased her: the little fish with the suction-cups on their heads, that attach to sharks and allow them to scavenge the bits and scraps of shredded prey to prevent parasites from bothering the ocean's apex predators.

It wasn't funny, when he said it. It was so pathetic now.

Now, she kept looking and looking and looking and saw no future. Not just emptiness ahead of her; a vacuum. A void.

Her inbox had filled with messages from friends and fans and trolls and the NRA ghouls who hadn't forgiven Mickey Madrid for being a gun control advocate, and they were quick to point out how he might still be alive if he had been carrying. Right? Strapped, onstage? Good guy with a Glock?

Fuck off.

Spin and Rolling Stone kept calling. Daily Mail, the Times and HuffPo. She wasn't returning, had no statement, wouldn't be giving interviews. What would she tell them? What can be said that wasn't vapid and/or stupid?

He was dead. She refused to even entertain the plaintive ask of "who would want to kill him?" ~ Mickey ~ because the answer was: pretty much anyone.

Turned out the one who did was a complete stranger, who blew his own brains out afterward.

"You okay?" Chemo's knobby hand tried to steady her.

No, Chemo. Not remotely okay. Vike was up there *playing* the fucking *song*. But she mumbled, "yeah," anyway.

Half turned from the small, restless crowd, head angled down, eyes on his hands and the frets and the strings that he tapped and bent the notes with a magic she'd assumed he would have lost. Vike could make the guitar sound like it was singing the lyrics.

A heartsick plea? For what, exactly?

Her cheeks burned, wet again. Crocodile tears, she told herself. The desert wind would dry them and leave a crusty jetsam. She gestured for a cigarette and Chemo, the band's dyspeptic bassist and only member of *All The Things* sober enough to escort her to the tribute, produced the skinny brown ones that would turn her already smoke-ravaged lungs into wheezy leather bags. She grasped for any help; the drugs were in the limo. At least the cancer stick gave her something to do with her hands.

Disappointed dozens of Mickey's hardest-core stans milled, restless, barely attending to the stage, Vike's acoustic version of the band's famous power ballad already disappearing in their fickle collective rearview mirror. The song had died with Mickey. Maybe they resented how much better Vike made it sound.

Because, yeah, it was his.

Or ~ she could almost hear Vike saying ~ hers. *Her* song. Fuck. Fuck that. Fuck Vike.

"Well then, isn't this an epic dreary?" Chemo bitched. His chipped, chewed fingernails were flaked with electric blue from last night's aborted show.

Emily smoked and watched the crowd. Wired and aggrieved, it stirred with an impatience, as if expecting something ~ as if craving something ~ as if in need of an even more violent encore to happen. Anything, really, as long as it was ... epic. Emily knew too well how that went. Chasing the high. Never quite reaching it again.

Poor babies. They'd seen a man die.

Mickey was history.

Next?

And Vike? Vike wasn't epic, she had decided, spike heels sinking into the hot asphalt as she blew angry smoke rings into the liquid ochre Hollywood half-light. Luminous black-brown smoke soared from behind Griffith Park. Another flare-up. Helicopters circled and strafed, leaving smears of their red and white running lights strung across the sky. Vike was a cautionary tale. Vike was a tragedy trope. Vike was debris from a catastrophic event of his own making. In her past.

Or so she liked to pretend.

***

Emily.

The song makes a point not to rhyme. Vike had always insisted that this was fundamental to its hook; she had always been a little paranoid that Vike was, in fact, making some kind of coded observation about her.

Thank you, narcissistic bleed.

They met in film school. She had fled Winston-Salem keen to make the kind of hyper-visual art documentaries Stan Brakhage did back in the sixties. Teetering on the edge of impenetrability -- frenetic, experimental, non-linear. She micro-dosed acid, embraced Kabbalah, read Danielewski, listened to the music of Björk and David Lang and pity-fucked most of her fawning, self-impressed, colorless professors so she could gaslight them later with sexual misconduct in the event it might prove helpful advancing her career. It didn't. They were useless. All she wound up with was depression and a bunch of unpronounceable STIs.

Quiet, shy, opaque, Vike was for a long time invisible to her. There had been nothing remarkable about him back then; not bad looking, but short on charisma. Someone who sat in back of class and sometimes offered to write the music for student projects but never got asked. To fulfill his crewing requirements he performed all the set shit-work that nobody else was willing to do. Booms, cables, crates, dolly puller and loading. Everyone else had a vision. Vike, it seemed, was just there marking time.

Now and then he spoke cryptically of a stint in the Army. As if it had been a hobby he took up for a while and then lost all interest in.

Emily had loved cinematography, but the visiting cameraman-professor was imperiously gay *and* a sexist asshole and therefore not only immune to her charms, but dismissive of her talents. Writing bored her. Producing was too much thankless work. She had no ear for sound. Careening toward graduation devoid of a specialty, Emily had designed some ninja outfits as a favor for a trans friend's meta Hong Kong chopsocky send-up. Just like that, she became the class costumer. Everyone begging for her help with their thesis films. It pissed her off but was "just as well," one of her other misogynistic faculty lovers had told her with poorly veiled condescension, since women don't make good directors because "all that power turns y'all into shrews."

Then, out of nowhere, recalcitrant Vike Maas approached her after a World Cinema lecture to ask if she'd consider shooting something on her iPhone. He had this friend who was a musician, he explained. They were going to make a video of one of the guy's songs.

"I've watched all of your class assignments," had been Vike's come-on. "They're not half-bad." Emily would learn that, with Vike, 'not half-bad' was his highest compliment, and pretty much all you could hope to achieve in this life.

Shoot some film for him? He was cute. He was new. He was unexpected and unknown. Her answer had been an emphatic, "sure."

If only she'd said no.

Vike, thanks to the GI Bill, was the only graduate filmmaker not going into deep student debt. Emily mistook this for a plan. Whether he ever aspired to score movies was debatable; Vike had talent but no drive. Something had been sucked out of him in during his deployment to the Middle East. He was a hollowed man. Recon and Intelligence was all he would offer Emily when she asked, later, repeatedly, what it was he had done over there.

And while the music video they made had been forgettable (seventy-one views on YouTube, and two likes), Emily found herself falling hard for the enigmatic ex-soldier even though his evident reciprocal interest in her was so veiled and guarded that seeing them together one could have mistakenly believed they had only just met.

Vike's musician friend was this slight, mouthy, overconfident and acne-challenged band camp refugee, Mike Mrdryk (buy a vowel, whydontcha?), who, yeah, would later change his name to Mickey Madrid, but not yet. First there had been for her the couplet of surprises: an indie bar band Mike and Vike had put together on a lark, and their shared dream of hitting it big with all the songs they wrote together. Which was to say Vike wrote them while Mike made suggestions, smoked dope, drank Mexican coca cola, did mushrooms, planned his acceptance speech for the Rock and Roll Hall of Fame and binge-watched *Bojack Horseman.*

It wasn't exactly a blueprint for success.

Meantime, psycho-pharmaceuticals were where Emily and the future Mr. Madrid had found a common ground. Vike took a hard pass on joining them. He'd watched a buddy get decapitated by IED shrapnel in Islamabad. The snick of separation, the slick of blood and flesh and bone bits still haunted him, he said, and left him reluctant to chance revisiting any of that memory at the urging of some perky recreational drug.

Emily had been totally cool with his decision. She believed she didn't feel the need to get baked so much when Vike was with her. Sadly, the addict who was squatting rent-free in her head would crave the shame and self-abuse Mike Mrdryk kept offering, like the serpent in the tree. Love never had a chance.

Helpless, heartbroken, Vike just stopped writing music, quit the band, dropped out of school and jumped at a *tres mysterioso* NSA job in the Cuban embassy proffered by one of his spooky former Army intel handlers. Set adrift from her anchor, Emily began chipping heroin and lost all interest in film. Mike became Mickey, stole Vike's girl and Vike's song and went viral as *Mickey Madrid & All The Things*.

Shit happens. What can you do?

***

"Em. Emily."

"What?" How long had Chemo been waiting for her to answer? And what had he asked? She looked blankly at him. His face was all planes and angles, almost cubist, under his poser's hipster porkpie hat. Was she losing her mind? A clutch of fans had gathered at a respectful distance, corralled by club security. She felt their anime-big eyes drill into her, predatory, needy.

"Emily, sign my shirt?"

The tranquilizer she had popped on the way to the tribute was waning. The smokey air seemed to be getting harder to breathe. She was cotton-mouthed, everything around her looked weak-shadowed, shot through a lens coated with petroleum jelly, occluded but shimmering. The mike onstage was open again, a new band hurried to set up. Where the fuck was Vike?

"Em?"

"Ms. Hooper!" A young tanning booth casualty in Laker shorts and torn fishnets waved a white wife-beater singlet with Mickey's face screen-printed on it. "Ms. Hooper!"

"Let's get out of here," she said to Chemo, shaking. She prayed there would be Ativan or Valium in the bag she'd left in the Escalade.

Chemo said, "I asked how you know that guy who was just singing?"

Emily shrugged, irritated. "Who says I do?"

"Em."

"What?"

"You were staring at him like you did."

Dismissive: "No. I spaced out."

"I don't think so."

"Do I care what you think?"

"Bloody hell."

"Please please please sign my shirt?"

Two girls cooed, "We love you."

"Chemo, let's go. This, coming here, was a mistake ~"

"~ Excuse me?" Vike's soft voice cut in from somewhere close behind them. Her breath caught, her heart did a two-step ~ oh Jesus ~ but she couldn't help turning, and there he was. The eyes she once drowned in. That sad, lost smile. Where was Austin, where was her security? She felt like crying again. Vike looked like he hadn't slept in days.

"Listen mate," Chemo growled, stepping between them, clueless of their history. He hadn't been in the band when Vike went AWOL. "You can just sod on off now, yeah? Step clear. Give the girl her space." Chemo is tall, a hopeless anglophile from Asheville, North Carolina, whose English Beat affect strays from East Midlands to the Home Counties, with a little Scouse thrown in as a tribute to the Beatles ~ but he only weighs about a hundred pounds, so the threat rang empty. And quite a bit hollow.

"I didn't know who else to give this to," Vike said, and started a reaching motion that got intercepted by the band's security guy, Austin. Big and scary, but a step late, as usual.

"Dude. Easy."

"Ow."

Arm pinned back, Vike was spun around and slammed against the backside of their Uber Black hired car, the guitar stripped off his back. He offered no resistance.

The fanboy with the singlet had whipped his phone out and was recording them.

"That's Mike's," Vike said, angling fraught eyes over his shoulder at the liberated Stratocaster Austin gripped in one big sweaty hand. "I mean Mickey's." She could see that it was. Mickey had half a dozen made every six months, because he liked to break them onstage. "I saw it lying there. On the stage. I don't know why ~" Vike stopped abruptly and restarted, "I picked it up after ..." His voice trailed off.

After Mickey.

Emily had already seen the dark spatter on the guitar's top edge. Blood?

Chemo grumbled, "bloody wanker," tipped his hat back and gestured to Austin, "get him out of here." But before Vike could be frogmarched away, Emily heard herself intercede.

"Wait. No. Wait."

The world stalled, hung idle. Slow connection, loading, loading, the little spinning wheel of limbo. Onstage the new band began playing the Kink's *Better Things,* as a shower of silver ash from the Malibu conflagration got blissed by the halo of a parking lot halogen light that was stuttering to life in the eventide.

To Austin: "let him go, it's okay." To Chemo: "gimme a second." But to Vike she said nothing. Thoughts raced, swerved and overwhelmed her. Where would she even start?

Shaking out his freed arm, Vike seemed determined not to look at her, not directly, anyway, and he frowned ever-so-slightly, elusive eyes empty. Where had he gone?

"I feel like I know you," he said.

Did he really not remember? She knew, then, that she should tell him that he did. That they had had something once, and she had let it go. Or was it that he had started going, and she had chosen not to stop him?

Did it matter? Would it change anything?

They had stared at each other, then, for what seemed like a long time. She had heard a rumor, maybe from Mickey, that Vike came back early from Cuba after suffering some kind of catastrophic mental breakdown. Now, she thought: that must be what this is. For a moment, she even found herself wondering how much else has he forgotten? And hoping that it was everything.

Did he even know who he was?

Or ⁓ and it disappointed her that she even thought it possible ⁓ was Vike, in fact, gaslighting her? Trolling her. Payback, for all the cruel, foolish choices she had made.

"I don't think we've met, no," she finally lied to him.

"Maybe it was Mickey."

She held her breath.

He shook his head as if to clear it. "No. Never mind. Yeah ... yeah." He seemed confounded. "I'm sorry." His eyes, coming alive, held hers for one moment longer and then again slipped away.

Had he felt the same punch of loss that she had?

"I'm sorry, I'm all twisted up," he confessed, and then he introduced himself: "Vike. Vike Maas. Aka Mucho. Sort of a stage name, but ~" He stopped short, reeled back the slack of his digression. "See, I was in Havana for a while not too long ago," he said. "Got shot through irradiated with some microwaves or something. Migraines, nosebleeds, tintinaites. And I'm not the only one. They're not sure what it was. Brought me back, brought us all back. Ever since, I'm not the same. None of us."

Same as what? She waits, but that's all it seems he wants to say about it.

"Nice to meet you," she played along, and felt ashamed.

But as if encouraged somehow, Vike perked up and rambled on, "It was, yeah, whoa. I mean. Pretty crazy. Scary crazy. And Cuba. Have you guys ever been there? The skies are this blue I've never seen anywhere else, and the people are amazing. But. Well. Anyway." He lifted and dropped his shoulders, as if to emphasize a powerlessness with which he'd made his peace. "Hope I didn't butcher his song." He took a deep breath, exhaled. "I love the song ~ well, didn't even knew I knew it, to be honest, but. I don't know. I guess I just have to ... just have to ..." His hand made vague circles in the air and again he smiled the tortured smile that broke her heart. It transitioned to a grimace as he seemed to catch himself, chagrined. "Sorry for your loss," he added, swerving his attention to Chemo and holding up the palms of his hands as if in surrender. "No worries, bro. That's all I got. Vike's out. Rock on."

He pivoted to walk away.

The fan girls started shouting again, a garbled white noise that got lost in the over-cooked percussion of the new band on stage.

"Vike." His name felt all wrong on her lips. Something she shouldn't have been allowed to say.

Emily took Mickey's Stratocaster from Austin and held it out for Vike. An offering. An apology. "I want you to have this," she said.

"Oh." Vike looked confused again. "Thanks, but it's cool, no, I mean I already have one. I just dabble, you know ~ local gigs, happy hour at the bar in Long Beach. Still learning. Still learning."

"Em. Car's waiting," Chemo said.

"Not yet." She offered up the Stratocaster to Vike a second time. "You sell it, then. Ebay, could be worth a lot of money."

He was shaking his head, backing away from her. "I could never do that."

"Why not?"

He looked offended by the question. Opened his mouth, but nothing got said.

"Please."

"He'd want you to have it," Vike insisted.

"I don't care."

His eyes clouded. A sudden turbulence he seemed determined to fly through.

"You've always been wrong about him," Emily snapped before she could stop herself, and then she started crying again.

Vike looked stunned. "What?"

"Never mind."

He blinked. His weight shifted, his head atilt like a dog that doesn't understand. "He was an artist. Mickey was an artist," Vike Maas said with a certainty, as if that explained everything. And then, his tone much gentler, clearly trying to sound reassuring but failing, he added sadly, "Everybody always gets artists wrong."

***

She quakes to consciousness unaware of how long she's been without it, feeling so shitty she wishes she could have stayed in the void forever. No new insight, for Emily. No life-changing revelations. Panicked faces float across her field of vision, a Greek Chorus ~ Chemo, Austin, the limo driver who still holds the cylinder of Narcan that has evidently revived her. The Escalade is on the side of the highway, doors winged, hell's wind chafing her. Downtown shadowed buildings mime a cut-rate Milky Way, headlights spray past like shooting stars.

The thrum of traffic is relentless.

A tatted female EMT with a reflective Dayglo vest, her raven hair pulled back in a work-bun and hooded cat's eyes flickering worry, tries to strap an oxygen mask over Emily's mouth but Mike Mrdryk's muse and forever girl

229

(isn't that what he always cooed to her after they'd fought?) flails and bucks and bats it away. Crying. Shivering. Debased. Trying to sit up in the limo's back seat but hands hold her down.

She declines the precautionary trip to the ER.

"I'll be fine," she whispers but knows that she's not, she won't be. Maybe ever.

Bad luck, Chemo keeps repeating, aloud, as if that was the explanation for everything: the homicidal fetty, the false hopes, the failures, loves, betrayals, compulsions. The relentless tears. The shooting of Mickey. The brush fires. The stubborn ghost of Vike.

He haunts her.

The ghost of Vike rocks on.

Not that the other Greeks are listening to what Chemo has to say on the subject, their stricken, distracted looks clouded with a conditional relief for her disrupted doom.

Better her than them. Right? But. Better story if she'd just stayed dead.

Tidier. Almost poetic.

Emily knows that luck has nothing to do with what has happened. She doesn't delude herself. Every song, every yearning, every life has its ineluctable refrain. There are no victims, Vike once claimed, only volunteers.

And, like him, she's way too quick to raise her hand.

STARLITE
PULP

NEON GODS

BY E.B. HUNTER

The last two nights were the worst of my life. Cross my heart and hope to die. I was in my usual dive, debating with myself if I should start a fight with another girl at the bar or just drink until I pissed myself, when I felt a hand on my shoulder. My will to self-destruct melted away, the loud blonde across the bar got to keep cheering on the Red Wings and keep all her teeth. I turned to see who'd tapped my shoulder and behold; an angel from heaven.

"Who the hell're you?" I asked, doing my best to not let my jaw hit the floor. I'd been up for 26 hours at that point and had hit a wall with the case I was working, so my brain wasn't functioning well at this point. Some would argue it never functioned well at *any* point.

A beautiful woman stood before me with honey skin, eyes like caramel swirls and curly black hair that framed the most symmetrical face I'd ever seen. She said, "I'm Isis." and smiled so bright I thought I'd die of radiation poisoning.

"That's quite the set of teeth you have there." I said, "what're they like, 100 gigawatts or something? You could get McFly back to the future with that smile." She laughed and I took a drink. "What brings you into a shithole like this?"

"I came to find you."

I pulled a cigarette out of my jacket pocket and sparked it, "No shit?" I said and took a long drag, exhaling through my nose. "What makes me so lucky?"

She smiled again and, I swear, the lights flickered. "You've got a reputation, Tracy. I've heard good things."

I look behind me, expecting to see a camera crew, but no such luck. "You sure you've got the right girl?" I said, "Don't get me wrong, I'm flattered, but I'm just some washed up dick living in my car and taking pictures of husbands doing the dirty."

"Now I know you don't believe that," she smiled her most beguiling smile and her eyes flashed before she said it, "Godkiller."

I took a drag, looked at the ground and uttered, "Shit." under my breath.

"I heard about your little tilt in Buffalo. I know all about what happened when you went up against that mongrel Tyr."

"He wasn't a mongrel." I said, muttering into my whiskey as I took a good long pull.

"What was that?"

"I said, 'He wasn't a mongrel.' You're thinking of Fenrir. That's the mutt, and so far as I know, he's still breathin'."

"Details, details." she waved her hand, "The fact is, you ki–"

"Look, lady. I'm not who you're lookin' for, so hit the bricks." I swiveled back towards the Red Wings, as hard as that was to do with her caramel eyes still boring into me. Fuck was she good looking. It's really not fair for Gods to be both immortal *and* so damned beautiful.

Her fingers crept onto my shoulder and I felt a twinge as her thumb pressed on a nerve cluster, deadening my arm and making me drop my glass. "Son of a b–look what you made me do!"

The bartender's head spun around at the sound of a spilled drink and I waved at him with my good arm to let him know it was all in hand. I stuck my smoke in my lips then threw some napkins on top of the sticky brown sauce.

"You may be immune to God-magic, but you are far from impervious." Isis said. Her saccharin voice trilled in my ear. "Help me, and I can help you."

"This is the same bullshit that got me where I am today. Homeless and living in a shithole like Dearborn." I swiveled back to face her, my arm still hanging at my side with pins and needles jabbing my fingers. "I can't get much lower than this, so you might as well turf me."

"Exactly." she said, and a cheer went up from the other patrons as Fedorov did a lap around the ice, bumping fists along the home bench as he passed.

"Exactly, what?"

She slid closer to me, damn near sitting in my lap and ran a finger down my cheek. "You can't get any lower, so why don't you let me lift you up, little one."

I know she meant little as in 'little mortal', so I didn't let it irk me. I may be small, but I get shit done. I shook the last bit of sleep out of my arm and rubbed my brow. It was suddenly very warm in that bar. I would be a complete idiot to take on any more God work. I was still in deep hiding after the dust up in Buffalo, so getting another pantheon up my ass wasn't on my to-do list.

"Lift me up, how?" I asked. What an idiot.

"Why don't you drive, and I'll fill you in along the way?" she said, leaning close so I caught the scent of her. Honey. She smelled like honey. Life really isn't fair.

I led her out to my home on wheels and felt more guilt than normal (she's a God after all) as I shoveled old newspapers and take-out bags off the floor of the passenger seat so she could ride shotgun. Thankfully, she was gracious enough not to give me shit about it, and soon we pulled onto the I-75 headed east as fast as my shit bucket Pontiac could carry us.

"Atlantic City?" I asked.

"Osiris has been running that town since the sixties. He owns the Golden Bird Casino with Ra, as well as other property in the area."

"Well, good for him."

"Yes, we do quite well for ourselves." She said, missing my sarcasm completely. "But it's time for this farce of a marriage to end. I need my freedom, and I will never have that as long as Osiris has something to say about it." A green sign whips by, almost too fast to see with one headlight, and I head for the exit.

"What're you doing?"

"Look, I'm not some sort of assassin." I said. "I've got a few morals, some lines I won't cross." I slow through the ramp and pull over at a little shit hole gas station with a flickering neon lamp declaring it *o-en* with aggressive blue and red light.

"You killed Tyr." She said, as though this answered everything.

I brought us to a screeching halt and slammed the shifter into park, laying into her before the car stopped bouncing. "Look, you think you know what happened in Buffalo, but you don't know shit." I shoved a finger in her face, "I wasn't there to kill Tyr. I got played like some sort of pinball machine, and I ain't looking to get played again, I don't care how beautiful or dangerous you are, I'm no one's hitman. You got that?"

She smiled and I felt about two inches tall as my insides turned to water. This heavenly creature beside me could flatten me like a penny on a train track, and I had the stupidity to yell at her and wave my finger in her face.

She clicked her tongue and said, "Such tenacity. I like a woman with fire."

I put my finger away as I felt heat creep up my neck.

"I don't want a hit-man. I want freedom. I want you there as insurance, so that Osiris doesn't get any ideas when I tell him our time is through."

I looked out the windshield at the dingy store before me. A pink plastic flower danced side to side on some sort of perpetual motion device behind the grimy window. Life felt like the biggest joke of all time, and I was the butt of it.

"So you need a bodyguard?"

She nodded, "Uh huh."

"Why didn't you say so?" I said, getting out of the car.

"Where are you going?" she said before I could shut the door behind me.

"It's a nine hour drive to Atlantic City, eight the way I drive, and I haven't slept in days, so I'm gonna need some cigarettes and maybe a couple ding dongs." I paused and asked as an afterthought, "You need anything?"

She laughed, and this time I know for *sure* the lights around us brightened. "Nothing for me, dear." she said.

"Easy to please." I said mostly to myself as I shut the door. "I like that in a woman."

***

The Pontiac roared into Atlantic City the next morning as the sun was starting to brighten the dim autumn sky. The clouds hung low and traffic was a breeze with it being off season. Isis directed me to a swanky hotel and Casino her

238

husband owned. We pulled up and a valet took my keys (I was only slightly less mortified by the state of my car when handing it over to them than when Isis had hopped in. I really outta clean it more often). They let me fetch my bag of meager belongings from the hatch of the wagon and we headed upstairs.

"I feel like a fly at a frog convention here." I said, looking at all the shiny marble walls, the plush indigo carpeting and the bellhops, chamber maids and other various working people whishing about on the whims of the hotel guests. I tugged my overcoat around me a bit tighter and fished out my cap to try and hide the rats nest on my head.

"Come. I have a room for you upstairs." Isis said, taking my hand and pulling me toward the elevator. "We'll get you cleaned up."

Isis produced a key and slipped it into the elevator panel, turning it and pressing the top button for the penthouse. The elevator binged out the floors one by one, moving so smoothly I could hardly tell we were moving at all. She took the key out and the doors slid open to show a room of glass that overlooked Atlantic City as it woke up. The sun was doing a good job of shining and the people below zipped back and forth, living their normal lives and not worrying about being used as a doormat by a God.

"Do you like the view?" Isis asked as we stepped off the elevator.

"It's sure something," I looked at her and said what I shouldn't have. "But it's nothing compared to you."

I felt heat creep up my neck as she smiled her gigawatt smile and pointed across the room to a gold door.

"Go get cleaned up." she said, ignoring my mind numbing stupidity.

I shuffled off to the bathroom, keeping my head down. The hinges glided and the door opened to a lavish bath that would have fit my Pontiac with room to spare. The door swung shut behind me as I said, "Fuck me blue, this is incredible!" and Isis laughed before the door clicked shut and killed the sounds of the outside world.

I opted for the shower function as I didn't want to wait three hours for the tub to fill, and was sudsed and clean in the time it took to whistle 'God Bless America'. Feeling slightly refreshed, I went to throw on some clean (mostly) clothes and came across a set of new digs sitting on top of my duffle. *When the hell did she put those there?* I thought and heat rushed up my neck.

Not wanting to cause a fuss, and because the clothes probably cost more than I made in a year, I put them on and found they fit perfectly, like magic.

I headed back to the living room in my new navy suit and wingtips. "This is nice and all, but don't you think it's a bit much?"

Isis laughed from her perch on the arm of the couch, "You're with me now, Tracy. There's no such thing as 'too much'."

She headed for the kitchen area as I tried to stifle a yawn. I'd lost track of the hours it'd been since I had a good sleep, and I desperately wanted to crash. Isis opened a cupboard and pulled out a jar.

"No coffee for me, thanks." I said, eyeing up the plush sofa. "I need some shut eye."

"This isn't coffee," she said, and opened the jar. A slight pop was followed by a golden light shining on Isis' face like sunbeams. "Come, try some."

My curiosity got the better of me, and I shuffled over to her. One day my curiosity was going to be the death of me.

She pulled out a stick with a knobby end on it from the drawer and plunged it into the jar, pulling out the golden contents and spinning it around the wood. She plopped the stick into a cup and sealed the jar back up, cutting off the warm yellow glow as she did. She went to the fridge, pulled out a glass carafe filled with milk, poured it over the golden liquid and stirred.

"Here," she said, handing it to me, "have this and you'll feel much better."

I raised an eyebrow, but took the cup, the glass cool and smooth under my fingers. "What is it?"

"Milk and honey." She smiled, but her eyes had a glint to them, like she was testing me.

"Bottoms up." I said, and drained the cup in one smooth motion. I have a knack for drinking things in a quick manner, and drinking a lot of it.

The liquid was cool and refreshing and when it hit my stomach, I felt a warmth spread through my body that was better than any alcohol I'd ever drunk. It was like all the tiredness, all the complete and utter exhaustion, had evaporated from my system. That was when the world shook into hyper focus. The colours became more vibrant, and details sharper. I looked at Isis and she smiled, that knowing glint still in her eyes.

"What did you lace this with, speed?" I asked, smacking my lips.

"No!" she laughed and touched my arm, "It really is just milk and honey."

"Stop shittin' me, Isis. What the hell was that stuff?"

She bit her lip and I nearly did a backflip. Had I mentioned this Goddess was a knock-out?

"Promise you won't be mad?" she said, as if I could get mad at that face.

"Sure, whatever. What was it?"

"Well, it was milk. But it was milk from Hathor, the Goddess."

My mouth fell open, but I think I kept my cool. "And the honey?"

"Well..."

"Isis...the honey?"

"Tears from Ra."

Then I kind of lost it. "The *tears*– what do you mean *tears* from Ra?" I put a hand over my mouth, but thankfully the incredible feeling of Goddess' milk mixed with tears of a powerful sun God sustained me and I didn't hurl.

"Well, it was an experiment of sorts." she said, looking out the window at the city below, not meeting my eye.

"What kind of experiment?"

She shrugged, like playing guinea pig with me was no big deal. "Mortals don't usually survive this drink. It's too much. But not you," she smiled, "you're immune to God magic, so you survived and are restored."

I thought I wouldn't get mad, honest. But when someone gives you a potentially fatal cocktail and smiles at you, it makes you want to give them a good hard shake. I balled my fists, and tried to focus on the up side. I *did* feel like I just woke from a two day sleep after eating a mountain of hot dogs and being pleasured by Daryl Hannah. I guess it wasn't all bad.

Isis sauntered back to the door and said, "Maybe this will make it up to you." She opened what any sane person would call a bedroom, but she called a closet, and pulled a maroon trench coat and black fedora from a hook on the door. My mind went racing back to the Dick Tracy comics my Dad read to me growing up (and named me after) and I thought I might tear up. *How did she have all this ready for me? Was she so sure I'd say yes, like some sort of lap dog that comes when it's called?*

She handed them to me without a word and I pulled the coat over my shoulders. Just like the suit, it fit perfectly. Isis placed the hat gently on my head and ran her finger along my jawline, pausing for a fraction of a second near my lip. A question flickered across her face, but it disappeared in an instant as she turned toward the door.

"Shall we get this over with?" she asked.

I cleared my throat and tried to push the emotions back down where they belonged. I didn't need to be getting all sappy over a damned coat and hat like some sort of snot nosed kid.

"Yeah, just a second." I said and went back to the duffle on the couch. I pulled out a sword with a broken blade, the hilt nearly longer than what was left of the pocked steel. I tucked it inside my coat to hide it from the looky lou's in the lobby, and followed Isis to the door.

The ride to the elevator was smooth, and I enjoyed the soft hum of the wires, accompanied by the buzzing motor. All sounds I hadn't realized were there on the way up, sounds I was too tired to notice, and I was grateful for the extra go juice (or should I say God juice?) Isis had slipped me.

We walked across the still deserted lobby and past crap tables and slot machines to the back of the building. I marked four possible exits as I jumped up the three stairs that led to the office, a pace behind the graceful steps of my Goddess. I guess that's what she was now, my Goddess. Can't say I minded much. I'd take that gigawatt smile over a shot of wine and a cracker any day.

There were no bouncers at the door (why the hell would there be? They're freakin' Gods) so Isis strolled right in, happy as you please. I don't know what I expected when I walked through that door, all I know was it wasn't what I got.

Instead of a usual business lookin' office, there was a throne sitting on an elevated stage in a spacious area with a desk tucked behind it like an afterthought. A man who must've been seven feet tall with coffee coloured skin stood next to the throne. Yellow neon light from the Golden Bird Casino sign that hung on the wall glinted off his shiny bald head.

Beside the muscle (who I bet was Ra) sat our main mark, Osiris. He looked relaxed, but I could tell from the crinkle in his brow that he was annoyed by the intrusion, though he played it cool. Ra, did not, and scowled at me with all the arrogance these Gods tended to throw around. Like we're all just ants to be crushed. I was happier than ever to have the weight of Tyrfing in my jacket.

Ra spat something in Egyptian, but Isis refused to answer, only nodding her head in my direction. Baldy took the que (pun intended) and repeated in English, "You bring this bitch in here unannounced?"

"Watch your mouth when you speak to me, Ra." Isis spat, "Tracy is my guest and will be treated with respect."

I kept my eyes locked on Osiris, sensing the rage swelling in his chest. He tapped a long finger with a large tiger eye ring on it against his charcoal armani suit and kept running his other hand over his curly black goatee.

"I think we'd best cut to the chase here, Isis." I whispered to her.

"Yes," Osiris said, "please do 'cut to the chase'." He leaned forward in his throne, looking down on us mere women with scorn. I guess he'd never heard about the 'hell hath no fury' bit. "You've been gone for months, Isis, and now you return here out of the blue and dragging around a mortal pup. Why do you insult me?"

I felt Isis tense, and knew she felt what I felt. All the hairs on the back of my neck stood up, and cold crept across my skin. The neon sign behind the throne flickered briefly and the room temperature dropped until I could see my breath.

"Your parlor tricks won't work on me, Osiris." she said. "You know why I've come back."

Osiris looked away, and the rage in Ra's face turned to confusion as he looked to his comrade.

"Sign them." Isis said, "Sign them, and we will leave without bloodshed."

The cold eased, and Osiris turned to Ra, "Bring me the papers from the top drawer of my desk."

My muscles relaxed and I let out my breath. This guy was fucking scary, and I didn't want things to go sideways.

Ra returned in seconds with a manila folder and handed it to Osiris. He took the papers out and sifted through them, tutting under his breath as he glanced at each page.

"I really didn't want it to come to this, Isis." he said without looking up. "I thought we would have it all."

"You mean you thought you would have it all." she said. "You wanted your cake and to eat it too, but you stopped loving me a long time ago, just like I stopped loving you."

He stopped sifting and looked up at Isis, his eyes glazed over with a sparkling inky black. He sat there, still as a corpse, for long enough that I thought nothing would happen, but then he bared his teeth and said, "I don't think you ever loved me, Isis." and I knew we were fucked.

I reached in my coat and pulled the shattered sword from its hiding spot. The cool steel sang in my hand and prickled my skin as the room grew cold again. Osiris tore the papers in two and bellowed a gut wrenching roar that

rattled my fillings.

"Time to go." I said, and grabbed Isis' elbow, but she didn't budge, only

responded with a wail of her own. The room lighting smile was gone, and in its

place were black veins that spidered across her throat and face as she screamed

like the dead. I know this because a moment later, the actual dead started to

swarm into the room, howling like in the old horror flicks. But I ain't no

Barbara, and these newly made corpses weren't gonna *get* me.

I turned to face the bellhop I'd just seen a minute ago (then, very much

alive. Now, not so much) and skewered him through the eye with the jagged tip

of the sword. He dropped like a sack of hammers and was immediately replaced

by the concierge. That one got me, flailing into me and knocking me to the floor.

I managed to hold onto Tyrfing and shoved it in her ear, cutting her shriek of

vengeance short and spattering my new coat with blood and brains. Good thing

it was red.

I rolled the zombie off me and sprang to my feet in time for Ra to knock

me back on my ass. I landed on my tailbone, the force knocking the air out from

my lungs. I only gasped a second or two, and managed to get the half sword up

to block a downward strike from Ra's ankh shaped brass knuckles. I risked a

glance at Isis as I got to my feet, swinging blind at Ra to keep him back.

He laughed at my clumsiness and muttered in Egyptian, waving his

hands at the dead hotel workers and making them form a ring around us. "No way out, maggot." he said, and laughed. "Now, face me. Show me what that little sword can do."

He bunched his shoulders and I widened my stance, holding the blade in front of me. I had no sword skills, though I was good with a knife, having won tournaments back in the marines. But this awkward blade wasn't a commando knife, and it wasn't a human across from me, it was a God. I had to throw him off, get an edge before he could sting like a bee. I'm allergic.

"Why are you running around fetching files for that son of a bitch?" I said, "I thought you were supposed to be, 'king of the Gods'." I put air quotes up to try and get his goat.
He shrugged, "It's God of Kings, ingrate, and in this new land, there are no Kings, so Osiris rules. There is always death."

I laughed, "Sounds like a lie you tell to keep from crying yourself to sleep every night." He dashed forwards with three quick strikes. I turned the first two, the brass hammering my steel, but the third grazed my side as I tried to twist away. The punch sent me reeling into the wall of undead ring zombies and they pushed me back towards Ra. The smell of their loosened bowels hit me like a freight train and my hands started to shake as I gagged on the stench.
Ra laughed, bouncing from side to side. This was just a game to him. A way to pick on the little guy. His friend and his wife just killed a whole god damned hotel full of employees, people with families at home and who had dates and plans for night classes at college. They were flesh and blood and infinite

possibility snuffed out in a marital dispute. Like they weren't worth more than a piece of chewed gum you'd scrape off your shoe.

I felt it then, the same thing I felt in Buffalo, and I knew things were gonna go from bad to worse.

My hands stopped shaking, and I set my jaw, planting my feet and waiting. Ra dashed forward again, and time slowed as fury took over. I felt the steel in my hands turn frosty as ice poured from the hilt and across to where the blade used to be, taking its full form with the icy rage of a God-killer pouring into the grip.

But Ra was already in motion, no turning back, and I swung the now full blade across his chest. He managed to get one knuckle up, but by then the work was done. With a splash, his blood hit the floor, followed shortly after by his thudding corpse.

My mind was clear, I needed to kill Osiris and get the hell outta there. The ring of dead around me were no longer in Ra's control, so they bum rushed me, trying to doggy pile with me in the middle. I flung forward, chopping through a kid who couldn't have been old enough to drink and jumped over his corpse in a full run to the battling spouses. I shook off the clamoring hands of the dead as I flanked them to find a way into the fight.

Then it was before me, an opening, and I took it. I launched myself onto the desk behind the throne and catapulted into the air with every bit of strength I had. Hoisting my sword up high, I brought it down point first into the base of

Osiris' skull, driving the sword down to the crossguard. "Die you son of a bitch!" I screamed in his ear as blood dribbled out of it.

In the fray, I hadn't noticed, hadn't seen Isis get the edge and move in close for the kill. Osiris dropped and pulled her down with him, my sword shoved into Isis' throat. The dead in the room instantly fell silent and dropped with their puppet masters, leaving an array of corpses scattered across the spacious office to be basked in the golden light of the neon sign. Isis gurgled, and all I could do was stare down at her. "I'm sorry." I said, and she reached out a hand to me as she drew her last breath.

I stared into her cold dead eyes, and wondered why the hell I had followed her here. I should've known this was how it would end. Just like fucking Buffalo. I wiped a tear from my eye, and came to the realization that I would've followed her to the ends of the earth. That's why I followed her. That gigawatt smile had me the second I saw it, and I believed her when she told me it would be a simple job. What can I say? I'm an idiot.

I heard sirens, and decided it was time to get out of there. No doubt someone called an ambulance when the circle of death extended from the casino, but I heard the bray of fire wagons and cop sirens mixed in as well. I tore the blade from my victims and stole the knuckles from Ra before running outside, weariness creeping back into my bones as the go juice burned through me. I went to the valet station, grabbed my keys from the near empty rack and raced across the asphalt to my Pontiac.

I threw Tyrfing on the seat beside me, the ice melted and back to its half sword status, then fired the engine. I kissed the steering wheel when it turned over without as much as a stutter, and hauled ass out of there.

Now I was wanted for two dust ups that would leave the feds with too many questions. I should've never trusted a God. Not in Buffalo, and sure as *hell* not under the sardonic neon lights of Atlantic City. I revved the engine to put more road between me and the hell that was the Golden Bird Casino, and I vowed then and there to never trust a God again.

GHOST STORIES
WRITTEN BY ERIC ESQUIVEL
ART BY SCOTT GODLWESKI &
RYAN CODY

Humankind has always believed in ghosts.

Our ancestors assumed they were the benevolent spirits of their elders, forsaking the rewards of Eternity in order to guide the arrows of their heirs.

Modern, pseudo-religious "spiritual" types have erected a macabre dogma around the phenomena, claiming that the apparitions they see are the traumatized souls of victims of violent crime.

I prefer to think of ghosts as dents in the fabric of space/time, inflicted by folks who lived their lives so hard they wounded consensual reality.

You'll notice there's no such thing as a boring ghost story. It's never "Sandra lived with six cats and died clutching her copy of Reader's Digest".

They're always tales of misunderstood outlaws, heroic gunslingers, and beloved local nutcases.

...the kind of people one wishes could live forever.

THE CANNIBAL OF SPACE CITY:

A CYRUS MAJOR MYSTERY

BY JIM TOWNS

(NOTE: RELEVANT MAPS ON PGS 293-296)

I.

Oyster Prong, Florida – 1962

Cyrus had to shield his eyes from the glare as the powerful Redstone rocket rode a pillar of flame and smoke into the air. Close at hand, Blackfoot growled, confused, at the shuddering earth beneath his large paws.

The two stood on a low marshy bank, just a few miles from where the rocket was lifting off. Already, it was just a tiny dark speck, and no matter how hard he squinted, Cyrus couldn't see the tiny cone-shaped capsule at the top, in which sat a lone man hurtling towards orbit.

But that was fine. Cyrus had more pressing problems. Over the last two months, young people had been going missing in the swamps hereabouts, and the local sheriff seemed disinclined to do a thing about it... the missing kids being the sons and daughters of poor working folk. So a collection of them—homesteaders, small business owners, salesmen, even some gator hunters—had collected enough money to hire Cyrus to find out what was happening, and hopefully bring back their missing children.

"C'mon, Foot."

Cyrus squeezed his frame behind the wheel of his airboat, and Blackfoot jumped eagerly into the craft after him. He was a dog of indeterminate breed—a good three feet at the shoulders and easily ten stone; fur black as coal with soft brown eyes and powerful jaws. The great fan chugged to life in its cage behind the seat, and Cyrus pushed the throttle forward, working the petals to pull out into the center of Oyster Prong's waters.

Cyrus wasn't young, but he was big. He'd grown up in this swamp, so he knew these waterways from long before the government had come and begun laying concrete to build their rocket launch platforms and gargantuan assembly buildings. He knew which tidal estuaries he passed ran through to the Indian River, and which ones dead-ended in impassible mangrove forests. He could read the shifting weather patterns coming across from the Gulf; or worse, those that came from the south up the peninsula.

Being a black man of his era and region, Cyrus had a well-earned suspicion of anyone in power—be it Brevard County's white sheriff with the Confederate flag on the sleeve of his uniform (who often visited the black girls at Mama Rosa's brothel on Highway 1) or the ever-growing population of polite NASA eggheads currently immigrating into the area. Power was something folks didn't always realize they had, but that didn't stop them from exploiting it whenever it benefited them. The whole Cape was under development, it seemed, and the way of life he'd known all his fifty-some years—and that of the people who employed him—was quickly disappearing.

He picked up speed as he hit the mirror-smooth waters of wide Moore Creek. Not far ahead would be his first stop: and it would be a dangerous one.

2.

The Seven Scimitars Gun Club, Moore River

Its grandiose name aside, the gun club was little more than a shack built out on a pier over the water: one big room, a small storage shed, and just enough dock for the club members to stand while relieving themselves into the river. It had been built near the turn of the century by shellfishermen, and over the last fifty years the sun and storms had done their worst to it. The gun club had taken over the abandoned building a dozen years ago to use firstly as a refuge from their wives, and secondly as a place to drink and shoot. Cyrus knew several of the club's roster to be active Klan members—so he cut off the boat's fan when he was still a hundred yards out. He would coast and paddle the rest of the way.

The worn boards of the pier creaked under Cyrus' weight. He couldn't hear any voices coming from inside the shack, but that didn't necessarily mean the place was empty. As he reached the door he shut his eyes a moment—it would be dark in there, and he wouldn't have time to let his vision adjust to the dim. He put a big hand on the weathered door and went in:

The gloom inside was worse than he'd figured. A pungent concoction of damp wood and sweat and old beer filled his nostrils. He could make out a decrepit bar towards the rear, and a few rickety tables scattered about. An elderly, wiry-framed man slouched over one of them with a half-dozen empty bottles neatly arranged on the table in front of him. As Cyrus took a step forward, the man's chin rose just a bit, and he looked up: his eyes were bleary and deep; set in a face mummified from decades of sun and hard drink.

"It's members only, big fella..." he slurred.

"I'm just looking for a guy." Cyrus held up a placatory hand, but even as he did he heard from behind him the telltale *chk chk* of a shotgun round being chambered.

A brittle voice spoke: "He said members only... that means no smokes."

Having a gun pointed at his back was not a new experience for Cyrus. He raised both hands, and smiled friendlily as he slowly turned to see a big sunburnt man with a prodigious beard and sagging belly, holding a single-barrel pump shotgun on him.

"If I'm not welcome, of course I'll leave. May I please just ask one question first?" The circular mouth of the barrel hovered before Cyrus' eyes.

"Make it short," the bearded man muttered.

Cyrus lowered his hands.

"Do you like dogs?"

The bearded man had just a moment to register the question, before Blackfoot's jaws closed on his calf, his teeth sinking deep into the muscle.

With a scream the man began to fall, and Cyrus was there to snatch up his gun as he did. The big fella thrashed and hollered up a storm, but Cyrus knew Blackfoot well: big as he was, the dog was really a gentle soul—when he was done playing, the man would probably still be able to walk—just not well.

Cyrus held the shotgun by the barrel as he approached the stringy old man at the table. At this range, the gun was more use to him as a club than as a firearm.

"I'm looking for Georgie Packart, old man. I heard he's a member here." He had to speak up to be heard over the man on the ground's caterwauling. The older guy took a look at the gun in Cyrus' hand, and glanced at the man writhing on the floor—and nodded.

"What'cha want with 'im?"

"His daughter's gone missing. His wife didn't know where he was."

"This time of year he'd be at his froggin' cabin, right on Banana Creek.

"How far?"

The old man nodded to his friend: "Mebbie you can call your pooch off mah nephew?"

Cyrus yelled "FOOT!" and Blackfoot immediately let go of the man's leg.

"It's just off the river, right side on the shore," the old man said. "You get to Skunk Island, you gone too far."

Blackfoot stuck next to Cyrus' leg as he walked out, stopping near the door and breaking open the shotgun, setting it down but taking the slugs with him. Once outside he chucked them into the water.

The smoke trail from the rocket still hung in the sky as they cruised back down Moore Creek towards the Indian River.

3.

Banana River

The Indian River ran north & south along the coast, just a few miles inland from the Atlantic. This far up, it was nearly a mile wide—a brackish pool covered in blooms of floating red algae.

Cyrus was starting to wish he'd kept the shotgun. His total armaments amounted to one big Bowie knife and an old Winchester repeating rifle he kept aboard for angry gators. Banana Creek was out of his home territory. Folk there didn't know him, and he couldn't always rely on his wits and Blackfoot's teeth.

After a while he spotted the little brush-covered nobs of Stony Island coming into view, and he knew he was close. Blackfoot perked his ears up over the gunwale, and Cyrus slowed the airboat as he turned starboard into the narrower channel of Banana Creek.

There was no mistaking where Georgie Packart had set up for frogging: just a few hundred feet from the main river Cyrus spotted the wreck of an old iron-hulled ship washed up on shore, likely during a hurricane years and years back. Someone (presumably Georgie) had taken a hacksaw to the hull and cut a little door into it to make a hut. He'd also added a crude wooden deck that ran out over the water, and an old ratty canvas tarp strung on poles above: the better for shielding one's shadow when catching frogs. An old rowboat was pulled up on the bank close by.

Cyrus took the airboat in carefully, and when he was perhaps a dozen yards from shore a tan, lanky man with a balding head and squinting eyes came out of the makeshift shelter, all filthy and ragged and looking for all the world like a castaway in a child's pirate story.

From the sandy shore, Georgie waved to Cyrus in a friendly manner.

"What's the word, friend?"

"You Georgie Packart, husband to Dottie?"

Georgie's eyes squinted further: "I am. Who might you be, besides a man who knows my wife?"

"Nothing of the kind," Cyrus said. "She sent me to find you. Your Girl Ellie's gone missing."

"Missing, you say?"

"I do. Last seen this past Tuesday on her way to the store."

Georgie was doing the math: "Tuesday... that'd be almost a week, now."

"It would. You haven't seen her? She didn't come stay with you or anything? Your wife thought she might."

"I wouldn't bring my girl to this hellish place. Waters are teeming with gators and there's horseflies big enough to chew a man to pieces."

Cyrus nodded. It had been a long shot.

"You're that guy helps people out, ain'tcha? Finds folk gone missing. Majors?"

"Cyrus Major. This is Blackfoot:" Blackfoot gave a little bark at the man.

"Yeah, I heard about'cha," a worried look came over Georgie's face: "My kid the only one you looking for?"

"Nope. Some six or seven, best we can figure. Maybe more. All in the last few weeks."

"Christ..." Georgie muttered to himself. He grabbed up a few things, and made a move towards his rowboat.

"I appreciate you comin' by to let me know, sir... I better go. Dottie'll be needing me."

"I'd say that's a good idea."

The lanky man tossed a few items in his rowboat, and paused:

"You been over on Skunk Island lately?"

Cyrus shook his head: "Can't say I have."

Georgie stared off across the water at a small speck a ways off:

"Queer things going on over there lately. Mostly at night."

"That so?"

"That is so." Georgie pushed off from shore. "Need any help?"

"You go comfort your wife. Hopefully your girl's just funning, and she'll show up."

"Hope so. Good luck."

Blackfoot gave a yip, and Cyrus fired up the engine and pointed the bow towards the far-off speck of land.

4.

Skunk Island

It was well after noon when Cyrus and Blackfoot neared Skunk Island. It was a large mound of dry land in the center of the wide creek—maybe a whole acre in area, maybe a little more, with its own little woods. Cyrus decided to circle it once before deciding on landing there, and as the airboat came 'round the lee side of the island, he saw a shiny new dock had been recently installed.

That was thoughtful, he thought to himself. He pulled the boat up to the aluminum dock, climbed out and tied it off. The elements of the swamp ate away at anything made by man with alarming speed, and he noted the metal of the dock was smooth and unpitted. It was very recent, indeed.

Blackfoot gave a snort, and Cyrus held up his hand.

"You stay with the boat, boy. I won't be long."

Blackfoot didn't appear happy with this arrangement, but he obeyed: hunkering down on the raised bow section where he could keep an eye out.

Before Cyrus a path led upwards a bit towards the center of the island, and he started up it. It was easy going at first; then the path grew narrower, occasionally crossed by fallen tree trunks he had to negotiate around, and in one place it dipped into a deep and narrow gully which he was forced to leap.

He'd been gone from the boat about ten minutes, and was just thinking he should have reached the center of the small island, when a flash of white off to the left caught his eye. Turning, he couldn't catch sight of whatever it was now. He waited a moment, listening—and then took a step off the path to the left.

The terrain led him downward along the edge of another gully; or maybe it was the same one he'd jumped across back on the path, just wider this further down. He continued on for a bit. At one point he was certain he'd seen another flash of white—again just on the periphery of his vision, and again it was gone by the time he turned.

Cyrus had just decided to head back up the hill and check the other side of the island, when he looked across the gully to see a young girl staring back at him. She was shoeless, wearing a white dress all stained with mud and damp. She was dark complexioned with straight black hair, and Cyrus knew she couldn't be the Packart girl—she had Seminole blood.

"Hoy, girl, what's your name?" he called out. "It's alright, I'm a friend." Cyrus tried to suss out a way to get across the wide gulf between them, but then he saw a shadow of fear cross the girl's face, and she turned and fled the other way.

"Wait!" he called out—and as he did he heard a heavy footstep behind him. He spun 'round, and his hand went for the Bowie knife at his belt. But what he saw when he turned froze him stiff:

It was a man, and he was dressed in the silvered pressure suit and mirrored helmet of an astronaut. In one thick-gloved hand he held a metal box the size of a toolbox, and hoses ran from it to his suit. His other hand held a great heavy wrench.

"—the hell are you doing here?" was all Cyrus managed to get out before the man swung the wrench up and caught him on the jaw, and darkness crashed in.

5.

NASA Launch Operations Center, Merritt Island

The first thing Cyrus felt upon waking was Blackfoot's tongue licking his face.

"They nab you too, buddy?" he asked the dog, who seemed overjoyed his friend was again conscious.

He was lying on a bed of some kind, in a small room that shook and jostled. The sound of an engine and the smell of gas were close by, and after a moment Cyrus realized he was in the back of some type of camper van, rolling along bumpy unpaved roads. Except for the two low cots, the interior was largely unadorned: stainless steel walls with rivets, and the only exit via a queer rounded-type door in the rear. He'd seen astronauts getting out of something like this on the news, and that reminded him of the space man with the wrench on Skunk Island.

Cyrus rose to a sitting position painfully—he had a nasty welt on one side of his face and his jawbone was tender to the touch, but he didn't think anything was broken. A touch confirmed his Bowie knife had been taken from him.

With difficulty, Cyrus got to his feet. Blackfoot dodged around his legs as he made his way to the rear door. He figured it would be locked and, turning the handle, he wasn't disappointed.

He sat back down on the cot, which bolted to the side of the cabin, and waited. He was going someplace; that was for sure.

. . .

When the vehicle stopped, it did so abruptly, almost knocking Cyrus to the floor. He heard the tires kick up gravel to pelt the inside of the wheel wells. That told him they were someplace near civilization, and not in the middle of a muddy swamp. That was promising, at least. It would be riskier to dump a body near where people were. Cyrus chose to be encouraged.

After a moment and some muted voices he couldn't make out, the rear door opened and the amber light of dusk shone outside.

"Please step out, sir," a voice requested, and Cyrus squeezed his sizeable carriage through the narrow door and down two steel steps. Blackfoot followed.

In the lowering evening light, he found himself standing in the middle of a gigantic construction site: gargantuan concrete blocks formed long walls on many sides, iron girders rose in grids all around—the skeletal structures of what would become buildings. Titanic diesel cranes sat dormant in the distance and, beyond them, the treeline of the forest waited on all sides.

Standing near at hand were three men—two of them wore the crisp blue and khaki U.S. Air Force uniforms and insignia he'd been seeing at all the local bars of late. They were both young and lean and white, with close-cropped hair under their bonnets. Both had gunbelts strapped to their waists.

The third man was shorter and middle-aged; he wore grey slacks, an ugly plaid short-sleeve shirt, narrow tweed tie and thick glasses.

Cyrus glanced at the two airmen, then at the spectacled man:

"You're in charge here, right?"

"In a manner of speaking," the man replied, "I'm Rob Talloway, I'm the acting Site Director here at LOC."

"LOC?" Cyrus asked, even though he was starting to figure it out.

"Launch Operations Center. We're brand new, still under construction, as you see. Follow me, please." Talloway turned and led Cyrus and Blackfoot towards a low-ceilinged, bunker-like building. The airmen followed.

The pale green hallway of the building was lit with bright fluorescent lights hung from the acoustic tile ceiling. Cyrus noticed the walls had hooks spaced at regular intervals, but any photos had yet to be hung.

Talloway took a left into one of the first offices they passed, and held the door for Cyrus. It seemed he made a point of closing it before the airmen could enter, so the two guards took up position in the hall. The office was wood-paneled, with what looked like a war surplus steel desk and a few uncomfortable chairs—one of which Talloway motioned Cyrus to take. Blackfoot settled down on the floor near at hand.

"Can I get you something—there's coffee in the mess."

"I'm okay, thanks," Cyrus was looking around at framed pictures leaning against the walls, not yet hung: supersonic jets, test aircraft, scientists and pilots standing in front of rocket assemblies.

"The new rockets, the ones that'll take us to the Moon, they're gonna be too big to be launched off the Cape. And we'll need bigger buildings to assemble them. So here we are: in the middle of the swamp."

Talloway seated himself in a chair opposite Cyrus: "We should probably discuss why you're here."

"One of your Astronauts clocked me upside the head with a wrench."

Talloway didn't reply for a moment. His hand reached out and picked a manila folder off the desk.

"Your name is Cyrus Alexander Major. As far as I can understand, you make your living as a bodyguard, general problem solver, fixer... sort of an independent contractor, one might say."

"One might say."

"And currently you are..?"

"Looking for several missing persons in the area... minors."

"There's mining around here? I'd thought with the high water table—"

"No, *minors*... as in children. Missing."

"That's awful," Talloway sat back.

"Yes," Cyrus was getting tired of this: "So how come you have astronauts messing around on little islands in the Swamp?"

Talloway smiled, and closed the folder. "We don't."

"My jaw says otherwise."

"Well, your jaw and the United States government are gonna have to agree to disagree on that."

"Fair enough. Can I go, then? Since, as you say, I never saw any astronauts on Skunk Island."

Talloway seemed to be considering something as he watched Cyrus. A mental calculation was happening.

"Mr. Major, we have a problem. The astronaut you encountered today—"

"—was the one that blasted off this morning. Am I right?"

"You are. We don't want the public to know."

"I can dig that. Would look bad in the papers…"

"And to our enemies. And we *do* have enemies, Mr. Major."

Cyrus sat back. Talloway was about to spill what was really going on.

"Our rockets use advanced computer technology during both launch and recovery. Hundreds of bytes of data per second—far more information coming far too quickly for even a hundred mathematical geniuses to calculate."

"I struggled with times tables, myself."

"Yes," Talloway grinned, "Well, our problem: someone is manipulating that data. The calculations, which are figured out ahead of time and then entered into the computer system, are being altered. Not radically, but just enough to throw off our guidance and telemetry systems."

"So instead of landing in the Atlantic Ocean, your space capsule winds up landing in Banana Creek."

"Precisely."

"You have suspects?"

The man shook his head: "The usual ones. The Soviets, the Chinese—"

"—Army Corps of Engineers?"

"Sorry?"

"Didn't they run the rocket program before the Air Force took over? Might be sore."

"I really hadn't thought of that." Talloway's face creased with new worry.

Cyrus leaned back in his chair: "Mr. Talloway I'm sorry for your troubles, but I'm a simple man trying to make an honest buck in this swamp."

"Of course. I hope I can rely on your discretion in this matter. Everything I've told you is of the utmost sensitivity to National Security."

"You can trust me not to spill the beans. I may be a bottom feeder, but I'm a patriotic bottom feeder."

"I suppose that'll have to do." Talloway rose and extended his hand. They shook. Blackfoot got to his feet, excited to leave.

"The guards will take you back to your boat. Apologies for any inconvenience we've caused, and as way of making it up to you..." he opened the door, and there stood the young girl from the island, now clean and dressed in oversized military fatigues.

Cyrus could only stare. Blackfoot gave a little yip that made the girl start, and then padded over to her, sniffing her hand until she reached out and gave him a pet.

6.

Three Cabbages, Florida

True to Talloway's word, Cyrus, Blackfoot and the girl had been taken back to Skunk Island in a lightweight patrol boat. The girl and dog both seemed to enjoy the evening ride immensely, while Cyrus sat in the back, keeping a wary eye on the military men escorting them—and their weapons. He had no idea how seriously NASA wanted their secrets kept, and he wanted to be ready in case any 'accidents' were planned to take place along the way. But the trip proved him to be overcautious: the boat pulled up at the Skunk Island dock, the men politely assisted their disembarkation, and, without another word, pulled away and sped off back to where they'd come from.

The girl didn't speak a word on the half-hour trip southward to Augie's Feed and General Store, and Cyrus didn't push—he had no way of knowing what she'd been through, and there would be enough questions coming.

When they'd landed at the port and the three had made their way along the dirt street to the old shop, it was old Senora Sanchez who'd recognized the girl, and sent a boy running down the road to fetch her folks. It turned out her name was Alice Halpatter. She was the daughter of a fisherman named Tall Shoulders Halpatter, and his wife Myra; Alice had only been gone three days, and hadn't been counted amongst the missing boys and girls Cyrus had been hired to find. After a tearful family reunion, the hard work of trying to find out what had happened to her began. A small group of folks gathered in Augie's store: Augie, Tall Shoulders and Myra, Senora Sanchez, her son-in-law Devron Miller, and Cyrus.

And, of course, Alice.

In a halting, nearly inaudible voice, Alice told them how she had snuck out of her house late at night to go meet a boy she was sweet on (of whom her father didn't approve). The boy lived a good hour's walk away, in a small town called Mitre. She had walked along the levee until she had to cross the new highway that connected Pine Island to the mainland. There she'd encountered a man fixing a flat on his old pickup, who offered her a ride to Mitre. Alice could only describe the man in broad strokes: he was neither tall nor short—strong looking, but not large enough to stand out. He had a high forehead, and a neatly shaven beard and moustache. Alice mentioned he sounded funny when he spoke, but Cyrus couldn't be clear whether she was referring to an accent, or a speech impediment.

She'd accepted the ride, but almost as soon as she'd climbed into the cab a smelly rag had been clasped over her nose and mouth, and she didn't remember anything more, until the feeling of being carried along a trail in the middle of a swamp.

While it was visibly obvious that she was nervous at all the attention on her, Alice had been doing pretty well up until this part of her tale. But now her words became hesitant, and seemed to choose her words with more care:

It was not quite dawn when she'd reawoken in the strong man's arms. She was groggy from whatever had put her to sleep, so she didn't struggle. In a short amount of time they'd arrived at what she was sure was his campsite. It was on a raised bit of ground, surrounded on all sides by water, and accessed only via a narrow wood plank bridge, which he pulled up behind them. She described a green army-style tent, a dug-in cooking pit, and what sounded to Cyrus like an old steel transportation container in the middle of the tiny island, and that's where the strong man took her.

"What was inside the container, Alice?" he asked her. "Were there other boys and girls?"

She nodded, and mentioned a few names of children she'd recognized—all of whom were among the list of the missing—but there was something more she was hesitating to tell them.

"Go on, child..." her mother Myra prodded her. "It's alright. You're safe."

Alice told them in broken words how the strong man had brought her food to eat—tough pieces of red meat on charred bones, that needed to be gnawed at to get any sustenance. Starving, she'd accepted the meat and eaten it, only afterward noticing the horrified looks of the other children—and the fact that most of them hadn't touched their dinner.

It was later, when the man opened the door of the stifling container to let them out to do their business, that she'd seen the pile of bones near the spit— reeking and covered in flies. Many still had the flesh on them, and within the pile Alice saw tiny hands, and the head of at least one girl she'd known: Ellie Packard.

Terrified beyond words, she'd been herded up with the others and put back in their steel prison for much of the rest of the day. In hushed voices, the others described to her how the big man would let them out twice a day for a few moments—reminding them that the water all around their little island was teeming with crocodiles. Occasionally, he would even demonstrate this, by pulling a piece of remains from the pile and tossing it out into the water, and they'd all see the green sinuous shapes slither towards it, and devour it. Sometimes several of the reptiles would fight over the body parts. Then he would press them back inside—but every other day or so he'd hold one of the kids back, and they'd never see that child again, unless it was a glimpse of what remained of them on the pile.

The children were left locked in the suffocating hot container for much of the second day, and it was after dusk when they were finally let out. They'd had a few moments to stretch their legs, and drink a little water—and then the big man was shoving them back inside. Before the door closed, however, Alice had felt his fingers grip the back of her dress and hold her back. The doors closed with her on the wrong side, and she'd known what this meant.

She'd screamed, and fought—but the Big Man was too strong, and he dragged her towards his tent. As he did, however, he'd suddenly crumpled up in pain, grabbing his stomach and crying out. Alice hadn't hesitated a second, and had sprinted for the bridge. The big man tried to give chase, but another wave of pain had made him stumble to his knees, and Alice reached the edge of the little island. The bridge was pulled up, and in trying to move it by herself, she only managed to push it down into the water. With a moment's consideration, Alice had jumped into the stagnant moat, and swam for all she was worth towards the land at the far side. She was a good swimmer, and several long strokes had brought her to the muddy bank opposite. It was only after climbing her slippery way out that she spotted several crocodiles closing in on where she'd just been in the water.

The man stood on the far bank, yelling threats at her as he tried to reach out for the makeshift bridge—but Alice had turned and fled through the dark, and before long the horrific island was far behind her.

She'd tramped through the swamp all night and into the next day—thirsty, hungry, covered in sweat and muck and mosquito bites. To her left she'd seen tall cranes working and heard people's voices, but could find no passable way to get to them. Then she'd heard a great clamor and seen the rocket rise up, up in the distance. Not long after, she'd seen a capsule come floating down from the sky on colorful parachutes, to land with a splash in a creek nearby. Before the strange thing sank into the shallow water, she'd seen a man in a shiny suit and helmet clamber out and swim to a tiny island. Thinking he could help her, she'd stripped down to her underclothes and swam out to the same island. There she encountered Cyrus, and witnessed the space man hit him. She'd turned and fled, only to run right into men in uniforms.

Alice finally paused, exhausted from her ordeal, and from the retelling of it. The adults present all shared a look at one another.

Something frightful was in their midst.

. . .

Cyrus sat one of Augie's small tables. Myra had taken Alice home, offering Cyrus many thanks, which he'd shrugged off. His mind was racing—going over the very limited information the girl had been able to convey, and trying to make it add up to a location.

"Think I could get some dinner, Mama?" he asked Senora Sanchez. "I need to leave soon." The old woman ducked back into the kitchen.

"You should get some rest, Cy," Augie said, "You're likely still concussed, and finding that fella's island in the dark'll be next to impossible."

"That little girl made it out of there on foot in the dark well enough," Cyrus grunted. "With her getting away, he'll likely pick another one'a those kids. That's one more that's not coming back to their mom and dad. Maybe that'll... fill him up... for a day... hard to know for certain. But I aim to get there before he takes another."

The Senora put a plate of slow-cooked pork and fried plantains in front of Cyrus, along with a mason jar of sweet tea.

"She said he had stomach pains..."

"It's called *Kuru*, I think—comes from eating human flesh." Cyrus forced a few bites of the food down. He was going to need his strength.

"What you do when you find this man, Mr. Major?" Tall Shoulders asked.

Cyrus shrugged:

"Figure I'll start by killing him."

7.

Gator Creek

It was close to one in the morning. Cyrus spent a few moments gassing up the airboat and checking the engine. He was going into real danger this trip, and he didn't want the craft failing him. Meantime Augie made the rounds with all the fishermen on the jetty, and returned with several lengths of strong rope, fishing line, a medium-sized boat anchor, and a multi-pronged fishing spear. Senora Sanchez brought him a burlap shoulder bag with some hard bread, bananas, chocolate bars and a thermos of strong coffee. Finally Devron Miller approached and handed him the antique Japanese *bolo* machete his father had brought home from the Battle of Okinawa. When Cyrus pulled the blade free from the sheath he took note that while it was rusted in places, it was still razor sharp.

As he turned to get aboard his airboat, he found Blackfoot sitting patiently, waiting for him.

"Not this time, old man," Cyrus rubbed the velvety fur behind the dog's ears. "This one's gonna be bloody. Best you stay put here with these good folks."

Blackfoot's tail stopped wagging for just a moment, as though he understood—then it started again.

"I said no, buddy..." He took a few steps towards the airboat, only to find Blackfoot shadowing him.

"No. Stay!" he waved a finger at the canine, and stepped into the boat. "Stay…"

Finally Blackfoot got the message. As Cyrus started up the propeller and cast off, he lay down flat, watching him and whimpering. Just as it started pulling away, however, the dog came to his feet and, taking three or four bounding strides, leapt the seven or eight feet from the end of the pier to the gunwale of the airboat. He almost made it—but landed in the water just short with a splash.

"Damn fool dog," Cyrus grunted, and shut off the motor, leaning over the rail and taking hold of the scruff of Blackfoot's neck. He had to use both hands to haul the dripping wet dog into the boat, where he immediately shook, dousing Cyrus.

"Your funeral," he muttered, and went back to his chair and fired up the propeller full speed. The airboat took a sharp turn, and roared up the Indian River.

The swamp was vast, and to an outsider it might have seemed a monotonous expanse of marshlands, cypress groves, Spanish moss, and deadly creatures. But the wetlands of Brevard County held a diversity of life that would have stunned someone unfamiliar with the land. There was a place near East Pepper Creek where thousands upon thousands of white cranes would gather, and the branches would echo with their calls. Close to Pine Island (where Alice's young boyfriend lived) there was a forest of old birch trees growing incongruously right out of the swamp waters, their peeling white parchment bark visible for miles up-and-downriver. Colorful purple flowers bloomed all along the banks of Lower West Prong, and Peacock's Pocket derived its name from the colorful birds that gathered there in the spring to mate—easy prey for poachers.

But there were very few places around where crocs nested. For one, crocodiles and alligators didn't get along, and gators pretty well dominated most of the large rivers and creeks in the county. One had to go a decent ways upstream to get to the still backwaters the creatures thrived in. Cyrus knew of one spot over on the east side of Merritt Island, but it was much too far away for little Alice to have traveled on foot in a day. The other two nesting areas were up north a ways: a pair of inlets known respectively as Gator Creek, and Catfish Creek. Both would be about a half-day's trek to Skunk Island for a lost young girl, likely not walking in a straight line.

Reinforcing this hunch was Alice's description of building cranes off to her left as she made her escape. The Government was currently clearing a large swath of land for a big landing strip just northwest of the Launch Center.

The thin moon shone down and made dancing lights on the river as Cyrus and Blackfoot made their way northward. Occasionally he'd see the headlights and taillights of cars traveling up and down Highway 1 off to his left, and before long he could see the twinkling lights of Titusville approaching on that same side.

Catfish Creek was the closest, so Cyrus checked it first. He remembered it being a very small inlet, so he figured it wouldn't take long. Indeed it was only the work of a few moments to find that fallen logs made any access by boat impossible, and the ground itself was so supersaturated, no one could have walked across this stretch of swamp.

So it was gonna be Gator Creek. Now that he was here, Cyrus felt his stomach give a little lurch, and he tasted acid in the back of his throat. He knew he had to mentally prepare himself for what he was going to see, and what he was going to do. There would be bodies. Little bodies, likely. And there would be violence and blood, most definitely. As he turned the boat slowly into Gator Creek's narrow inlet, Cyrus felt warm breath on his leg and without looking, his hand found Blackfoot's head and gave it a good rub. He was glad his friend had demanded to come along. This could easily be their last trip, after all.

. . .

Gator Creek was a narrow channel that ran along steep banks covered in lush grasses. Even in the dim pre-dawn light, Cyrus could see tall cabbage palms leading off across the flat floodplain to the east—if this was where Alice had run from, that would have been the path she'd have taken.

Cyrus came to a spot where he could tie up to some mangrove branches and pull the airboat close enough to the bank to get off, and killed the idling engine. He wasn't too worried about sound—sound didn't carry far at all in the swamp—but he wanted to make sure he had the element of surprise working for him. Blackfoot jumped ashore easily enough, and Cyrus made sure he had the anchor and rope, the three-pronged fishing spear, and bolo knife secured to his person—then clambered ashore.

He followed the creek inland for about a quarter mile, 'Foot keeping at his heels and occasionally sniffing to the left and right. It was cool at this hour—as cool as it would be all day. Soon the sun would come up and the temperature would start climbing. Fighting in the heat was hard, and tiring: based on young Alice's description, Cyrus figured he had a good ten-to-twenty years on this fella. If he was lucky, Cyrus figured, he'd be able to catch the ghoul sleeping; but his luck being what it was, he wasn't counting on it.

After a ways he sensed Blackfoot tense at his knee. He paused and glanced down, and saw the critter going low on his front legs, while keeping his hindquarters up—he knew this meant he'd caught a whiff of something he didn't like. He moved forward cautiously.

The island soon revealed itself through a dense thicket of tall grass. It was precisely as Alice had described it: surrounded by the creek on all sides, it was separated from the land around it by a good twenty feet of stagnant water. The rickety narrow bridge had been set back up since she'd tossed it in the water. Cyrus didn't spot any crocs, but that didn't mean they weren't there sleeping on the bottom, or floating all still and looking just like harmless logs.

In the blue early light, a kind of throbbing glow lit the island with an amber tint, and Cyrus realized it was coming from a fire pit burning low—the kind local folks used for roasting pigs or ribs in hot coals. He didn't want to imagine what was roasting in there now. An acrid smell had now reached him, and he recognized the sharp odor of hair burning, and the sour reek that rose when blood was cooking off.

There was no sign of the man Alice had described, but Cyrus saw the tent clear enough, as well as the old shipping container sitting near the fire pit. No sound came from the hellish place.

"Okay, 'Foot... we're going in. Ready?" Blackfoot gave a little shake of his head.

Cyrus tested his weight on the wooden plank connecting the island to the land—it might support a girl or even a medium-sized man, but he was a bigger animal. The bridge creaked, but held his weight. He made his way across rapidly, all the same. On the far bank he paused again. He should be able to hear something—snoring or breathing from the tent, crying or whispering from the container. There was nothing: even the swamp was quiet, and the swamp was never quiet. This was a forsaken place. The animals knew it, and stayed clear— all of them, that is, except for the crocodiles. Dumb brutes.

Cyrus got ready. He'd chosen his weapons carefully. He'd intentionally not brought a gun—there were kids here and if things got crazy and he fired wild... well he couldn't have that on his conscience, no matter how noble his goals. He planted the spear point-down in the soft earth, and dropped the coiled rope next to it. Making sure the bolo knife was tucked tight into his belt, he uncoiled the anchor rope and made sure it was free and loose. Planting a foot on the end, he began swinging the anchor in a wide vertical arc, letting it gain its own inertia, before flinging it at the tent. It landed in the center of the sloped roof, and he yanked hard. The tines of the anchor caught on the pole, and the whole thing came down as he pulled, the ropes coming loose from their pegs as it slid free before tumbling into the fire pit—where the canvas quickly caught aflame.

Cyrus had already grabbed up the spear and got ready—but even as he did he realized that no one was in the tent. Blackfoot had moved forward and now sniffed around the low cot, a trunk and some odds and ends, but he just looked up ruefully. Had the flesh eater fled after Alice had escaped, convinced she'd bring back the authorities? Was he still out looking for her?

Blackfoot gave a sharp bark, and Cyrus turned. He'd let his guard down.

8.

Hell Island

The two men stood opposite one another: the heat rising from the burning pit between them making each appear distorted to the other.

"I assume you came here for the children." The man was shorter but stocky, and had the short beard and mustache Alice had remembered. He wore shirt sleeves and duck cloth trousers, and had a Colt revolver tucked in his belt: the kind highway cops carried.

"Not just the children. You."

The bearded man looked Cyrus up and down.

"You're not the police. They wouldn't have colored police down here."

"You misunderstand. I'm not arresting you."

"I see. It's an assassin come here to finish me, then."

"If you want, yes. No more kids for you, monster."

The man's hand moved towards the grip of his gun: "No, I think I'll have a few more before moving on. I think you should have come here better prepared. I think you're not a hunter, so much as you're a custodian... someone who cleans up other people's messes. And I think you've made a great mistake coming here, boy."

They stood there a moment, then the man pulled out his gun and shot Cyrus.

It seemed to Cyrus he was flat on the ground before he'd even heard the gun's report. Scorching pain lanced from his neck and he instinctively put a hand to it—it was wet. He knew if the bullet had clipped his carotid artery, he'd be dead inside a minute or two. The world spun and he could hear his pulse in his ears, but he struggled to stand. Even as he did the dirt near him kicked up, flying into his eyes, and he heard another shot from what seemed like far away—then the man's voice sounding close by:

"Stay down, partner. Make this happen easy."

"Easy my eye," Cyrus gritted through his teeth. "FOOT!"

The man had barely a moment to turn and let off a wild shot before Blackfoot was on him, tearing at his leg, rending both cloth and flesh. The man screamed and lowered his gun to kill the animal, when the bolo knife slashed across his forearm, severing its tendons.

The gun fell to the ground to the left, and the man fell to the right.

Cyrus hollered: "Foot! Let him go!" and Blackfoot immediately broke off, licking at the blood dripping off his fangs. Cyrus was on one knee from where he'd thrown the knife. His neck was still bleeding, albeit slower now. Still he had to use the spear for support to stand.

The man lay there, moaning, trying to hold the pieces of his leg together. As Cyrus approached, he could clearly see the twin bones of the shin exposed. Sure, Blackfoot was the kindest of creatures, but a fella didn't want to take that for granted.

"See, unlike some folk, Blackfoot here knows what he's allowed to eat, and what he ain't."

"It hurts..." the man just moaned.

"Yeah, I bet. Along with those cramps, right?"

He stood looking down at the killer.

What's your name? So's I can tell folks."

"Cooper..." the man hissed between locked jaws. "Edmund Cooper."

Cyrus nodded. "You come down here for the Space City?"

"Just a job. Two weeks. But I liked it. I stayed... plenty of easy pickings... kids no one would miss much." he smiled hideously through teeth red with blood. Cyrus glanced over at the shipping container.

"Any of them alive in there?"

"Some."

Blackfoot glanced over towards the container, and took a few careful steps towards it, sniffing.

"Right, then:" Cyrus said, and laid the three points of the spear on Cooper's chest—then shoved it in. The bearded man gasped. Between the leg and the forearm, he'd lost enough blood that he was likely in shock, and probably past feeling much pain: but Cyrus was going to put that to the test. Using all his strength, he leveraged all hundred and fifty-odd pounds of the man off the ground, shoving him back a few feet, his heels dragging in the dirt—a few feet more, and those heels rested on the edge of the flame pit, the rest of Cooper's body hanging from the spear over the smoldering coals. Cyrus let him hang there a moment, the big muscles of his arms shaking with the effort. Cooper's eyes stared at nothing and his head lolled on his shoulders.

"Hey. Hey, Edmund? You still there?" Cyrus hollered.

The man took a breath, and nodded.

"Good. I want to make sure you're awake for this."

He shoved, pushing the man down into the coal bed. Sparks flashed from the coals and a sizzling sound rose. There was a moment Cooper seemed to come back to awareness, and then he screamed. Instinctively, he tried to claw his way out, his hands digging at lava-hot coals, scorching their flesh away, but Cyrus pressed down with the spear, holding him down to the flaming bed. The cannibal's screams grew in pitch and frenzy as he held him down, slowly seeing his clothes catch fire and burn away, then the flesh burn to black and shrivel, the eyes melt in their sockets. Somewhere during that process Edmund Cooper died, but Cyrus didn't want to take any chances, and held him down for a while to keep cooking—even as he felt the hairs on his own arms singe off from the heat.

Finally, as the sun rose on a new day in the swamp, it was done.

9.

The Airboat

Whatever else he was, Edmund Cooper had not been a liar. When Cyrus opened the door to the container he'd found six scared and malnourished children staring at him. Scared, but alive. They'd heard the cries.

It was some little doing getting them all back to the airboat. Blackfoot was a great help in calming the kids' fears of the tall dark stranger. As they left, a few of them glanced briefly into the pit, where the blackening bones of their abductor were still smoking.

There was little talking on the way back to Augie's place at Three Cabbages. Some of the kids whimpered, and the bigger ones held their shaking shoulders. Cyrus tried to talk calmly to them, to reassure them that things were going to be okay, but he was no good with kids. He never had been. And anyway, he wasn't sure if what he said wasn't a lie: would any of these kids be whole again, given what they'd been through—what they'd seen? He hoped they would be. He hoped to God they would be.

They'd heard his boat coming at the docks, and Cyrus found a group of people waiting for them. Word had been spread, obviously, and many families with missing little'uns had turned up with hope of seeing them again. Cyrus knew some of them would be elated. Others would be devastated. That was life in the swamp. It gave; but it took, too. Even though everything around them seemed to be changing, that still remained true.

10.

Switchgrass Point

It had been a long forty-eight hour day, and Cyrus was looking forward to sleeping clean through to the next one.

His house sat at the very tip of a small promontory at the end of Moore Creek, right where it split to become Middle Prong and Oyster Prong. It was of spruce and poplar, with a roof that sloped in one angle from right to left, and it was set up on stilts above the ground a good couple feet, in case the waters rose. A little dock floated near at hand, and behind the house a path led into the dense grass, which Blackfoot enjoyed exploring.

When he came 'round the bend from the Indian this morning, however, Cyrus' hopes for a well-earned rest were dashed. Tied up to the dock where he normally moored his airboat was a familiar military patrol boat.

Skilled from long practice, Cyrus cut the engine and coasted the last dozen feet to the other side of his dock, where an airman in fatigues caught his line and secured it. Cyrus climbed out onto the dock, and the airman cocked his head up towards the house. Blackfoot chose to hop out the far side into the water and splash his way onto shore.

Reaching the top of the steps, Cyrus opened his front door to find Rob Talloway sitting at his table cleaning his thick glasses on a handkerchief—a blue folder with the words "EYES ONLY" next to him.

"Hello again, Cyrus. We need your help."

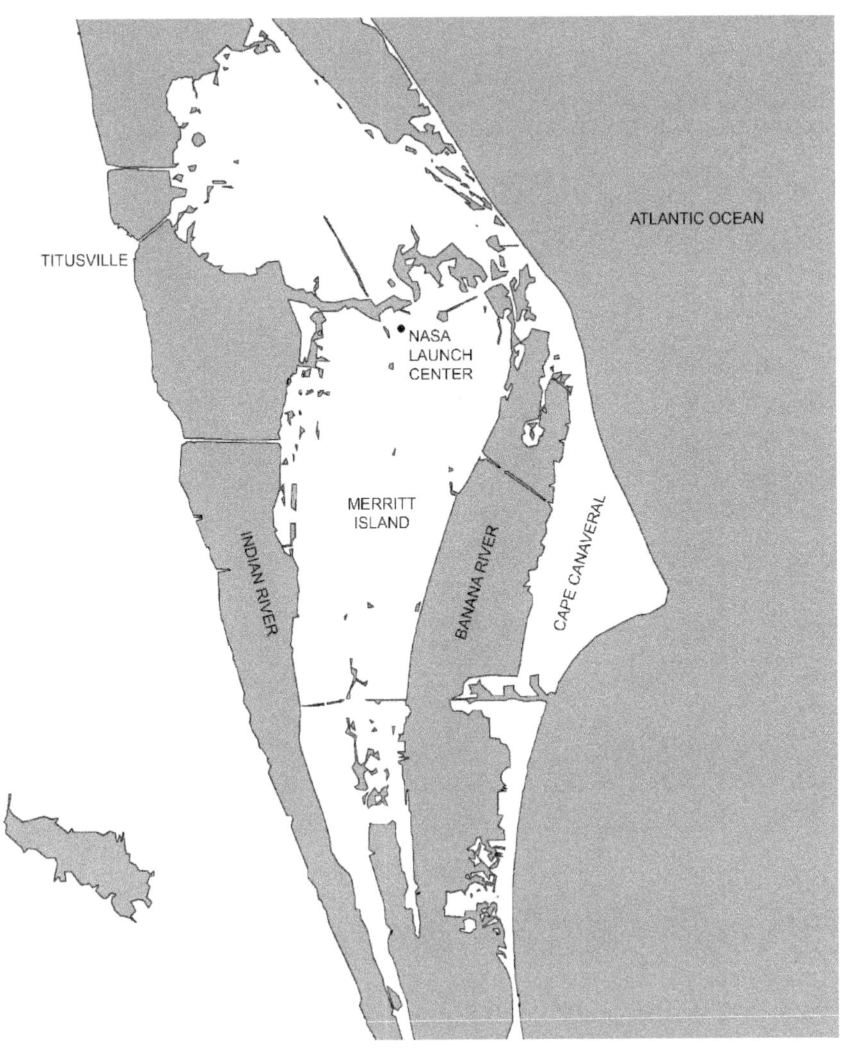

ATLANTIC OCEAN
TITUSVILLE
NASA
LAUNCH
CENTER
MERRITT
ISLAND
INDIAN RIVER
BANANA RIVER
CAPE CANAVERAL

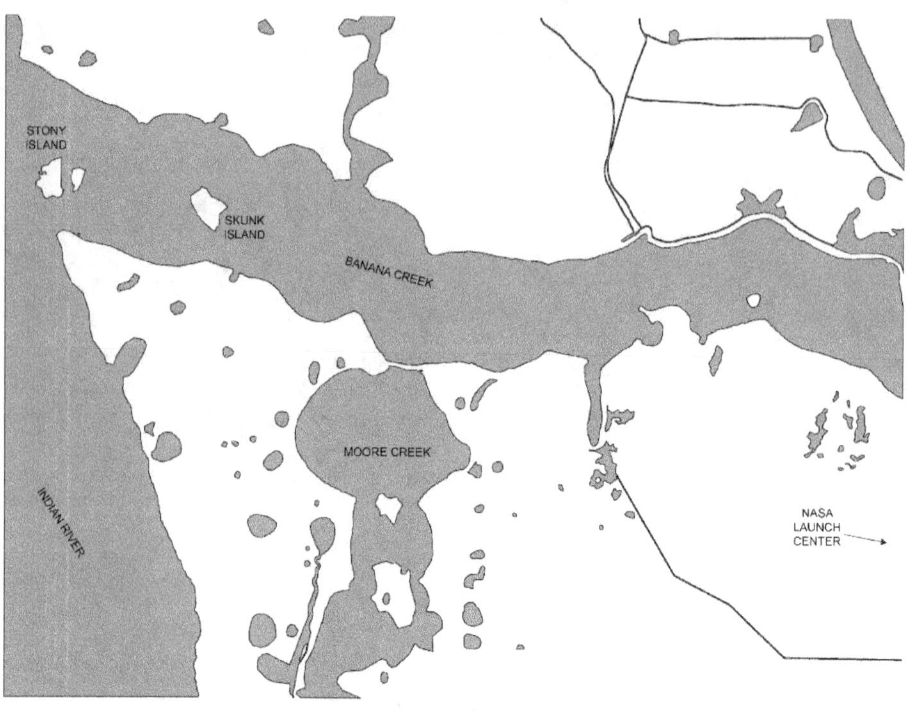

STONY
ISLAND
SKUNK
ISLAND
BANANA CREEK
MOORE CREEK
INDIAN RIVER
NASA
LAUNCH
CENTER

GATOR CREEK
CATFISH CREEK
INDIAN RIVER
BANANA CREEK
SKUNK ISLAND

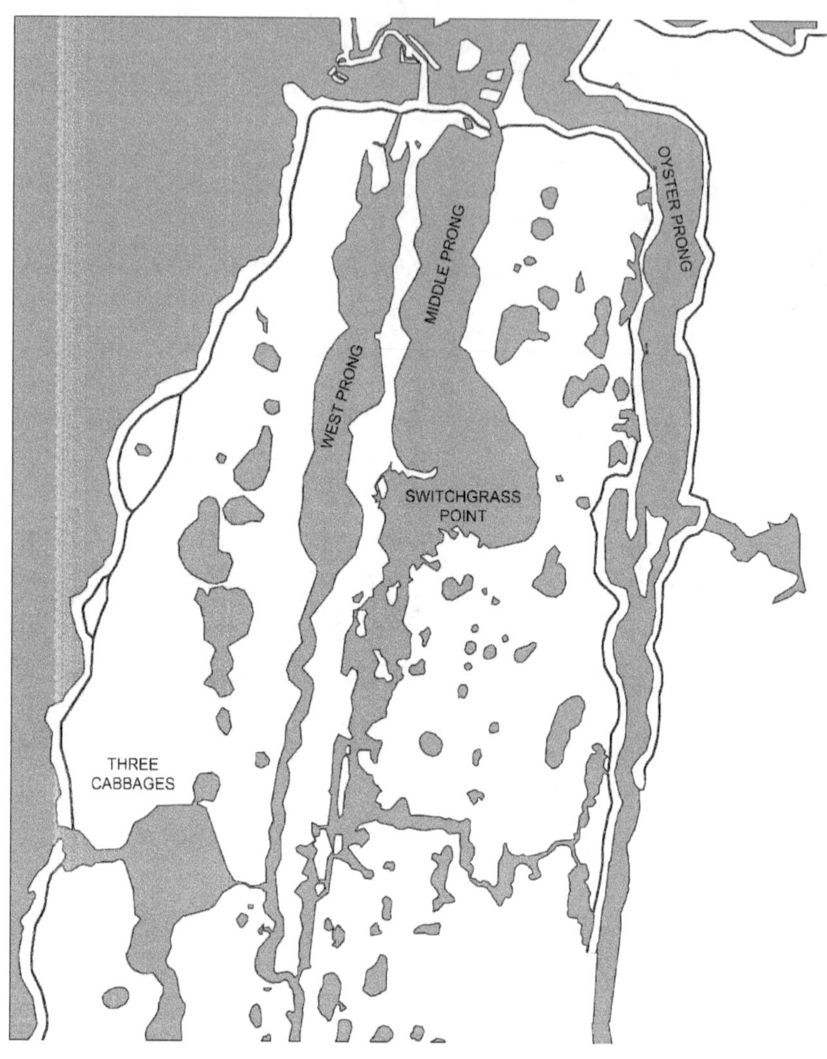

Note: these four maps represent the main land areas and waterways in the Cyrus Major story.

ABOUT THE AUTHORS

MICHAEL BRACKEN is the Edgar Award-nominated, Shamus Award-nominated, Derringer Award-winning author of more than 1,200 short stories, including crime fiction published in *Alfred Hitchcock's Mystery Magazine*, *Ellery Queen's Mystery Magazine*, *The Best American Mystery Stories*, *The Best Mystery Stories of the Year*, and many other publications. Additionally, Bracken is the editor of *Black Cat Mystery Magazine*, associate editor of *Black Cat Weekly*, consulting editor for Level Short (an imprint of Level Best Books), and editor or co-editor of thirty-two published and forthcoming anthologies, including the Anthony Award-nominated *The Eyes of Texas: Private Eyes from the Panhandle to the Piney Woods*. His stories have been translated into several languages, released in audio format, and adapted for animation.

ALEC CIZAK is a writer and filmmaker from Indiana. His collection of crime fiction stories, *Nobody's Coming Home*, is currently available from ABC Group Documentation. He is also the editor of the digest magazine *Pulp Modern*.

ERIC ESQUIVEL is a pulp hack from Los Angeles, California. In his short and weird life, he has produced work for the theatre, video games, comic books, magazines, newspapers, and paperbacks, like the one you hold in your lucky little hands.

JEAN-PAUL L. GARNIER is the owner of Space Cowboy Books, producer of *Simultaneous Times Podcast* (2023 Laureate Award Winner, BSFA Finalist), and editor of the SFPA's *Star*Line* magazine. He is also the deputy editor-in-chief of *Worlds of IF* magazine & the soon to be relaunched *Galaxy* magazine. He has written many books of poetry and science fiction. https://spacecowboybooks.com

E.B. HUNTER lives in a remote town in Northern Alberta, Canada with his wife and daughter. He spends his days working, and his nights crafting stories to entertain himself through the long, harsh winters. He hopes these stories portray people as they are, flawed humans capable of great and terrible things, and you can see yourself within his body of works. If he ever stops writing, there are strict instructions for him to be put out of his misery. You can find his short stories in anthologies with Dragon Soul Press and Starlite Pulp, as well as on Vocal Media.

MEAGAN LUCAS is the author of the award-winning novel, *Songbirds and Stray Dogs* and the collection *Here in the Dark*. Meagan has published over 40 short stories. She has been nominated for the Pushcart, Best of the Net, Derringer, and Canadian Crime Writer's Award of Excellence multiple times, and won the 2017 Scythe Prize for Fiction. Her short story "The Monster Beneath" was listed as Distinguished in the 2023 *Best American Mystery and Suspense*. Her novel *Songbirds and Stray Dogs* was chosen to represent North Carolina in the Library of Congress 2022 Route 1 Reads program, and won Best Debut at the 2020 Indie Book Awards. Meagan teaches Creative Writing at Robert Morris University and in the Great Smokies Writing Program at UNC Asheville. She is the Editor in Chief of *Reckon Review.*

JOHN MCNALLY has published 19 books. His first thriller, *The Pinned Butterfly*, was published in 2023 under the pen name Johnny Mack. His most recent story collection, *The Fear of Everything*, was published in 2020. The 20th anniversary edition of his novel *The Book of Ralph* will be published in September 2024. His short stories have appeared in dozens of magazines, textbooks, and anthologies, including *Shadow Show: All-New Stories in Celebration of Ray Bradbury* (Morrow), *New Sudden Fiction: Short-Short Stories from America and Beyond* (Norton), and *New Stories from the Midwest* (New American Press). He presently lives and teaches in Louisiana.

GREG MOLLIN is a fiction writer and the owner/bookseller at Artifact Books, an independent bookstore in Encinitas, California. His stories have appeared in numerous print and digital publications, including *Weird Tales* magazine, *Crime Factory* magazine, *Thrillers, Killers, 'n' Chillers, Burial Day Books*, and *Dark Moon Digest*. He is a member of the Horror Writers Association, the International Thriller Writers Association, and the American Booksellers Association. www.gregmollin.com & www.artifactrarebooks.com

J.D. O'BRIEN is the author of the novel *Zig Zag*, a 2023 Southwest Book Of The Year. His writing has appeared in *Maggot Brain*, *The Lowbrow Reader*, *Arthur Magazine* and elsewhere. He has a dog named Lefty.

DANIEL PYNE is a writer and filmmaker who drifts back and forth between Los Angeles and Santa Fe on the I-40. He's got a decent resume of movie and TV credits and has published six novels. For many years he had a rowdy pair of mixed-breed dogs, but now there's just the stray white cat that climbed up under the Honda's hood one night to get warm and agreed to stay.

ALEX SLUSAR writes crime and neo-Western fiction. His stories have previously appeared in *Grain*, *Saddlebag Dispatches* and *Starlite Pulp Review*. He is a member of the Saskatchewan Writers Guild, and was selected for the SWG Mentorship Program in 2022. Apart from writing Alex works in national politics and serves as a reserve Navy officer. He lives in Canada and divides his time between Saskatchewan and Quebec.

MANNY TORRES is an Atlanta, Georgia transplant from Brooklyn, New York. His crime-noir novels and novella's include *Dead Dogs, Father Was a Rat King, Perras Malas*, and his reggae and salsa crime-comedy, *Cabrones Perros*. His short story "Bet" was featured in Starlite Pulp Review #3, and his novel *A Simmering Dissonance* is slated for a Spring 2024 release through A Thin Slice of Anxiety.

He was a programmer for Step Outside: The Strange and Beautiful Music program on WMNF 88.5FM in Florida and enjoys painting, photography, and the music of King Crimson, and taking care of several cats. You can find him on Twitter @_MATorres_ and Instagram @_m.a.torres

JIM TOWNS is an award-winning filmmaker, writer and artist: his feature films include *House of Bad, End Times, The Possession of Anne, Killer Ex* and *Mandromeda*. He's the author of the novels *Bloodsucker City* (Castle Bridge Media), *Braddock's Falls* (Anxiety Press), the nonfiction book *American Cryptic* and *Whiskey Stories*—a collection of his poetry, writings and photography (Uncle B Publications). His short fiction has been published by dozens of small presses, and he is the creator and co-host of the popular "Borgo Pass Horror Podcast." He currently lives in San Pedro, CA, with his wife and several mysterious cats.

BRIAN TOWNSLEY is an award-winning writer, as well as a podcaster and the Executive Editor at Starlite Pulp. He is the author of three collections of poetry, as well as the Sonny Haynes crime fiction books *A Trunk Full of Zeroes* and *Outlaw Ballads*. His short fiction has appeared in various publications, including *Mystery Tribune, Quarterly West, Black Mask, Berkeley Poetry Review, Connecticut Review, Frontier Tales*, and many others, and he had a Sonny Haynes story make the distinguished list in *Best American Mystery Stories, 2019*. He is a graduate of the Professional Writing program at USC and is also an alum of the mighty California Golden Bears. He lives in Southern California.

Also from Starlite Pulp:

Starlite Pulp Reviews #1-3

Praise for the Review:

"Pulp fiction in all its glory."

"An excellent first Review!"

"Starlite Pulp is the most exciting new publisher on the block."

Outlaw Ballads by Brian Townsley
A Sonny Haynes collection

Praise for *Outlaw Ballads*:

"Sonny Haynes deserves a seat at the bar next to Marlowe and Spade."

"Townsley takes readers on a film noir-style tour to the early '50's in Palm Springs, California, that bears little resemblance to the Los Angeles many of us know so well. The Sonny Haynes series acts as a mental time machine, and is worth every minute of the trip."

"Sonny Haynes did what other men boasted of."

Visit **Starlitepulp.com** for your pulp books, hoodies, tees, decals, submission guidelines, & so much more!

www.ingramcontent.com/pod-product-compliance
Lightning Source LLC
Chambersburg PA
CBHW070504160726
48003CB00004B/1410